D1204012

[Bellwood]

[Booklet]

Books by Elisabeth Ogilvie

BELLWOOD
WATERS ON A STARRY NIGHT
THE SEASONS HEREAFTER
THERE MAY BE HEAVEN
CALL HOME THE HEART
THE WITCH DOOR
HIGH TIDE AT NOON
STORM TIDE
THE EBBING TIDE
ROWAN HEAD
MY WORLD IS AN ISLAND
THE DAWNING OF THE DAY
NO EVIL ANGEL

Books for Young People

THE PIGEON PAIR
MASQUERADE AT SEA HOUSE
CEILING OF AMBER
TURN AROUND TWICE
BECKY'S ISLAND
THE YOUNG ISLANDERS
HOW WIDE THE HEART
BLUEBERRY SUMMER
WHISTLE FOR A WIND
THE FABULOUS YEAR

[Bellwood]

Elisabeth Ogilvie

McGraw-Hill Book Company

New York   Toronto   London   Sydney

[Bellwood]

[1]

A July Sunday at Bellwood. The chatter of goldfinches and catbirds around the birdbaths; the scent of new-mown grass and roses carried on a breeze from the sea that glittered like blue diamonds; gulls riding the air currents far overhead. Eighty years ago the house must have been a monstrosity in its glaring newness, but now the bricks were faded, and tree shadows danced softly across them, ivy climbed the chimneys, and torrents of red and pink rambler roses splashed the walls. In the heat of the day they gave off the warm fragrance of raspberries.

I sat on a lawn chair under the birches and watched the boy playing with toy boats in the pool set in the fold of ancient gray ledges. The big yellow cat Tristan sprawled near us in the shade, gazing out into the sun with blinking golden eyes, a lion in repose. Far off in the deep woods thrushes called the fine sweet chiming that had given the place its name: *Bellwood*. Everything was the same as it had been a week ago, except that now I was so frightened that perspiration sprang out on me, and a deathly faintness seized me. I fought it silently; wanting to give in to it was like a compulsion to jump off a high place.

The boy talked to himself as he played. He was several people all at once. Sun lay across the innocent nape and skinny shoulders. I concentrated on him; for him I had to stop being afraid, or at least gain control of my terror. But all the time I could feel my head wanting to turn and my gaze traveling inexorably toward that opening dark in the brilliant day, that shadowed leafy tunnel in which the thrushes sang, the way through the woods that led to the small stone house.

Four weeks ago there had been no terror.

"Listen, I know why you want to go away," my brother Elliot had said to me. "But Caro, it'd only be worse when you came back. Face it out now, get over the worst of it, and *then* go, if you want a change."

"But it's *now* that I want to get away from," I said.

My sister-in-law was practical. "They're likely to say you're going to have a baby, and that's why you disappeared."

"I don't care what anyone says."

"Well, I can see how she feels," Mindy said to Elliot. "And why shouldn't anybody run if they feel like it? It's nobody's business but Caro's, anyway. Of course, dear, if *you* should go to jail I'd stick around to bake cakes for you with files in them and things, but I don't think Paul deserves that much attention from Caro."

I was grateful to Mindy for being open about it, and not tiptoeing around me the way everyone had been doing since Paul had been sentenced last week to a year in the state prison, for embezzlement from the bank where we both worked.

2

"Look," I said, "I'm thankful to have you two on my side. I know you're here if I need you. But this is something I have to manage on my own, don't you see?" I tried to laugh. "Get away and lick my wounds, so to speak."

"But good Lord, Caro!" A new thought struck him. "Do you realize that if you leave now it'll look as if the bank had quietly let you go?"

"Leave her alone, Elliot," said Mindy. "Do you have plans, Caro?"

"Yes," I said. "First, I'm leaving the bank. And they didn't want me to go. I think they'll make it clear if there's any talk. And I'm going to see about a job down east, near Somerset. I found the ad in today's *Patriot*, and called, and the man's coming here to interview me tomorrow."

Elliot looked stunned and began to fuss with his pipe. "What kind of job?" Mindy asked.

"Taking care of a child in a beautiful coast setting, no housework, etc., etc." I showed them the ad. "I don't know how intelligent and sensitive I am, seeing that I hadn't any idea what Paul was up to, but I'm a healthy young woman who doesn't mind a quiet life—I can say that with all honesty. The quieter the better, right now."

"I don't like it," said Elliot stubbornly. "What do you know about this man?"

"He has a lovely voice on the telephone," I teased him. "No, he has good references. In fact, one of them is Mr. Hayward at the bank."

"I'm glad it's in Maine, with summer coming on. How could you stand it in Boston or New York?" asked

3

Mindy. "And it's so beautiful up there—down there—which is it? Anyway, I just love that part of the coast. We'll come and see you."

"Wait a minute, now," said Elliot sternly. "Before I agree to your going to work for him I want to see him."

"I'm to meet him at the Wainwright Hotel for dinner. Perhaps I can bring him here afterward."

"For coffee and dessert," said Mindy at once. "That's it. He shouldn't object, if he's what you think. He should appreciate the fact that you have a protective family." She tried to look stern and protective, quite difficult since she's shorter than I am, and has a lightly freckled gamine look while I have long bones and my Brewster grandfather's nose. A feminine version of it, of course. Mindy admires that nose no end. She calls it aristocratic, and was happy when her baby girl began to develop an unmistakable edition. I am tall enough and have the other features to go with it, so I'd look peculiar with any other sort of nose but this thin and slightly aquiline one.

"That nose will lead you straight into trouble, Caroline," my Elliot grandmother used to tell me. "It's the sign of a restless character, with too much curiosity for its own good." She reiterated this every time I got into a scrape, blaming everything on my nose, and thus, by implication, on my Brewster blood.

I was glad she had died long before the business with Paul. She'd never have believed that what had led me into our association wasn't a nose for disaster. But who would have suspected disaster? I'd seen Paul around for most of my life, and he was always the same likable, charming boy. His widowed mother gave him a brand-new car when he got his first driver's license, and even

4

the really well-to-do in Limerock didn't go that far with their children, but none of us held it against Paul; he was so witty, so kind even to the plain girls, he got such good marks when he exerted himself, and he won so many basketball games for the school.

I went out with several boys in high school and while I was attending business college in Boston; I wasn't closely acquainted with Paul till I went to work in the bank where his father had once been an officer and where Paul, with infinite tact, arranged loans for nervous fishermen and farmers, and sent them away shaky with relief and convinced he was the salt of the earth.

The first time he took me out it was to an auction far back in the country, and we had so much fun that I came home feeling my whole life had been burnished. Paul had that quality of turning the simplest expedition into an adventure.

I had begun to believe I was in love with him before I found out that this magic quality, his delightful manners, his charm, were all there on the surface—skin-deep. Underneath there was an almost pathologically self-centered creature who saw insults and offenses where there were none, who required of a woman what he had been receiving from his mother for years: an absolute subjugation. The slightest opposition meant that you didn't love him.

It took a heart-breaking and mind-warping effort for me to keep that charm of his going. At first I tried to find out why he reacted as he did to an amiable difference of opinion or even an imagined glance, but he was having none of that. After a while I realized that he was terribly afraid to look into himself, and that

5

beneath the smile, and the ability to turn the simplest occasion into a festival, there was a cringing insecurity.

But it took me a long time to discover this, and I was emotionally worn out by then. Festival or debacle—he could produce either out of nothing. If there was a woman for him besides his mother, it certainly wasn't Caroline Brewster. I pitied him, and it was pity that kept me from breaking off with a brutal suddenness more than once. Then, when he came to apologize for a scene, he would seem so reasonable that I would believe he had begun to change. Until the next evening, or even in the next hour, when a tantrum would come like a tornado.

When I finally made the break he wouldn't accept it at first. In my relief I could afford more pity, enough to save his pride, so only Mindy and Elliot, with whom I lived, knew that it was all off. Paul and I had never joined in with a group. (He had given in rather ungracefully to having Mindy and Elliot go with us just once, when I wanted to treat Mindy to dinner and a summer theatre for her birthday.) And at the bank we both played up well, but then Paul was always somebody else at the bank; perhaps his father. So there were no comments or even lifted eyebrows about a broken engagement.

Later, when the facts of the embezzlement came out, I almost wished I'd had cards printed and sent around months before, or even put a notice in the paper saying, "After this date I am no longer engaged to Paul Rideout." Because Paul's sick pride had kept him from telling his mother we'd broken off, until he blubbered it out to her in the police station the day he was booked.

Mrs. Rideout weepingly called all her friends to

6

describe how I had egged her son into crime and then broken off with him the instant he was caught. My friends and my employers didn't believe it, but Elliot wanted to drop her a legal word of warning just the same. I wouldn't allow that. She was suffering enough. However, my compassion was no help to me when Paul told the same story in court. Evidently he'd decided that it went over so well with his mother, taking the onus off him, that he'd believe in it too. It must have been a marvelously comforting pacifier.

I'd been so dirtied that I would never be clean again, I used to think in the middle of the night, sitting up in Elliot's kitchen. Worse than that, I felt guilty. Paul's theft had shocked me terribly; I tormented myself with wondering if he'd stolen as a kleptomaniac steals, to compensate for the loss of me. Then I decided I was turning as neurotic as he was. Whatever his motive was, it had come into existence long before I ever came into the picture.

After one of those nights I gave my notice at the bank. I didn't know where I was going; I only knew I was getting out.

Then I found the ad in the *Patriot*, and without giving myself time to think I called the number and spoke for the first time with Rees Morgan. At dinner I told Elliot and Mindy, and that night I slept better than I had any night since Paul's arrest.

I kept busy all the next day with Mindy and the children, and at night Elliot drove me to the Wainwright Hotel. Paul and I used to go there often for the Sunday night buffet, and as I walked through the lobby I was weakened with grief for the good part of being with Paul; there'd been a lot of fun and some unexpected

7

patches of beauty. They had been as authentic as the shoddiness.

I saw myself in a long mirror panel; a tall girl in tangerine linen, walking well and swiftly, her short brown hair in loose curls around her head. If her face seemed a little thin, her dark eyes a little more deep-set than usual, her tan was smooth and warm, and the lipstick had been applied with a hand much steadier than it had been for a week.

Caroline Brewster. Twenty-three years old. Where is the Brewster nose leading you now, Caro? I asked. And then I was there, on the first step to wherever it was.

[2]

Three men were standing up, smiling at me. Two faces slowly became familiar, as one's bedroom slowly asserts itself after a bad dream. Mr. Hayward, vice-president of the bank, pink of cheek and silvery of hair, everybody's picture of the Good Uncle, and Judge Carver, lean and leathery, just retired from the Superior Court bench. He and my father had been hunting and fishing friends. I shook hands with them both, and then the third man and I looked questioningly at each other, not quite smiling. I was suddenly and illogically excited, out of all proportion to the occasion. After all, I was being considered simply as a babysitter, not as a female secret agent.

"This is Rees Morgan, Caroline," the judge said. "Rees, Caroline Brewster." I put my hand out to him, saying, "How do you do?" It was firmly held, and dark blue eyes looked into mine, the kind of eyes I always thought of as Irish, with peaked black eyebrows and the thick black lashes that manage to look completely masculine because of their setting above rugged cheekbones and strong high-bridged nose. So the Welsh have those eyes too, I remember thinking.

This was all in an instant, while the voice I remembered from the telephone, even warmer and deeper than it had been then, was saying, "Miss Brewster, this is a pleasure. I hope very much that you'll accept these two gentlemen as my references, and consider the position seriously."

"If you'll accept them as mine," I said. I had been desperate for the job even before I'd seen him, and I still would have been, even if he'd been short, stout, and had a squint. Yet, standing there in the lobby of the hotel, I had the strangest sensation of having been transported bodily into another world, where I could gratefully and eagerly forget the old. I knew I was experiencing this even while I was very much the same Caroline Brewster who had come in.

There was a little more conversation, genial and joking, and then the other men left, and Rees Morgan and I went in to dinner. He had a quality—of which I'd never met much in Limerock—of making one feel at once graceful, poised, extremely feminine, extremely precious. Yet he was not a glib talker. I'd seen men like him from a distance on those Sunday evenings with Paul, travelers from one exotic milieu to another who had stopped here for a night. I'd wondered who they were, what marvelous things they did and thought, composed and wrote. And here I was having dinner with such a man. Because of Paul.

"That's an odd little smile," Rees Morgan observed. "Is it ironic or wistful?"

"A bit of both," I said. "I imagine Mr. Hayward has given you my history—the recent chapter."

"Yes. A tragic situation for the man, but not for you. You are sound and basically untouched, simply bruised a bit, but he's flawed and he'll never be otherwise."

"I don't like to think that," I objected. "Paul has many good qualities. But he's immature. He may grow up some day."

"When at twenty-five he's both liar and thief?" He smiled and shook his head. "I doubt it. . . . Am I treading on your toes? Will you be waiting for him at the prison gates?"

"No," I said. "Paul and I broke off months ago, but we didn't make a big thing of it. Consequently, when it did come out, it looked as if I'd deserted him in time of trouble." I heard myself saying more than I'd intended. "I should have made the break even earlier, but Lime-rock is a small place and Paul was fun; I fooled myself into thinking any doubts I had were just some sort of female vapors."

He nodded. "You saw him as what you wished him to be. Well, you're not the first to do it, and you won't be the last. And sometimes it works, you know. Sometimes the loved one becomes what the lover sees." He stopped short and his face became expressionless, and so bleak that the cold reached me like a killing frost. I paid attention to my food, but hardly knew what I was eating.

After a moment he said in his originally pleasant voice, "I don't imagine Mr. Hayward and Judge Carver have filled you in on me. To make it brief, they were both my wife's trustees. Did you ever hear of the Martyns of Hatch's Cove? The ship-building and lime-stone dynasty?"

"Who hasn't?"

"My wife was Valerie Martyn. She was left an orphan in her teens, and the Haywards and Carvers were more family to her than any of her cousins. I had to be approved of by them before I could even begin to *look* serious." He smiled, as if at a young and happy time. "I should add that they couldn't consider me a fortune hunter, because my own family's coal and steel interests in Pennsylvania were moderately impressive."

"Where did you from Pennsylvania and Valerie Martyn from Maine ever meet?"

"In London," he said, and we both laughed. "But I already knew Maine as a youngster, when my family summered on Mt. Desert. I loved the coast, especially, the long wild fierce stretches of it to the east. I could see nothing more ideal than to settle down with Valerie on a headland facing three thousand miles of ocean, live as good a life as possible in the world today, with children, books, my studies and research, music, the sea." He shrugged and the curtain of ice slipped over his face again. Whenever this change appeared he was a totally different person. His intensely blue eyes saw me without interest, and shifted beyond me. After a moment he said in a colorless voice, "To make a long story short, my wife died in an accident three years ago, and our first and only child, a boy two years old, was injured at the same time, both physically and mentally."

I couldn't pretend to eat any longer. I laid down my fork. "I'm sorry," I said. It sounded pale and feeble. "Is that the child—"

"Yes. He's five now."

"I haven't had any experience with children who—"

My face burning, myself on the edge of desperation, I began again. "Mr. Morgan, I thought I could handle this job because I've earned my pocket money by taking care of children ever since I was fourteen. I helped to put myself through business school in Boston by my earnings. But I've never handled a handicapped child. I don't know if I could."

"Let me assure you that you can handle Tim. He will be madly in love with you at first sight, and then you can do anything with him."

I felt only slightly better. He went on, "Tim wears braces and it's a simple matter to learn how to put them on and take them off. The brain damage is—well, Tim's a personable little boy, good to look at and to be with. The specialist in Boston tells me that he is probably at the peak of his powers right now, at five; and I can only hope that he'll be the same sunny five-year-old for the rest of his life. It's a strange situation," he added matter-of-factly, "when a man hopes devoutly to outlive his child."

"In your case it's understandable," I said. I was still upset, all the more because I wanted to take the job. As if he read my mind he said, "In a few years it will become noticeable that Tim is slower than other boys his age. But for now—well, he's not too different from any other five-year-old, only much nicer than most." His smile was at once persuasive and appealing. "Please come and give us a try."

It took all my Yankee reserve to keep me from blurting out, "Oh yes, I'll come!" Instead I returned his smile and said, "My brother and his wife would like very much to meet you. Would you go there for coffee?"

13

"Certainly," he said promptly. "I want to meet your family and I expect them to be very thorough about me."

Mindy was charming, her coffee superb, her strawberry mousse elegantly simple; but Elliot asked so many questions I was embarrassed. Rees Morgan seemed to take it as perfectly natural, and sometime during the hour I became aware that the two men had slipped into an entirely normal masculine conversation, the kind possible only when a couple of strange males take a liking to each other. Mindy and I took the dishes out to the kitchen and she shut the door with elaborate caution and then mouthed to me, "Wow!"

"*Wow* what?"

"He's so *nice!* And distinguished, and cosmopolitan, and intellectual, and let's see what else I can think of. Look, I *adore* Elliot, but I immediately turned into Cleopatra when that man came through the door. No, not Cleopatra, but somebody lovely and heart-breaking and fatally female."

I was laughing. "Yes, he's nice. I know exactly what you mean. He also lives as far away from everything as he can possibly get, out on the edge of a cliff. He doesn't have close friends who come there, and I must expect to do my socializing elsewhere."

"With him for a boss who needs a friend?" demanded Mindy. "He'd be friend enough for *me*. And the way he looks at you already—"

"And he has a retarded child," I said. "In braces."

She ran out of words for an open-mouthed moment. Then she said, "Difficult?"

"He says not. I told him I had no training."

Mindy blew upward hard enough to lift her soft curly bangs. "Are you going to try it, Caro?"

"Yes," I said.

In a little while Mr. Morgan left. When I had told him I'd take the job, I felt as if I'd lifted a ten-ton granite boulder from his shoulders, the way he looked. "Timmy will be frantic with delight, but Jason and I will try to contain ourselves," he said. "We'll merely simmer. When can you come?"

"I have another week at the bank," I said. "I'm breaking in my replacement. I can start—oh, a week from next Monday? I can make the trip on Sunday afternoon, if there's a bus."

"We'll drive you up," Elliot said.

"Good!" said Rees Morgan. "Get there in time for lunch on Sunday. You can meet my son, and see where your sister will be living. I assure you, it's not a bleak raven-haunted castle clinging to the edge of a cliff, all honeycombed with secret passages and with a locked room that flashes a mysterious light at night." We all laughed and he looked modestly pleased. "Maybe I should write suspense stories instead of sociological monographs," he said.

And so the evening ended, and with it a whole section of my life fell away like a section of shore weakened in a hurricane. An earlier piece had gone when my mother died, another when my father died; the wonder was so many Carolines existed—no matter how many disappeared, there was always a Caroline left. Now Paul's Caro and the bank's Miss Brewster had just disappeared, and I was on my way to be born a new Caro-

15

line, so I was temporarily in a sort of unborn state.

Paul's mother called me up in mid-week. She was a plump, very pretty little woman who'd wept ceaselessly during the trial. Now she was even more breathless and agitated than usual. "I hear you're going away!"

"Yes, Mrs. Rideout, to a new job."

"How can you go so far from Paul? When he hears about this he'll be just sick!"

"There's nothing I can do for Paul by staying here. I'm sorry, but that's the truth."

"You can see him every Sunday. I'd gladly stay home and give you young people the chance."

I was burning hot, but sweat was chilly running down my back under my dress. "Mrs. Rideout, you know Paul and I have broken off." I felt so sorry for her, but I was suffocating with this needless sense of shame.

"You mean you're really *deserting* him? *Now?* You haven't thought over what a terrible thing you've done to him?" She rushed on like a spring flood. "After all, he got into this horrible trouble because of you, wanting to give you nice things, to take you out in an expensive car—"

Out of self-defense I stopped listening. It wouldn't lessen my hurt and the humiliation if I shouted at Mrs. Rideout that Paul had lied and lied. Paul was all she had. Maybe she'd helped to make him what he was, but it wouldn't help *me* any to tell her so.

When she had stopped listing my sins against her boy I said gently, "Mrs. Rideout, you know I'm not the right girl for Paul, and he knows it, and I know it. I hope he'll find her some day and I wish him all the luck in the world." And he'll need it, I thought. Because he's

16

got nothing else going for him, not even himself. At the other end there was an ear-shattering clash as the telephone was replaced and I turned away, sick with the longing to escape.

[3]

In early June the apple trees and lilacs were full of blossoms and birds. We walked among them, Timothy and I and Tristan the golden cat. It was hard to believe, looking down at Tim's swiftly turning red head, that he would never be any older than he was now; that even when he was gray-headed he would still be this child who talked to me so eagerly. His eyes were a glistening sea-blue behind black lashes; freckles shone like endearing little gold stars across cheekbones and nose that were a baby reflection of his father's, and the perfection of his mouth delighted me.

"Enjoy him as he is," his father had said. "With no regrets or reservations." And I did.

"That's cedar waxwings eating the apple blossoms," said Tim.

"I see them. They're in that tree that looks like a big dish of pink strawberry ice cream."

"Does it *taste* like pink strawberry ice cream to them?"

"I'll bet it does," I said. "But it wouldn't to us."

"No, because Jason said worms taste like roast beef to

robins, but I ate one and it didn't taste like roast beef to me."

"What did it taste like?"

"It tasted like worms."

"Logical," I said.

"Logical," Tim repeated with pleasure. "Logical, logical, logical." He chanted it under his breath.

The pay I was getting seemed a blatant deception on somebody. I was with Tim all day, certainly; but I could read or knit or simply sun myself while he played. We ate breakfast and lunch together, served by Jason in some pleasant place out of doors when the weather was fine. We liked the little terrace where we could sit under the apple trees and look across the green lawn, and the rose hedge at the rim of the cliff, to the glittering sea and the lobster boats. On the lee side of the house, we could watch birds splashing and feeding, and listen to the chorus from the woods that made a leafy green wall all about the place. Mr. Morgan sometimes appeared unexpectedly in a break from his work, but half the time I never knew whether he was around Bellwood somewhere, or had driven off early to Bangor to work in the big library there.

I'd been rather intimidated by the idea of a manservant, but any question as to my attitude toward Jason had been skillfully resolved by Jason himself. He was small, immaculate, and as light and quick as an acrobat, his bony face ageless, his black hair like patent leather. He was devoted to Mr. Morgan and Tim, and if I suited them I suited him.

"Come on, Caro," Tim said. "I'll show you where Daddy works."

"But I've already seen the library," I said.

"No, I mean the other place, the stone house in the woods." He looked back at me, bright and eager as a little terrier even if he couldn't run like one. "It's down there." He pointed across the lawn toward the wall of trees, and after a moment I saw the dark opening splashed with sunlight. "Come on, Caro," he teased.

"All right." I started after him, and the yellow cat rose and stretched himself and followed me. *Paul, Paul,* I tested myself. Nothing, not even remorse, and not even guilt because of no remorse. I was happy. The thrushes sang in chimes.

"Miss Brewster, Miss Brewster!" It was Jason's voice sharp in the sunny hush. I stopped, but Tim with an effort went a little faster, and he reached the dark hollow among the trees. Jason was hurrying across the lawn toward us, in his shirtsleeves, a cleaning cloth in his hands. "Don't go that way. *Tim!*"

Tim stopped. "I want to show her where Daddy works."

"You know how your father feels about that," Jason said. Gently he turned the boy back. As we walked on either side of the child, holding his hands, Jason said, "Mr. Morgan has strict rules about his study, Miss Brewster. No one is to go down that path without invitation."

I felt myself blushing. "I hope you don't think I was prying, Jason."

"Not at all, Miss Brewster," he assured me. "It's simply something that hadn't come up yet. That is the only part of the establishment that is out of bounds; a scholar needs an inviolable retreat."

"Of course," I agreed. "I promise you, I shan't even *look* toward the path." We both smiled.

"Now any time you'd like to go down onto the beach," Jason said, "I'll carry Tim down the path. It's a bit steep, but we're used to it, aren't we, Tim?"

"Can we go to the beach now?" Tim asked at once, well over his disappointment.

"If Miss Brewster wishes."

"I do wish," I said. "I've only looked down at it over the rose hedge."

A shadow passed over Jason's face. "Heights like that don't bother you, Miss? They make me a bit queasy, especially with the rocks below."

"I wasn't especially fascinated with the view straight down," I admitted.

"None of us like it, even the boy. Well, the way down to the sand isn't half bad."

"Let's go, Caro," Tim squeezed my hand. "I got new trunks. Blue!"

"Oh, I have to see *them*. Let's go change."

"And I can sit in the water and have my braces off!"

Though the straight drop from the cliff beyond the rose hedge was a steep one to ledges below, the meandering diagonal track we followed after we went through the gate was easy to travel.

Tim sat in the gently swirling water, free of his braces. To keep an eye on him, I confined my swimming to heading in toward him again and again. His laughter rose like a young rooster's crowing as I paddled into shallow water and said I was a crab wanting to eat his toes.

Afterwards, as I was drying him on the big beach towel, he kept wiggling his feet and said, "I hate those old braces."

"Some day you won't have to wear them."

21

"Some day" to a five-year-old is "never." He rolled out his lower lip and watched dolefully as I fastened them. He shrugged off my assistance with his sweater and I reached for my beach coat, looking up at the path to see if Jason was coming. But I saw, instead of his dapper little jockey figure, a taller one on the diagonal track. I felt a jolt in my midriff; it was Mr. Morgan, and I hadn't even known he was at home. I wondered how long he had been watching us and, as a woman does at such times, I ran a lightning check of my overall appearance. Relieved rather than vain to know I was presentable in a swim suit, I pulled on my beach coat and said to Tim, "Look who's here."

"Daddy!" shrieked Tim, forgetting his bad mood. As Rees Morgan approached us, I was ready to blush at my self-importance for believing he'd noticed *me*. He had eyes only for the boy, and I looked away, moved and depressed, and suddenly so lonely I could hardly bear it. For the first time since I'd come to Bellwood my new serenity was flawed, and I saw myself as a woman who had failed in love and would always be alone. Even if I tried again, I would make wrong choices, and each time the loneliness and defeat and sense of inadequacy would be worse.

Everyone else had something; Tim and his father had each other; Jason lived out his life for them. I was an outsider and always would be.

"Miss Brewster."

I glanced around. He was looking at me with concern. "You look sad," he said. "Are you unhappy here?"

"No, no," I said quickly, managing a smile. "I was thinking, that's all. And I'm probably hungry. That always makes me sad."

"Then we can relieve your depression very quickly. I was afraid you were thinking of going away."

Tim suddenly grabbed me fiercely around the legs. "She's never going away, are you, Caro?"

I was touched and embarrassed, and Mr. Morgan saved me.

"Come on, son, let's take her home and feed her so she'll cheer up."

[4]

I had dinner with Rees Morgan that night, in the glassed-in porch that looked out over the sea straight to Spain. Candle flames barely flickered in the still air that brought a scent of honeysuckle through the open windows. Moths bumped softly against the screens. It was a simple meal, but it was most elegantly cooked and served, with wine and with piano music floating dreamily from somewhere out of sight; Rubinstein playing Chopin nocturnes. It was like a setting for a play, but it was real; people *did* live like this, Jason with his white coat and deft hands and silent feet existed, and Rees Morgan existed; oh, he certainly did. *Paul*, I tested myself, and felt again the shock of realizing he was in prison, and the familiar ache of regret. But not for long. I couldn't dwell on it here, even if I'd wanted to.

After dinner we had our coffee in the living room, where a small fire burned. I remember a great vase of white rose-scented peonies, and how sometimes a petal dropped to the polished table. Tim was asleep long ago, Jason had retired to his own quarters above the kitchen. Outside the night was silent as only the coast can be silent; the hush of the sea was like a hush laid over all the world. Above the mantel there was a portrait of a girl with fair hair and a delicate narrow face. In the shifting light the eyes seemed to move, watching first one of us and then the other. Rees didn't refer to the portrait, so I tried not to notice it.

"Do you feel sad now?" Rees asked me with a smile.

"No," I said.

"Happy?"

"I don't know," I said honestly. "Happy is too simple a word. That's for playing in the sun like Tim, swimming when the water's just right, settling down with a good book when it's raining outside, making a perfect run down a perfect slope."

"And this isn't like any of those things."

"No . . . you see, those things are *touchable*. You recognize the joy because you've felt it before, and you'll feel it again. But this is different. It's like a dream when you know you're dreaming and it won't last." I was embarrassed. "Listen to me. It must be the wine."

"*In vino veritas*," he said lightly. The firelight came and went on his face. "We'll have other evenings like this. Many of them, I hope."

"But none exactly like this."

"No, you're right. This is the first. But each one should be in a class of its own, don't you think? . . . You know, it's very pleasant for me as well as Tim, having you here, and Jason's positively outdoing himself. Our last lady was suspicious of him. She'd never encountered such perfection before."

"Perhaps she thought he was really a robot," I said. "Or a secret agent, or—let's see, what else does TV provide?" We both laughed. "By the way," he said, "Jason told me about Tim taking you to my study."

"He explained that it's out of bounds. He said a scholar must have an inviolable retreat."

"Jason's language is a lot more high-flown than mine. It's simply that I need a place where I can be sure of being absolutely undisturbed. It also serves as a repository for my rare books, and some valuable old manuscripts that wouldn't otherwise fare very well by the sea. The climate is controlled as efficiently as possible. I wish I could do the same for the house." He got up and went to the small grand piano, and ran a scale with one hand. "For this we have to import a tuner from Bangor several times a year. But if I kept it in the study I'd be defeating my own purpose."

"I hope you play it sometimes."

"I do by spells. If you want to amuse yourself that way anytime, help yourself."

"I wouldn't have the courage to perform 'To a Wild Rose' on that beautiful instrument. At least not the way I played it at the age of twelve. Even my mother could hardly stand hearing me, and she was prejudiced in my favor."

He laughed and came away from the piano. "Do you like music?"

"I love it, but I don't know if that's the right word any more than *happy* was, a while ago."

"You're very meticulous," he said. "Do you always look for the right word? No generalizations?"

"I don't want to misrepresent myself, that's all. Of course Elliot calls it being relentlessly literal. . . . I love some music because it makes me peaceful, or cheerful, or ready to dance or laugh. But some makes me want to cry, or at least makes me very sad and nostalgic for I don't know what, or it tells me that there's a whole world of experience I'll never know. It must be the wine," I said angrily; "I haven't talked this much about myself ever since—" The first knowing of Paul, I almost said. As if he knew, he nodded.

"Oh, the wine's worn off long ago," he said, "and I'm glad you feel like talking. There's been a sad lack of conversation around here for a long time. I'm going to say one more thing, and then I'm going to do a few hours' work." He stood looking down at me in the glow from the fading fire. From up behind his head the portrait watched me. "I won't be like Tim and demand you stay forever. I can't hope for that. But I can hope that you'll stay a long time with us."

"I hope so too," I said huskily.

"When I started down to the shore today, and saw you there drying Tim off, for a moment it was as if nothing had ever happened three years ago, and we'd all been here safe and sound ever since, she and Tim and I."

There was nothing I could say to that. After a moment which seemed to go on forever, in which he appeared to look far beyond me into a past that was also a future that would never be, I said awkwardly, "Goodnight," and went out into the hall.

"Goodnight," he said absently.

If the wine at dinner had stimulated me, the effect had quickly gone and I felt tired and depressed as I went up the stairs.

I went in and looked at Tim. He always slept hard

and restlessly, as if he were playing in his dreams with other boys or with the rough, whiskery pup he had told me about one morning. Tris sprawled on the foot of the bed, purring at my presence; he was a very amiable cat. He lay draped over my arm like a fur piece as I straightened out the clothes with one hand. When I put him down again he collapsed as only a cat can do. Then I went through the connecting bathroom to my own room.

Jason, though unseen, was everywhere; my bedside light was on, my bed turned down, and there was a Lowestoft bowl of black cherries beside my book. As I stood looking at it I heard the front door shut softly below, and I switched off my light and went to the window. I saw a flashlight moving across the lawn to the particular rhythm of a man's long stride, toward the place where in daylight the dark opening would show.

My depression deepened. I couldn't explain it any more than I could explain my guilt about Paul. I wondered if I'd made a serious mistake in coming here. The atmosphere of Bellwood, Rees Morgan himself—wasn't the whole thing too great a contrast to the places and people I was used to, and especially after this recent sordid business? I'd always kept my poetic tendencies and romantic imagination well in check, but in my present bruised state I could very well conceive an emotional crush on a man like Rees Morgan. And I didn't want to be that sort of imbecile!

Furiously I wished he'd been a decent but humdrum personality, maybe a little pudgy, with chronic foot trouble or indigestion, a nine-to-five position in Ellsworth or Bangor, and a tearing urgency to get to his evening paper after dinner each night.

My depression went in the night like a coastal fog before a change in the wind, and didn't come back the next day. I basked in the sunny, detached peace of life at Bellwood.

We had worked out an arrangement where I would have a free afternoon once a week. It would begin right after lunch and go on till whenever I chose to go to bed that night. Every four weeks I'd have a long weekend at home. Now, settling into this tranquil existence in which the hours dropped as soundlessly as the white peony petals, I was glad that the first long weekend was still three and a half weeks away, and in the meantime I refused to think about it. But here was my first afternoon coming up, on Wednesday.

Rees Morgan ate breakfast with Tim and me that morning, on the flagged terrace under the apple trees.

"Now, Miss Brewster," Mr. Morgan began over his second cup of coffee.

"Call her Caro, Daddy," Tim urged. "I do."

"You're a privileged person, Tim," said his father. He smiled at me. His eyes were the color of the sea behind him. "What are you going to do with your afternoon?"

"I don't know," I said. "I hadn't thought about it. I might write letters, read, swim. But I don't think I *need* an afternoon off. Must I take it?"

"No," said Tim loudly. His father shook his head at him. To me he said, "Yes, you must. It's important for you to get entirely away from the house at least once a week. We want to keep you—that's why you must have a change from us."

"Couldn't I disappear into the woods for the afternoon, just wander and explore by myself? Or go for a long walk along the shore?"

He shook his head. "I'd prefer you didn't go off into any strange territory alone. I have about a hundred acres, left in a wilderness state because I'm by way of being a conservationist, and they aren't marked for walking. You could easily become lost. And the shore line is very rugged; there are places where you can't get past the foot of the cliffs when the tide is high."

Gentle as his manner was, he made me feel not much older than Tim. I poured coffee I didn't want, and took another warm muffin from the covered dish; I didn't want that either. My cheeks were flaming. I couldn't look up from my plate.

"I'm also by way of being a dictator, I'm afraid," he said. "You'll have to forgive me that, but I'm responsible to your family for your safety." He waited, and I didn't look up from my plate. I was wretched with embarrassment.

"*Caro?*" he said softly, and my head flew up. He laughed, and Tim did without knowing why.

"That's better. Now, there's a car for you to drive, and Somerset is ten miles to the west of us. It has a beautiful little harbor full of lobstermen's boats and yachts, a summer theatre, good shops, painters, musicians, very friendly local people. I think you'll be able to find something to do and see."

None of it impressed me, but obviously I was under orders, so I put the best face possible on it. "Well, I do need some things," I said cheerfully, "and I do like to look at boats. And I do like to investigate strange towns where the natives are friendly. I'm beginning to look forward to it."

Mr. Morgan approved, and I was ridiculously pleased by that. Tim sulked at his plate, but as we began our morning activies he seemed to forget about it. He and I ate a picnic lunch out on the ledges beside the pool, and I told him stories of being a little girl and visiting my grandparents. He seemed to long for other children, and couldn't get enough of their adventures. So I drew on Elliot's life too, and everything else I could think of.

All was peaceful till we went upstairs to get ready for his nap. When he was settled in his bed with the various stuffed animals who kept him company when Tristan was out, he gazed up at me with unblinking intensely blue eyes and said, "Don't go away."

"Darling, I'm not going *away*," I said. "Just to town for the afternoon. And Jason's going to take you down to the beach to play, remember?"

"I want *you* to take me." Without any apparent effort on his part his eyes shimmered with tears.

"I'll be back before you go to bed," I promised. I had not promised his father that I'd stay away all evening, only that I'd get away from Bellwood completely for the afternoon. "And if you've been a good boy I'll bring you something."

"What?" he said suspiciously.

"I don't know yet, but when I see just the right thing I'll know that's what Tim would like."

"No you won't," he said. "You'll go away and you won't come back."

"Why won't you believe me when I promise I'll come back?" I asked, and then thought, Poor little devil, he can't understand; this is where his retardation must truly show up. He couldn't imagine even a near future, because only the present was real to him. Yet he enjoyed stories about me as a little girl; he'd asked intelligent questions about how tall I was, did I have hair like a girl in one of his books, was I ever spanked? It was as if he could really *imagine* me as a small child like himself. It was all very curious. But his father had told me of brain-damaged children who were capable of great mental feats.

"Look," I said to his worried, wet-eyed little face. "When your daddy goes away you know he'll come back, don't you?" He nodded soberly. "Well, then, you know *I'll* come back."

"*She* didn't," he said.

"You mean Mrs. Partridge?"

"Not *her*," Tim said with masculine impatience. "I knew she was going away. I said goodbye to her and gave her flowers." He yawned suddenly, and his eyelids drooped.

"I'll see you by and by, Tim," I said softly.

"Mm." He gave me a glazed look, and then he was off. Relieved, I tiptoed out of the room.

The car for my use had been brought around from the carriage house and it waited in the drive outside the front door. It was a cocky little MG and Jason obviously expected me to show ecstasy. I tried to, but I felt a little sick. He thought I was apprehensive.

"Don't you think you can drive it, Miss? The stick shift is very simple. Look, I'll show you."

"Oh yes, I can drive it. I've driven one just like it." Up to the top of Cadillac on Mt. Desert; out to the wild surf on Pemaquid Point. To Friendship to watch the sloops race. To dances, auctions, festivals, concerts, and just to park.

I feel like a bird when I open her up, Paul said. Paul in prison. It was incredible. [And in June too. . . . He deserved it, he should have known better, and he had to go through this alone, if he was to have any chance at all. But I couldn't help feeling sadness at the waste.]

"It's a marvelous little car, Jason," I said, sliding behind the wheel.

His smile came out like the sun. "That's fine, Miss. Have a good afternoon," he said. "The gates will be open when you get to them."

They were; in fact they opened as I approached them, some ten minutes later, along the narrow road winding through Mr. Morgan's small wilderness. They were heavy wrought-iron affairs, controlled from the house, swinging back without sound from their solid cement posts. After I drove through they closed as silently. There was a bell set in one of the posts to press for entrance.

I turned right to go to Somerset. For about a mile a six-foot brick wall ran along beside me. I stopped the car where the wall turned a corner into the deep woods. As the brilliant noonday sun struck down through the spruces and some huge old pines, I saw that the wall wasn't as tall on the side; apparently it was high on the road boundary to discourage picnickers. A little way beyond the side wall an old wood road lost itself in the trees.

I started up again and drove on toward Somerset.

[5]

Somerset, like the other harbor towns along the coast, had its own individuality; a harbor steep-shored with massive slabs and chunks of tawny rock, and wharves taller and heavier-built than the ones I knew around Limerock, showing that the tide was higher and stronger here. The summer people weren't yet in full force so Main Street wasn't crowded, and I poked around in the gift shops, visited the library, bought myself a few things I needed, and then went down to the Public Landing to sit on a bench and contemplate the harbor like a tourist. In fact, I rather felt like one; free, not lonely, not knowing anyone or being known by anyone, and not caring. Watching a blue sloop skim gracefully among the moorings, the activity on a wind-jammer tied up a little distance from me, and then a lobster boat coming swiftly up the long harbor with the bow waves flashing back from the stem, I felt that a major miracle had taken place in my life when I answered Rees Morgan's ad.

There'd been a bad moment when I saw the car in the driveway, but that was long gone.

A tiny dinghy scooting around under a red sail made me think of Tim, and I decided to go back to one of the gift shops where I had seen toy boats. As I walked across the broad landing I came face to face with a large old barn of a building, decorated with the words SAIL LOFT in faded gold letters. There were big windows let into the lower floor, and a hanging sign over the door announced GALLERY . . . COFFEE . . . GIFTS.

I went in. It seemed empty at first, though I smelled fresh coffee and baking from an invisible kitchen, and I wandered around looking at the paintings on the walls and the shelves of gifts at one end, most of them hand-made. As I examined the little dories that came in different sizes, a woman's voice called from behind me, "Can you find something there you'd like?"

She came between the tables, tying on a fresh apron, a stocky blonde woman with a squarish tanned face and a pleasant smile. I held out the dory I'd selected and she said, "Aren't those the cutest things? One of the fishermen whittles them in the winter time. He does real well out of them too. . . . I'll put it in a box for you."

"That coffee smells good," I said. "I'll have a cup, I guess."

"Would you like something with it? Fresh rhubarb turnovers?"

"Mmm!" I said. I was suddenly starved. We both laughed, and I took a table by one of the big windows that looked out on the harbor. When she brought the coffee, and two still-warm turnovers on a blue willow plate, she said, "You staying around here or just visiting for the day?"

"Oh, I'm staying around here. At Bellwood," I added

35

experimentally; I hadn't said the name aloud to anyone till now. It sounded very nice, I thought. Of course if she'd never heard of the place the effect would be spoiled.

"*Bellwood?*" The smile went so quickly out of her eyes that they looked like two blue glass marbles. Her face became stolid. Adjusting the bachelor's buttons in the bowl on the table, she said with what I guessed was a careful indifference, "You a guest there? Don't tell me Rees Morgan's about to be married."

"His affairs are no business of mine," I said coldly. "I'm concerned only with the little boy."

"Oh, you're *working* there." She couldn't act indifferent any longer; her face was very much alive now with a kind of feverish eagerness. "How long have you been there?"

"Just since Sunday. This is my first afternoon off." I sipped coffee and stared out at the harbor, hoping she'd go away. From the corner of my eye I could see her there, or rather the bright stripes of her apron; I could *feel* that eagerness, charging the atmosphere with a disturbing energy. I knew I shouldn't have come in here; I didn't know why I knew it. Yet I couldn't get up and walk out, leaving the food untouched, the dory not yet wrapped. I couldn't get up and walk out without knowing why a very few accidental words had this effect on us both. The Brewster nose, I thought in resignation.

I turned my head and looked at her. She flinched, and then blushed. "I guess you think I'm nosy," she said. "The fact is, I'm interested because I worked out there for a few months. I guess you're my replacement. I'm Phyllis Partridge."

I heard myself stammering. "I wouldn't have come in if I—"

"Don't worry, I left under my own steam. I was glad to. It was over a month ago but I still have dreams about it now and then. Bad ones."

"Did you have trouble with Tim?" I asked. "Or was it because it's so far from everything, so quiet and cut off? That wouldn't be everybody's cup of tea, I know. But to me it's fine. It couldn't be better."

"You haven't been a week yet," she said. "You got any relatives around here?"

"No, I come from Limerock. I'll be going back there every fourth weekend."

"You'll be heading for home before your month's up," she said defiantly.

"Won't you have a cup of coffee with me?" I asked her, with all the charm I could gather. Her glance was ironic, as if she saw through it.

"All right." She went and got it. A young girl came in just then, heading for the kitchen like a homing pigeon, and Mrs. Partridge called to her, "It's all yours for the next ten minutes or so, Sharon. This'll be the first time I've had a bite since I started the baking."

"Okay!" Sharon's voice floated back. "Hey! Lemon-cheese tarts! Can I have one?"

"You can have a couple." She turned to me with a good-natured grin. "That kid has hollow legs. But she's a fine little waitress, Merry Sunshine herself." She passed a package of cigarettes to me, I shook my head, and she lit one for herself.

"All right," I said pleasantly, "Now tell me why I'll be heading for home before the month's up."

"I don't know what it'll be with you. But it'll be

something. I can only tell you why *I* left. I had to, or I'd have gone out of my mind. One thing, it was lonesome, you guessed that; I was only ten miles from home but it felt like a thousand. Once you go through those gates it's like losing yourself in space, or . . . remember those Twilight Zone shows on TV?"

I nodded, and she said gloomily, "I never wanted to miss one, but they always scared me half to death. And whenever I'd go back to Bellwood after my day off I'd feel as if I'd got lost in one of 'em. That Jason!" She shuddered. "It's not natural for a man to move so quiet and so fast from one place to another. You never knew where he was going to pop up. And as for *him*—"

Rees. She didn't have to say his name. *He's a wonderful man,* I wanted to say, but that would have dammed the flow. Feeling like a traitor to him, I said, "What about him? What's he really like?"

She frowned into her coffee cup. "He was always polite. As if he couldn't bother to be anything else, because he was walking around up there somewhere and I was down under his feet. . . . He wouldn't go out of his way to step on a cricket. It was that kind of politeness. I was just something that was *there*." Her face flushed, and she said doggedly, "Not that I expected him, a man like that, handsome as he is and educated and rich, to make a pass at me! Only to recognize me as another human being, if not a woman. . . . But that wasn't the main thing."

"Tim?"

"Oh, no!" She looked up at me then and smiled. "He's a nice little kid. Retarded kids often are a lot sweeter than some normal little brats. Though Tim's not bad enough so you'd notice it much yet."

"No," I agreed. A party of men and women came in, and Sharon went to meet them. They sat down at a table by the next window, talking and joking with the girl.

Phyllis Partridge spoke in a low rapid voice. "It was like being in a straitjacket all around. Nobody to talk to but the youngster for all week, and I couldn't have someone come out to call on me of an evening once in a while, when I'd be all soul alone from the time I put Tim to bed till I went myself. . . . I'm a widow," she explained swiftly. "I have friends. *Adults,* not kids who'd wreck the place. What was the harm to have someone come to play cards sometimes, or even to play records on the stereo and dance a little? The butlers and maids in the big places entertain their friends like that when the family's gone, and I wasn't hired as a *maid.*"

I nodded sympathetically. "And for my time off I couldn't have my dates come and get me and bring me home," she hurried on. "Perfectly decent, respectable men couldn't come to the door for me and deliver me back again. . . . And sometimes I was real nervous driving home late. . . . Those woods between the gate and the house were the worst part of the trip. I tried to tell *him* once, and he said he'd have Jason meet me at the gate and drive up with me." She shuddered again. "I'd sooner have Dracula!" Her voice started to rise, and she glanced quickly at the next table and went on in a lower tone. "What did he think my friends would do, case the joint and then break in later? I'll tell you, I was some mad. . . . But that wasn't all."

How could there be more? It sounded as if she'd been in a constant ferment of indignation from the start. "It was the dreams I had. I never had so many nightmares in my life. I'd wake up drenched with sweat, thinking I'd heard someone crying out, once even a shriek. I'd rush in to Tim but he'd be sleeping sweetly, only once *he* heard something too." She rubbed her arms, where the gooseflesh showed. "Or else it would be too cussed quiet in that house. Unless he was playing the piano, that creepy kind of long-hair music, you know. And that was worse than the quiet."

"Well, I guess the whole place was wrong for you. You like to be where there's something going on, and I'd say this was perfect," I said.

"You're right, I love it. I manage the place for my brother-in-law, and bake the pastry, and I'm happy as a clam at high water."

"This pastry is marvelous. You belong here, all right." My sympathy was honest; I knew it was torture for some people to be quiet, to be alone. Paul was like that. Silence—or Rees Morgan's "creepy kind of long-hair music" falling through that silence like the peony petals —was as much torment to them as incessant racket was to somebody else. No wonder she'd had bad dreams. I said, "You suffered from a form of claustrophobia, I'd say."

"Well, it was *something*," she said gloomily. "But the work was easy and the pay was good. I liked the youngster. I kept hanging on, the way anybody does, thinking things would maybe be better. Then one day—oh, boy!" She stared out at the harbor, shaking her head. "You may think you've been bawled out by some experts in your life. But the day when Rees Morgan lights into you, you'll know that until then everything else has been just a little kind advice. *That's* when I left. I couldn't get out of there quick enough." Her eyes grew wide with astonishment and outrage. "And I didn't do anything so terrible! It wasn't anything I'd been told not to do! It certainly didn't harm the boy!"

At the other table the women were exclaiming over the gifts they'd chosen; there was a good deal of laughing and joking as if the two couples had been close friends for years. Phyllis Partridge picked up her coffee cup in both hands, and when she drank from it I heard it bump against her teeth. "It was a lovely day. Too hot for April. You get those still days sometimes, when the ocean's like a big blue glass, you know?" I nodded and she went on, "I got Jason to take Tim down to the beach for me, to play in the sand. Well, the sun got so hot I was afraid we'd both burn, so I lugged him over onto the rocks, in the shade of the cliff. You know, where it drops down steep from the lawn. There was a tide-water pool there, and he was sailing shells around and talking to himself the way he does, happy as could be, and I was reading. It was *nice*," she said to me indignantly. Her eyes watered suddenly and grew bloodshot. "Then the *Marster* came. Him and his bloody stuck-up ways. He was so mad he was feather-white. But never a word to me then, no, he didn't trust himself, I guess. Just lugged Tim back up the path to the house with me trundling after and my stomach heaving. He still didn't say anything till the boy was in bed that night." She lit a cigarette with a shaking hand. "Look at me, even now, two months later! You talk about being skinned alive by an artist! There wasn't any blood, but the raw places still hurt."

It took all my will power to keep my eyes earnestly on hers. I simply couldn't imagine Rees Morgan's deep, gentle voice saying cruel things, attacking a well-meaning woman's character, and humiliating her so that she trembled now to remember it. I couldn't imagine his dark strong face transformed into a mask of icy rage. I could only see it as I had seen it turned toward Tim, and I realized with shock that I was imagining that look of tenderness turned on *me*.

For a moment I heard nothing, saw nothing but that. Then gradually Phyllis Partridge's voice became distinct again. I seemed to have made a remark because she was saying angrily, "But couldn't he have told me *politely* he didn't want Tim on the rocks? Couldn't he have just said, 'I'd rather you didn't take him over there again'?" This was all delivered in a low, passionate tone as she leaned across the table toward me.

Young Sharon was being gently kidded by the men as she served coffee, and some new people were coming in. Their greetings all sounded so ordinary; they were like signals from a cheerful, sane, far-off world. Because I was sure this woman, if not insane, was on the border-line.

"But *no!*" she said in that hushed, yet penetrating voice. "What it boiled down to, was 'You are never, as long as you are in my employ, to take that boy to that place again.' Well, I tried to defend myself. I mean, I have my pride. I said, 'Mr. Morgan, I wouldn't let Tim walk on the rocks in his braces; I carried him,' and he said, 'That makes no difference. He is never to be anywhere near those ledges under any circumstances.' Then he said—he said—" Her face turned an ugly, blotchy red. "He said, 'You stupid woman, whatever possessed you even to *think* of it?' And I—" She drew a long breath and smiled slyly and coldly past my shoulder at nothing; I thought with a chill, she *is* mad. "I said, 'Mr. Morgan, I don't know whatever possessed me to take this job!' Thank God he never knew what I felt like inside. Like throwing up, or bawling, or both. I could hardly wait to get out of there. After what I saw in his eyes down there, I was scared to be in the same house with him."

Mad, mad, mad, I thought behind my deceptive face. And I wanted to be out of here and back there with him, or at least back in the house that was full of him even when he wasn't in it. She was staring at me and I was afraid it was all on my face. I gave her a crooked little smile and said, "Tim brought you flowers when you left."

"Yes." She groped for a handkerchief, and wiped her eyes and blew her nose. "He said, 'Philly, didn't we have a nice time at the pool yesterday? I wish you wouldn't ever go away, Philly.' Poor little boy. What'll happen to him I don't like to think."

"If Mr. Morgan cares for anyone, it's Tim," I said.

"There's all kinds of caring," she said. "Some isn't good. It's worse than not caring."

I could agree with her there, even though we were talking about different cases. "Well," I said, "I'm sorry you had such a bad time out there. But this must make up for it, a little."

"Oh yes. Lucky for me my sister got pregnant and couldn't run the kitchen this summer." She laughed, beginning to recover. "They feel lucky too; they've been waiting a long time for this."

"Then it worked out well all around."

"I hope it works out well for you," she said darkly. "One thing, you'll know enough not to take Tim over to the ledges."

"Yes, I'm glad you warned me about that."

"And if you get to having those dreams—" She sprang up. "Here, let me get you fresh coffee—I've kept you from drinking that."

I protested, but she took the little pot and started away, straight into the path of a big young man in dirty white duck trousers and a striped jersey. He grinned at her. "Hi, Philly. Still spinning around like one of those dervishes, I see." He looked past her at me, and I smiled politely.

"Oh, Eric, this is the new girl out at Bellwood," she said. "Caroline Brewster, from down Limerock way. This is Eric Allenby. He's a summer complaint, but we like him just the same."

"You and your smiling insults," said Allenby. "Summer complaint indeed! I've been coming here twenty-five years and *you* never moved into Somerset till you were twelve, my girl. Hi," he said to me. "Can I sit down?" He was tanned darker than his yellow hair, and he had a wide grin and big white teeth. His eyes were a lighter blue than Rees Morgan's; a sunlit, innocent, youthful blue. True, I was younger than he was, but I felt a lot older, sitting there across from him; my experience with Paul had put years on me, and now my association with Rees Morgan and his tragedy was adding depth and dimension to my knowledge of life. And then this mad—well, at least neurotic—tirade that I'd had to listen to without showing my distaste. . . . Well, at least Eric Allenby was a pleasant change.

"How do you like it out there?" he was asking me.

44

"Very much."

"Philly thinks Morgan's the devil incarnate."

"Do you?"

"I don't know him, except by sight. Nobody does. I guess he was a retiring kind of guy even before his wife died, and now he's even more so. Handsome devil," he added with innocent admiration. "I remember when his wife died, there was this little cult sprang up, my mother was in it, all wanting to comfort him. You know, invite him to dinner, take him calves'-foot jelly—not really, but that was the idea. Well, whether they went to call or tried to get him on the telephone, they never got by Cerberus."

I laughed at that. "What a name for Jason."

"According to them, it fitted him perfectly. Anyway, they gave up. But the romantic mystery's still there, ready to flare up any time, and you're likely to find yourself the cynosure of all eyes, as they used to say in old novels."

"That won't worry me. I'll only be coming to town when it's absolutely necessary. I'm here today because Mr. Morgan insists that I leave the house and grounds on my time off."

"In a horror story," said Eric, "that would be when the mad scientist conducts his fiendish experiments."

"That's it!" I snapped my fingers. "What do you suppose he's making down there in the stone house?"

"Stone house?" he said at once, his head cocked. Instantly I was chilled and ashamed, as if Rees Morgan himself had heard me discussing him in this light, foolish manner.

"His air-conditioned library," I said off-handedly, "where he keeps his rare books." I welcomed Phyllis

Partridge back with the fresh coffee as if she were an old and valued friend. She had powdered her face and looked cheerful and healthy once more. She went off to give Sharon a hand with the customers, some of whom had just come in from sailing or from working aboard their boats in the harbor.

"Well, I'm glad he makes you leave the place and that this is the nearest town," said Eric. "Have you ever sailed?"

I'd sailed with Paul, about a hundred years ago. "Yes," I said reluctantly. "But—"

"We've got a Friendship sloop, an original. She's the fastest thing around here, by the way. Look, about once a week several of us sail in company with each other, race if there's a good wind, or go out to one of the islands and picnic and sail home by sunset or moonrise. If we go on a Wednesday sometime, will you go?"

"I—I—" I was stammering, all my poise gone. Don't be a fool, just say *No*, I told myself, but I'd never been able to be brutally frank even when it was necessary. I'd only been so with Paul, finally, for self-preservation.

"Of course you will!" he said jubilantly. "Look, I'll call you next Wednesday morning if it's a good sailing day, so you can come dressed for it. And if it's not fit for sailing we'll do something else. Now I've got to go; I see somebody looking for me."

He sprang up from the table and went out, greeting and being greeted from all sides, but without slowing down, and I wondered if his spontaneous departure were really a studied move to keep me from refusing him then and there. I saw him cross the public landing and join a big man who was very much like him except for graying hair, and they went down the ramp to the long float and dinghies. So there was someone after all. Maybe he *was* just what he seemed; a huge and enthusiastic boy, in spite of being at least twenty-five. How did it happen he wasn't in the Army? Pull? A perennial student, going from one graduate school to another? Anyway, I knew Rees Morgan, and I wasn't about to be swept off my feet by an overgrown setter, and when he called he'd find that out.

Phyllis Partridge was busy at the gift end when I paid Sharon and left. I was glad of that. When I went out I didn't think I'd ever go into the Sail Loft again.

I wished I could go home to Bellwood right now, but I'd only upset their arrangements; Tim would be having dinner with his father tonight, and I had no place there. I'd used up an hour or more on my shopping and harbor-viewing, another hour in the Sail Loft. So I went back to the library where there was an art exhibit going on, and studied every entry with close attention. I took out a summer card, because it might come in handy on my afternoons of enforced exile to spend some time choosing books.

I walked around to the movie theatre and examined the stills for the Coming Attractions, then over to the summer theatre in the Opera House and contemplated photographs of the actors. By being very deliberate and merely strolling from place to place, I finally reached a decent hour for eating, and had dinner in an unpretentious place where the specialty was seafood, and some fishermen ate at the counter. The baked haddock with lobster sauce was all anyone could ask. I saw Eric Allenby go by the window while I ate, but fortunately he was in animated, arm-waving conversation with another young man and didn't see me.

At last it was time to go home, if I was to see Tim before he went to bed at seven-thirty. The little car and I sped out of town as if we were taking off through star-sprinkled space, with a due regard for the local speed laws. The sense of glad homecoming was in itself a wonderful experience for me; for too long my life had been weighed down with a smothering load of depression. To be able to feel this sharp brilliant pleasure in anything was like being reborn.

When I pressed the button in the gatepost, the thrushes and white throats were singing their vespers in the Bellwood forest, and far up overhead, in the last blue light of day, gulls were flying in slow splendid arcs with the late sun shining on their wings. I watched them as I waited for the gates to open. If it were not for them, I could imagine the house set deep in a fold in distant inland hills, far from everything familiar to me.

The gates began to swing open. Then the drive appeared before me, glimmering in the early dusk under the trees. I drove in, and the woods seemed to close in behind me as silently as the gates had done.

[6]

When I drove around to the graveled parking area in front of the carriage house, Jason was watering the kitchen garden and Tristan sat immaculately on an overturned bushel basket, watching him. At sight of me Jason's bony face creased into a smile, and Tris got down off the basket and came to welcome me with his tail waving over his back. "I should have brought you something," I told him. "Next time I will."

"Tim's awake and waiting for you, Miss," Jason called to me. I went in through the spotless kitchen; Jason's housekeeping was immaculate. There was a back staircase, but it led to Jason's quarters, and I felt that to use it would be trespassing on his privacy, so I went along the narrow passage into the wide front hall. The open front door showed the shadowy lawn, with robins on it, and there was a pervasive scent of honeysuckle. I ran up the main stairs. The carpet made me noiseless, so I felt like a ghost. Tim's door stood open and I went straight in there as I was, with my light coat over my arm and my bag and my parcels, smiling because Tim would like the little dory.

Rees Morgan sat on the side of Tim's bed, reading

aloud. I hadn't heard his voice as I came up. Now I stood there stupidly staring at the line of his shoulders in the blazer and the back of his dark head. Tim's eyes were unblinking on his father's face.

I'd felt until this moment a little like a mother rushing home to kiss her child before he went to sleep. It all went in this moment, like the dreams that leave you wide awake and too sad even to feel dissatisfied. *These two,* I thought incoherently. *These two....* I began to back soundlessly out of the room, but Tim's eyes moved as quick as a little animal's, and he cried out in delight, "Caro! You did come back!" He bounced up in bed.

Rees closed the book before he turned his head. Miserably I thought, He's angry at the intrusion. I braced myself for coldness, remembering against my will Phyllis Partridge's words.

"So there you are," said Rees. His gaze moved over me as if I were a painting on a wall and he was enjoying what he saw. I remember an odd sense of helplessness, a beseeching somewhere deep in me, but beseeching for what? I was in love with him, I knew it then. The worst had happened. I was going to be that kind of imbecile.

"What did you bring me, Caro?" Tim clamored. Rees stood up.

I said, "I didn't mean to interrupt the story."

"Tim's been listening with only one ear, the other was cocked for you."

I gave Tim his package and the two of us watched him dig into it. You nut, I told myself savagely. You silly, soppy, sentimental, teen-age female. So he's lighting his pipe; didn't you ever see anyone light a pipe before? Why is it so ravishing when *he* does it? Just because he's the first mature and sophisticated male you were ever this close to, do you have to fasten onto him like a limpet? Good Lord, in your own way you're as neurotic as Phyllis Partridge!

It helped, like a cold shower. Brutal but restorative. We discussed the workmanship in the little dory; in fact we got a lot of mileage out of the whole subject of dories. We watched Tim's raptures, now and then exchanging a little smiling glance. Finally I said, "I'd better settle him down, hadn't I?"

"Perhaps you had. Then come down and have a drink with me." He kissed Tim, was violently hugged, and left us. I went into my own room and put my things away, leaving Tim to play with the dory a few minutes. When I'd tidied myself up I went back to him.

"I love my dory, Caro," he said happily.

"Tomorrow you can sail her," I said. "And for tonight we'll put her right on the stand beside the bed. You'll see her the first thing in the morning when you open your eyes."

"All right, " he said. "I'll put her there myself." He arranged dory and oars carefully by the lamp.

"Do you need to go to the bathroom?"

"No—well, maybe," he conceded. He sat up and swung his legs out of bed. I went to pick him up, and with an impish little grin he slipped away from me and scampered across the floor. He burst out laughing at my expression and went into the bathroom. I remained where I was, astonished and speechless. It had been a wobbly scamper, like that of a very young kitten, but a scamper none the less. When he came out of the bathroom his eyes were still dancing. He walked more cautiously to his bed, touching things now and then.

I covered him up. "I didn't know you could do that," I said.

"I do it lots of times."

"Does your father know you walk around without your braces?"

He looked guilty and whispered, "I'm not supposed to."

"Then you'd better not," I said. Whatever the precise form of his physical handicap was, no one had told me, but there'd been mention of an orthopedic specialist in Boston. "Have you said your prayers?" I asked him.

"I'll say them by and by. I like to talk to God when it gets dark. Then I'm not afraid."

"That's right, " I said, kissing him. "But there's nothing to be afraid of."

"Yes, there is, and God keeps them away."

"What's *them*? Those lions and tigers you like to hear about?"

"I don't now what they are, but they cry. One night they woke me up." He looked toward the side windows, and his eyes grew round. "Out there," he said in a husky little whisper. "Tris heard it. And Philly did, too."

Or else she'd infected him with her nightmares. "Well, anyway, God takes care of you," I said. "Good night, Tim."

"See you ... morning," he mumbled. "Say ... prayers now." His yawn made me sleepy. Smiling, I left him and went downstairs. But whereas I'd felt completely in charge in Tim's room, now with each downward step my self-confidence disappeared. I wanted to go where

Rees was, I wanted to shut myself in my room and lie in the flower-and-sea-scented dark and think about him.

He was waiting for me in the shadowy hall. "Let's go out."

"I'd better get a sweater."

"Take one of mine." He laid a cardigan over my shoulders. Like one resigned to drowning I thought, Paul's lightest touch never affected me like that.

Outside there was the clear blue light before dark, silent except for a sleepy twitter now and then from the woods. The only lights in the house were from Jason's room over the kitchen, the orange squares turning the twilight even bluer. We walked without speaking on the lawn overlooking the sea. The turf was springy underfoot, and white moths fluttered around the small glimmering moons of the nicotiana. Beyond the rose hedge the sea reflected the last light in the sky, but it was darkening fast, as if the dark were coming in like the tide.

What did he want, simply a shadow to accompany his pacing? Was I supposed to talk? I couldn't think of anything to say that wouldn't sound stupid, so I said nothing.

Suddenly he said, "What did you do with your afternoon?"

I listed everything but the visit to the Sail Loft, hoping I didn't sound too breathless and juvenile.

"You see, you did find something to do after all," he said kindly. That indulgent tone touched my pride.

"I forgot to say where I got the little dory," I said. "I bought it in a place at the public landing, called the Sail Loft."

Nothing interrupted the rhythm of his walking or

pipe-smoking. Angry now and enjoying it—at least it was better than being abjectly adoring—I said, "The woman who runs it used to work for you, Mrs. Partridge."

"Oh?" That got the pipe out of his mouth. "I wondered where she'd got to. I'm glad she's situated. Does she seem happy?"

"Very happy." She likes meeting and talking to people, I thought.

"Good. This was a hard place for her. She has many friends, and she felt cut off from them."

"She told me that."

"What else did she tell you?" The question sounded lazy and desultory.

"Oh, that she was very fond of Tim, but she felt claustrophobic. I told her I didn't feel that way, and that was about all. Then I met—" I never got a chance to reach Eric.

"Are you sure that was all?" Rees asked. He stopped our pacing and turned to me. "You've left something out, Caro. Already I've got to know that much about you—when you're lying in one way or another."

"I'm not a liar." I stepped back, rigid with anger.

He laughed, not cruelly but as he sometimes laughed at Tim, and that was almost worse. "Yes, you are, but only to be kind. I know. I know a great deal about you, Caro, and it's all to your credit, believe me." He took my elbow and we began walking again, toward the hedge and the darkening plain of water beyond it. "I'm curious, that's all. She left here under unpleasant circumstances and I wondered if she mentioned them."

We reached the roses, rugosas that hid a tough woven wire fence, and gave off a cool fragrance in the dusk. I

54

wished for the poise to say indifferently, "She didn't tell me anything about that. I met a man who's taking me sailing next week." Instead I heard myself begin, "She said you reprimanded her for something, and she was so upset she left."

"Yes. She needn't have, but it was bound to happen sooner or later. She wasn't happy here, as I've said. Did she go into details about the reprimand?"

I wouldn't give him those, no matter what. "Only the reason for it. She'd taken Tim somewhere you didn't want him to be, where he might have got hurt."

"Where he had already been hurt beyond repair." His voice was as gray and lifeless as a dead fire. "I lost my good judgment with Mrs. Partridge, but perhaps you'll understand. The place was almost directly below where we're standing. It's a spot that I'd blast out of existence if I could. This is where Tim and his mother went over the cliff. There was no fence there then. The ledges where that cretin took him to play are the ledges where his mother died, shattered like a child's doll, and where Tim became the way he is. Her body took the brunt, so he wasn't killed too. And the five-year-old that he's always going to be won't ever know enough to wish he *had* died with her."

I didn't know what to say, but I couldn't have spoken anyway. I just wanted to get him away from the fence so he couldn't stand there reliving that moment, seeing whatever horror he saw. I took his arm and tugged gently, then I put my other hand on his shoulder and tried to turn him. He was like rock, and for an instant my own boldness appalled me, but suddenly he gave in and came away. I didn't release his arm until we were halfway back to the house, and then I said, "Excuse me for doing that. But you shouldn't have stayed there any longer."

"I know. Thank you. If I'd been alone I'd have stayed there for hours. I've found myself there in the night sometimes, and not been quite sure *how* or *when*." He took out a handkerchief and wiped his forehead. "Many, many thanks," he said with a half laugh. "Let's go in and get that drink."

When we reached the door he said swiftly, "Look, if you're afraid I'll climb the fence and chuck myself over some night, and leave you exposed to a nasty investigation, never fear. Death's going to have to seek me out and drag me away from Tim. I'll never go looking for it."

"I wasn't afraid of that," I said. "I just couldn't bear for you to go on seeing what you must have been seeing."

I felt that he was trying to see my face in the dusk, or into my mind; knowing his eyes by now, I wouldn't have been surprised by the latter. He said abruptly, "Now for the drink."

I was a little shaky—other people's tragedies always move me, and this was closer than most. While Rees fixed the drinks, I moved around the long living room, fastening my attention on various lovely or intriguing objects, my cure for steadying myself. The room wasn't cluttered, but it held many things to delight the eye, from the child's very old rocker by the hearth (where Tim like to sit and watch the fire, he had told me) to the glowing colors of the old Oriental carpets, and the ivory carvings a Martyn sea captain had brought from China.

And then, finally, the portrait over the mantel. I came to a stop before that. Her youthful serenity made me feel much younger than she must have been when she was painted. Would I ever be that wise?

The longer I looked into the delicate narrow face and the calm dark eyes the farther I went into my own shortcomings. When Rees Morgan spoke beside me I jumped. He didn't smile, but handed me my drink. "You're rather like her."

"Oh no," I said. "Well, physically perhaps, but she's forgotten more than I'll ever know."

"It's all gone now," he said. "All of it. The goodness, the gentleness, the spirit, the deep intelligence. The beauty. Wiped out in an instant, as a bird or a butterfly is destroyed by a cruel child." He lifted his glass to the portrait, said something under his breath, and then drank. I felt like an intruder, and turned away and walked across the room to where the piano stood in its shadowy bay. I sat down on the bench and sipped my drink. Over there by the mantel he was as far removed as he had been out by the cliff. I could have gone off to my room and he'd have never noticed.

I *would* go, quickly and quietly, with no backward glance; the efficient and tactful governess who would be an embarrassment neither to her employer nor to herself. I was here to look after Tim, not to fall in love with his father. When I reached my room, I could once more become the Caroline Brewster I knew. Meanwhile, I was in sort of limbo between identities.

Just as I stood up, Rees Morgan spoke. *"Caro?"*

"Here I am," I answered.

"I owe you an apology. I'm poor company tonight."

"You needn't feel that you have to entertain me to keep me contented," I said drily. "I didn't come expecting that as one of the fringe benefits."

"I thought it might be one of *my* fringe benefits." he said. "But I realize that I've fallen out of the knack of talking to a woman. I'm intolerably self-centered, it seems. If you're as patient with me as you are with Tim, I may improve."

There wasn't any answer to that which wouldn't sound coy or silly, so I smiled and said, "Goodnight, and thank you for the drink." There was still time then for me; as yet nothing was irretrievable, and I would find myself again at the head of the stairs.

He took my glass and walked with me to the hall. "Tim's very happy with you. And as for Jason, he's never approved of anyone else to this extent,"

"He's certainly been very pleasant and helpful."

"If you should leave us tomorrow I think Jason would go into as deep a slump as Tim."

"I don't intend to leave tomorrow. We have to sail Tim's new dory."

"Look," he said, "don't let Tim con you into bringing him a gift each time you go away."

"It's no trouble, and it reassures him. He thought I was leaving for good today, but when I promised him something he was relieved. . . . It may be nothing more than something from the five-and-ten the next time, but I couldn't resist the dory today." I went up a few steps. "Goodnight."

"Goodnight, Caro. Sleep well." The memory of his smile went with me, and the way my name had sounded in his voice, especially when he had called it there in the living room when he couldn't see me.

Just as I reached my room the piano began, a Chopin nocturne. I left my door ajar so I could listen. A mistake. If my own Caroline was hovering, she never had a chance to reclaim me. Lying in the dark listening to those reveries, longings, and griefs flawlessly expressed, I felt all my doubts resolved by the certainty that I was meant for something in Rees Morgan's life. Not to be loved by him; there was only one woman, and she was dead. But to be *there,* a presence to recall him from those frozen moments by the cliff's edge; someone, not a small child or a manservant, to answer when he called out. It seemed a sad, rich, and wonderful purpose in life. Devotion and self-sacrifice. . . .

On the very brim of sleep I had one of those diamond-sharp hallucinations peculiar to that state; Paul was regarding me with that wide, serious, gray gaze that seemed now to carry the same essential innocence as Tim's. He was wearing a heathery sports jacket I'd always liked, and his hand kept fooling nervously with his cigarette lighter, a habit of his, but his eyes never left mine; this was also a habit of his, in those moments of fervent apology after a scene.

"But that was all *I* ever asked," he said now in a clear and wondering tone. "Devotion and self-sacrifice. Why was it so different?"

"It's not the same thing *at all.*" My own voice woke me completely. Paul was gone, the music had stopped. What insanities one displays on the edge of sleep, I thought, and this time I slid over that brim without any visitations.

Something woke me again, not myself or an astral projection, but a cry. I sat up staring into the grays and blacks of the room, my heart beating so hard that it made me a little sick. The echo of the cry seemed to be shut in with me, bouncing from wall to wall.

I slid out of bed, grabbing for the flashlight which I used to check on Tim, and went into his room. He slept hard. I straightened his covers and went to first one window and then to the other to listen. The rising wind blew through the trees with a soft rush, now and then accented by the percussion of surf crashing on the ledges. *The ledges.* My shudder had nothing to do with the damp gusts blowing throught the screen. I closed the window toward the wind, and went back to my own room.

My windows were in the lee, yet some trick of the wind baffling around the odd gables and leaves set up a small fine keening at one screen, so I shut that window. Wrapped in my robe I sat by the other, which looked over the lawn toward the place where the study path began. There was nothing to see except the not-quite-darkness of a midnight when the moon is behind the hurrying clouds, and nothing can be heard but the wind in the spruces, the loud rustling of maple leaves, the sea on the shore. I wanted to go back to bed, but the memory of the cry was too vivid. Had *I* cried out after all? I didn't remember dreaming, but I could have been affected by Phyllis Partridge's nightmares, just as Tim had been; and I could have been influenced by what Rees had told me tonight. Valerie must have cried out when the turf broke away under her feet, or the sudden strong gust of wind caught her off balance, whatever it was that threw her off the cliff. I pressed my folded arms tight across my midriff to fight the sickness there. My forehead and neck were clammy under my hair.

I wished I could go down to the kitchen and make myself something hot to drink. I'd done it many times at home after Paul's trouble. Sip and read, and wait for morning to come. Then I might get a few hours' sleep before it was time to go to work. Now I had to deal with a five-year-old who woke with the birds. I drank some water, and ate a couple of English biscuits from the flowered tin box that Jason had put in my room a few days ago; I read for a little while, and then tried to settle down again. I was convinced now that I'd cried out in my sleep, or else it was an animal in the woods. Porcupines could make some pretty weird noises, and bobcats could really freeze your blood. I pounced on that. Phyllis Partridge could have heard one! Tim could have heard one! Of course!

I went back to sleep again.

[7]

July brought in the best of coastal weather; my next day off began with the diamond sparkle of dew across the lawn, diamonds trembling on twig and leaf and in the hearts of flowers, and a sea that glittered to the sharp azure line of the horizon. After breakfast I got Jason to carry Tim down the cliff path. The tide was out, and there was a marvelous expanse of damp firm sand for castles. We spent a rapturous two hours there. Sandpipers ran fearlessly near us, and Tim watched them with his heart in his eyes. I wouldn't let myself brood about his limited future; it tortured me to think that he would always be a little boy even when he was physically a man. I hoped that he would always have someone who truly loved him, but Jason and his father couldn't live forever. I knew, and experienced with him, Rees Morgan's constant fear for his son.

But fear and dread had no part in our lives this morning. "I'll make a tower on this side," I said, packing a pail with damp sand. "See?" I upended it. "Now you make one on your side." I handed him the pail and he began loading it with both hands. Out to sea a sailboat was coasting along before the light northwest breeze, and I remembered that Eric Allenby was going to call me this morning. It had gone completely out of my mind since last week; so had the town and all I had seen there.

"Look!" Tim crowed. I praised it and said, "Make another one. We have to have four, one on each corner."

"One, two," Tim counted.

"The next one will be three."

"And then four!" He shouted it.

Good sailing weather. I might as well go. It would be a pleasant way to use up my time. Since the afternoon away was inevitable under Rees's orders, I would make the most of it. I began to look forward to sailing and wondered if Eric's friends would welcome me or be merely polite. There might be a girl or two who'd resent his inviting me. Well, they needn't worry. I was an entirely disinterested party.

Tim made the fourth tower, and the man who built the Brooklyn Bridge couldn't have been prouder. We began terracing the grounds and planting an orchard of seaweed fronds.

"This is my day to go to town, Tim," I said. "Remember how I went last week, too?"

"Mm," he said, busy with his orchard. "And you brought me the dory."

"And I'll bring you something this time too," I said, "but I may not be back before you go to sleep."

"I'll stay awake for you."

"I may not be back until it's time for me to go to bed. But I'll come in and put your present beside your pillow, and you'll find it there when you wake up in the morning."

He looked enchanted. Then he said, "Take me to town with you sometime."

I considered, while he watched me as expectantly as a puppy. Perhaps we could go and do errands sometime, or ride along in the station wagon with Jason when he did the marketing. "Well, we'll talk to your father about it," I said.

"We could go for a walk sometimes too," he offered. "Out the gate, and along the road."

"There's nothing much to see out there, Tim. Just the wall and the woods."

"There's the road," he pointed out. "Cars go on it, and people. Sometimes there's a dog in the car. We could wave."

"But Tim," I said reasonably, "you can't walk very far in your braces. Maybe that'll have to wait till you don't need them any more."

"I've got a go-cart! It folds up."

"Well, we'll see," I told him, then hoped he hadn't caught on to the eternal certainty of most children that "we'll see" means "yes." But his isolated existence had apparently kept him free of it. He merely nodded co-operatively.

At eleven Jason came down to fetch us and to tell me Eric had phoned; would I call him back. The tide hadn't yet reached the castle, so it was there for him to admire. Tim counted the towers for him, and Jason was suitably astonished. Tim went round the towers again and brought the count up to eight, and Jason gave me a sidewise glance. When Tim began bubbling that maybe he could go for a walk out on the road, and ride into town sometimes, Jason said, "Sounds like you two have been having quite a chat this morning. Counting, and now all these plans."

I was a little annoyed. "Believe it or not, Jason," I said, "the plans are the private and absolutely unencouraged project of the Young Idea. As for counting, when someone asks me what comes after four, I'll be darned if I say I don't know."

Jason gave me a puckery smile. "No offense meant, Miss Brewster. But Mr. Morgan's afraid of putting pressure on the—er, Young Idea. Well, my boy, are you ready to mount your trusty steed?" He bent over and Tim, giggling, climbed onto his back with an assist from me. I gathered up the beach bag and sweaters and followed up the path.

When we came into the house Rees met us in the kitchen. In slacks, open-necked shirt, and pullover he looked young and relaxed.

"Hi, daddy!" Tim was incandescent. He started to meet his father, trying to go fast in the constricting braces, and Rees came to him, dropping down onto his heels; he took the little boy by the middle, shook him gently, and kissed him. Then he made a face. "That was a sandy one."

Tim laughed. "I've got sand in my *hair!*"

"I guess you have. But what's a little sand in our young lives?" He stood up, and Tim began to tell about the castle, pleading with him to go and see it before the tide took it.

"I shall go to see it," Rees promised him, "while Caro returns her telephone call."

Jason moved into action. "Come along, Tim, and we'll shower that sand off." He led the way to the small downstairs bathroom. Tim followed, talking the whole time.

"You can go into the library to call your young man," Rees said to me.

"He's not my young man," I said too quickly.

"I'm sure he would be, with any encouragement."

"Well, I'm not about to encourage him. He asked me to go sailing within five minutes after he was introduced, and never gave me a chance to refuse. But I'll refuse now."

"Why?" he said, following me into the library. "I can vouch for the Allenbys, if that's what you want. They've been summer people here for years, long before I ever came. I understand Eric distinguished himself in Vietnam, not only in action but in working with the people. He had the whole town here taking part after a while, shipping blankets and clothing for the refugees."

It certainly gave Eric new dimensions, but I was unwilling to concede anything; this morning Rees wasn't the desperately tragic, lonely man, but the one who could always make me feel childish and inept, and as a defense I turned prickly, even antagonistic.

"I'll go and look at the sand castle," Rees said behind me. His arm reached by me, his hand turned the note-pad on the library desk, so I could read the number he had written.

"Before you go," I said formally, "there's something I'd like to discuss with you." I turned around to face him.

"Certainly," he said, also formal. But I felt he assessed my flush as more than windburn. I tried for what I fondly imagined was a crisp governessy tone.

"Well, Tim brought a book to me a few mornings ago and wanted me to tell him some of the letters. He knew some, and he wanted to know more. We spent only about fifteen minutes at it, but he was very eager and picked them up as rapidly as—well, any child, I should say."

Rees's face was attentive but otherwise without expression. I went on.

"Jason seems to think I shouldn't encourage Tim, and he said you'd feel that way too. I wouldn't want Jason to think I didn't believe him, but you're Tim's father so I wanted to consult with you."

He heard me out without moving. Then he made a gesture toward a chair, and went around behind the desk to his own. I sat down, saying, "I wouldn't encourage Tim to the point of pushing him, of course. But shouldn't I answer his questions?"

He began to fill his pipe. I recognized the signs of male intransigence. Elliot did the same thing to Mindy when she wanted a simple answer. *Don't you patronize me, Elliot Brewster,* she would flare at him. *Save that for your two-year-old daughter!*

"Caro," Rees began. "You said yourself, when we talked in the hotel, that you knew nothing of retarded children. Well, the parent of one, in his journeys to clinics and specialists, and in his meetings with other such parents, becomes in time an expert. He knows that no two of these children are alike, just as no two normal children are alike.... Tim has rare charm and spirit; if nothing had happened, he would have become a brilliant man, because he was born with a great intelligence. You see flashes now of what might have been. Simply flashes. That's all." He was as detached as a doctor, but I wondered what the effort cost him. For an instant we heard Tim's squeals of laughter in the shower, then a door was shut.

"So," Rees continued with a slight shrug, "these things he wants to do can't go any farther than the desire."

"He remembers the letters from day to day, Mr. Morgan."

"Would he, if you weren't there to help him?" he asked gently.

"Well, the average five-year-old has to see and name the letters several days in a row before he remembers them."

"And then he goes on to something more," he said. "But Tim can't go on to something more, Caro. His reach outstretches his grasp, and we've been very careful not to let him realize that. If he ever does, he'll be heartbroken. It could set him back—" He got up and strode over to the windows. "I don't know how far. He has the passion to accomplish and not the means. Eventually this could wreck whatever happiness his life could bring him."

"Then what am I to do when he comes bringing a book? You've surrounded him with books. He recognizes characters in them, and the letters are characters to him like Peter Rabbit and Jemima Puddleduck and Christopher Robin."

"But some day, perhaps sooner than we think, he'll know the difference."

He didn't turn around, and, gazing at the back of his neck, and his shoulders in the blue pullover, I wished I had the right to go to him and massage those rigid muscles, let my compassion flow into him through my hands. But, having no such rights, I should make this discussion as easy as possible for him and get out. As he said, it was his child and he was the expert.

"Then I won't encourage him in any way, but if he points to a letter and asks what it is, what shall I say?" He didn't answer, and my throat constricted. I said distantly, "I seem to have brought you more problems than I'm worth. I think I'd better resign."

He turned quickly then, and came toward me with his hands out. "Caro, for God's sake, don't talk like that. We need you here." I thought he was going to take my hands, but suddenly he put his into his pockets. "Look, when he wants to know, tell him, but tell him only that one thing and then try to divert him. Will you do that?"

"Yes," I said. I would have promised anything.

"Good!" His smile came on; it had that quality of sudden light and heat warming your cold bones. "Now make your call. That young man must be pretty impatient by now."

He left the library and closed the door behind him. I looked at that closed door. *Caro, for God's sake . . . we need you here. . . .* If only he'd said *I.* But surely that was implicit. I heard the words again, the timbre of his voice, saw the strain and anxiety as he came toward me, felt the response in myself to give and give. Paul hadn't actually needed me, for all his demands. He was like an infant wanting to be sure of food and warmth, and sheltering arms. Almost anyone's would do.

But this was a man with a man's genuine needs, and for this *I* was meant; no one else. My conviction came back like a spring flowering as I turned to the telephone.

[8]

It was superb sailing weather, with just enough wind, and so clear that the distances seemed carved in crystal. *Kingfisher,* the Allenby sloop, raced *Phoebe,* of a more modern design, on a triangular course from the black can buoy outside Somerset Harbor, from there around a high crag of ledge marked with a spindle to the foot of Samson's Light, and then back to the black buoy. *Kingfisher* won, as effortlessly as a gull rides the summer winds.

"You've brought us luck, Caro," Eric said. "How'd you like to be our mascot?"

"I thought *Kingfisher* always won," I said.

"She does," Mark Webster said. "That's just his idea of a subtle approach." He was short and studious-looking. His glasses didn't hide a quiet smile which was almost completely in his eyes. "It's a secret test. If you make the right answer you get the prize."

"That's a special blanket to wear," his wife explained. "Like the Marine Corps bulldog."

"Oh?" I said, lifting my eyebrows. "I thought it was Eric."

"Well, now," said Eric, sprawling back by the tiller,

70

"we might revise the rules and change the prize." His blue eyes stayed on mine with just the right degree of warmth; there was no pressure, no hint of the wolf, and I thought, He likes girls. Plural. He doesn't intend to be tied to *one* any sooner than he can help; he might invite you out but he wouldn't consider it binding. Well, that's fine with me, Chum, I told him silently, and gave him a forthright gaze right back.

"Come on up forward," Helen said to me, "and I'll give you some helpful hints." We lay on the deck as *Kingfisher* plunged softly through the blue swells toward Bannock, the island where we'd have supper. *Phoebe* came steadily behind us.

Helen was the mother of three, but didn't look it. She had a freckled insouciance and directness that reminded me of Mindy. "I'm so glad Eric met you," she said. "He hasn't taken up with any one girl since he came back from Vietnam, and it's such a waste."

"But why?" I asked. "Why should he be anchored until he's ready? He's young yet."

"He's older than he looks," said Helen, "and I don't know why he doesn't *look* older than he is, after a couple of years in Vietnam. I *hate* that blasted war over there! But let's not get onto that! Each day we go out like this I try to squeeze every moment dry."

"Of its golden juice," I said, lying on my back and watching the sails against the sky. I was floating weightless through a world that was neither here nor there, but a marvelous suspension in between.

"Eric's the greatest, as the kids say," said Helen. "And when I say it's such a waste, I mean it. He's the kind who ought to be founding a home. Think what additions to society his kids would be." Then she burst out laughing. "I just heard myself, as if it was somebody else mumbling on. You must think I'm some kind of a nut."

"Well, a nice one."

"Thank you—I think. No, I'm not really on a eugenics kick. I haven't picked you out for the perfect mother of Eric's children."

"After all, you don't know my case history," I said. "I could be a psychopathic personality behind this tranquil exterior. I may do murder when the moon is full. Or I could be a vampire."

"No, they have red hair and blue eyes," said Helen. "Or is that how you can tell if a woman's a nymphomaniac? Anyway, I read all about it once." We were laughing again, and I was happy. Aft by the tiller the men were quiet, Mark smoking his pipe, Eric squinting up at the sails and smiling to himself in pure pleasure. I remember what Rees had said about his war record and his work with the people; I imagined him, a blond giant in Army fatigues, respectfully trading courtesies with the headman in a Vietnamese village; squatting on his heels to talk to a baby; followed by small boys wherever he went, because he was that kind. Even I could feel it; it had nothing to do with sex, but with a kind of serene strength and an uncomplicated honesty.

Yes, he would be a superb father, I thought. Anyway, I'm glad he survived Vietnam. I'm glad he wouldn't take *no* for an answer in the Sail Loft, so I'm sailing out here today. And I'm glad I'm going back to Bellwood tonight. . . . And at what that name conjured up I turned over on my stomach on the warm deck and shut my eyes.

I hadn't met the crew aboard the other sloop, since *Phoebe* was out sailing among the moorings in the harbor when I'd arrived at the yacht club to meet Eric. When we all reached the island and rowed ashore to a scrap of sand beach tucked away between points of black volcanic rock, I got to know *Phoebe's* owners. The two Gillespie brothers were both sandy-haired and pleasantly craggy of face; they could have been a couple of native Hebrideans on their own northern island as we explored Bannock's treeless beauty. Peter was a medical student and Burr his father's partner in the family lumberyard. Like the Websters they were Somerset natives. Peter's date was Nancy Allenby, Eric's cousin. She was a very tall girl with wonderfully long, slim, brown legs, and shoulder-length yellow hair that kept falling over her face like a curtain whenever she tilted her head forward. Then she would toss it back with a motion that could have become tiresome to watch after a while, except that her beauty was always such a surprise; with the right clothes and the right expression she could have stepped out of a Sargent portrait. Instead, she had sunburn, a grin like Eric's, short shorts and a basque shirt, and a pitching arm that would have gotten a high school boy a talent test with the major leagues.

Burr Gillespie's girl was Tamara O'Neill, half-Irish and half-Russian, stocky and round-faced and with wonderful smoky eyes whose true color I couldn't make out.

"Isn't she gorgeous?" said Burr at supper, clasping one big hand possessively around her ankle. "And she's all mine. The only trouble is I can't get her to admit her

Romanoff blood and put in a claim for that fortune they keep telling about."

"All that and hemophilia too," said Peter.

"Oh, we'd adopt a few dozen kids, wouldn't we, honey?"

Tamara smiled. She was even quieter than I. Nancy waved a flaming marshmallow in the air and said, "That's what I'm going to do even when I have my own kids. The nonadoptables are what I want. Mixed-blood babies, and homely ones with squints. Peter, why don't you specialize in eyes so you can operate on my children's squints?"

"Nancy's a female Catcher in the Rye," Eric said. "She wants to save all the little kids in the world." He took his cousin by the nape of the neck and shook her gently.

"Well, look who's talking," said Nancy. She ate her marshmallow. "Hey, who's going to play catch again?"

"Nancy's house will resemble a training gym," said Helen. "All her babies will swim at three months and do twenty pushups before breakfast." She fell back onto the sand with a sigh. "Now me, I never pass up a chance to collapse."

"Oh, in time I'll probably give up and turn into a mountain of flesh while the kids do all the housework," said Nancy. "Come on, Peter. I'll settle for a walk if catch is too strenuous. You're not being very gallant."

"I never pretended to be," said Peter. "Not in daylight, anyway. However ..." he groaned and got up from where he'd been lying with his head against a driftwood log.

"Come on, my smoldering Slavic beauty," said Burr, hauling Tamara up, "we'll go in the other direction."

"What are you going to do," Mark asked Helen, "stay here and chaperone these two?"

"Lover!" Helen scrambled up. "You mean *you* want to go walking like a courting couple?"

When they'd all disappeared we stayed where we were, lounging on a natural bench of rock that still stored heat from the sun, though the day was cooling now toward a clear and windless sunset. A mile to the west, the land was black between a glittering sea and polished sky. Eric put a few more chips on the small driftwood fire in a crevice, and said, "More coffee?"

"Please." I held out my mug. He poured for us both and sat back on the ledge.

"You had a good time today," he said. "I could tell. You quietly radiate."

"That makes me sound like a computer, all little flashing lights."

"You know that corny joke about the Martian getting into a joint by mistake and saying to the juke box, 'What's a lovely girl like you doing in a place like this?' "

It was exquisitely silly and we both laughed. "What do you think of them?" he asked.

"I like them all. It's a good mixture, full of contrasts."

"They like you too. How are you getting on at Bellwood?"

"No complications yet."

"You sound as if you expected them."

"It's only my inborn fatalism. Everything's so perfect"—I knocked on a piece of driftwood—"that I keep expecting something to spoil it. The place is beautiful and Tim's a darling."

75

"And is your boss a darling too?" He grinned at me. "Well, I can't help a healthy curiosity, can I? Is he a combination of Heathcliffe and Mr. Rochester, or is he really a gentle and scholarly soul?"

"That's it!" I said in the same bantering tone. "He *is* gentle and scholarly, and he's so busy with his studies that I don't see much of him. So that takes care of my employer for today."

"Takes care of me, too," said Eric. "Consider me flattened. I asked for it."

"You don't sound a bit squelched."

"They don't call me the Unsinkable Allenby for nothing."

"I'd call that expression smug if I knew you better."

"Go ahead, call me smug and I'll figure we've known each other at least a year. It'll cut out a lot of the preliminaries. Then we'll be set for all summer and fall, skiing in the winter—if you don't ski I'll teach you—and ice-fishing, and—"

"Don't you go somewhere else for the winter?" I interrupted. "Home?"

He beamed. "Nope. The rest of the family does, but not me. I've got a job beginning in September. Teaching. You didn't know I was a scholar as well as a gentleman, like your sainted boss, did you?"

"Nope," I mimicked him. But I was surprised; it gave him another dimension. "I don't see you as a teacher. As a bridge-builder, yacht designer, architect—but never a teacher."

"And never in the kind of school I'll have," he told me with gusto, sitting up so he could wave his arms better. "You know there are a few one- and two-room schools left in the state, and I hope to God there always will be. Well, there's one back in the country about fifteen miles from here, and the last teacher retired in June. They've been having a hard time to get someone. So I applied, and was taken."

"Good! But did you train as a teacher?"

"No, the family business is paper. But I've got a degree, and I like kids, and the town up there is so desperate to keep the school going as long as possible that they'd have taken me if I had two heads. The old teacher says she'll give me all the help she can. So what do you think?"

"I think it's marvelous," I said honestly. "And I think those kids up there are very lucky. How does your family feel about you deserting the family business?"

"There's a maverick or two in every generation. My father wasn't the one in his, but he seems pleased that he's raised one. Besides"—he leaned forward and added wood to the fire, and something about the way the shadows changed on his face made him much older for a moment—"I came back from Vietnam apparently in one piece. It wouldn't matter to them if I wanted to be a barker in a circus midway."

"You said *apparently*. Why?" I asked bluntly.

He gave me a sidewise look and the corner of his mouth lifted in a smile that never touched his eyes. "Are you unsinkable too?"

"I'm sorry," I said at once. "I guess we can still overstep, even if we have known each other a year."

"It's just leaped ahead another six months." We both laughed, in warmth and relief; and if time hadn't actually leaped ahead, my comprehension had. Eric, no matter how seemingly uncomplicated, was no flat portrait in poster paints.

The sun hovered just above the black rim of the land, reddening the rocks, our hands and faces, changing the sea and the sky even in the east to rose and amethyst, turning the gulls' wings pink as they flew over us toward their nesting ledges. Voices sounded nearby in the cool hush, and a wild whoop rang from up on the crest of the island.

"Nancy," said Eric. "She looks like the Blessed Damozel and sounds like Tarzan. She's the other maverick in our generation. She went South on a civil rights march instead of coming out. My aunt was very brave about it, and my uncle was relieved. The thought of a début unnerved him completely, but he didn't turn a hair when his daughter spent a weekend in a Southern jail."

"The Allenbys sound better and better to me," I said. "Both seniors and juniors."

"She's halfway to being a biologist right now. She'll probably go into the Peace Corps when she graduates."

"You know, that makes me feel awfully wishy-washy and ineffectual," I blurted out. "I never even *thought* of the Peace Corps when I was—" I stopped short. When I was wallowing around in self-pity, I almost said.

His head came up. "When you were what?"

"When I finished business college," I said lamely.

"That wasn't it," said Eric, "but since we've founded this rich and rewarding old friendship on minding our own business, I won't crash in."

"Thanks, old friend," I said. The sun was a thin melon-rind of fire behind the hills where Eric's school was. And then it was gone, with only the reflection of its flames in the sky.

We sailed home under the first stars, leaving a phosphorescent wake behind us. Eric's arm draped over my shoulders as we stood by the tiller meant nothing, and to move out from under it would make something of it. *Phoebe* rode abreast of us, her crew singing. Aboard *Kingfisher* the Websters sat silent and close, Helen's head on Mark's shoulder.

"*Phoebe*'s a ghost ship," I murmured. "White hull, white sails glimmering in the starlight, white water gleaming along her sides."

"And we'll all feel as free as ghosts until we're ashore again. It's a queer thing how, if you love being afloat, you can give up to it completely. Everything else loses its weight and its significance until you put one foot on that landing again."

"I suppose it's like being born," I said. "The instant you're in the world your troubles begin."

As the sloop lurched slightly in a tide rip, Eric's arm drew me closer to him, but it was more a steadying gesture than a pass; at least I chose to treat it that way. From across the water the singing came.

" 'Speed, bonny boat, like a bird on the wing, over the sea to Skye. . . .' " I saw Helen Webster fumbling for a handkerchief. Eric said in my ear, "The combination of salt water and stars and beer always makes the Gillespies revert. Bring Bonnie Prince Charlie back right now and they'd be off in a cloud of claymores."

I laughed without sound, so as not to disturb Helen's sentimental mood; besides, my own happiness was perilously close to tears. Eric was as solid as a rock against the sloop's motion. It was curious to like someone so well, without any complications, and to be in love with someone else. It wasn't necessary that Rees love *me;* it was enough for me to exist at this moment in the blessed state of being in love.

The mainland lights twinkled like jewels, and at the public landing there was the sociable atmosphere of a town enjoying summer so much it didn't ever want to go to bed. The big windows of the Sail Loft were alight, and *Phoebe*'s crew wanted to go in for something to eat. But Mark and Helen had a babysitter to think about, and I didn't want to meet Phyllis Partridge again and smudge the exquisite bloom of this day.

"Jason waits up for me," I told Eric, "and he puts in a long day. So do I, come to think of it. Tim wakes early."

"Look," Helen said urgently at the yacht club wharf. "Next Wednesday we're having a clambake for Mark's birthday. So will you come, Caro?"

"You'll have to," said Mark. "My birthday's really Tuesday, but she's making it Wednesday for your sake."

"I'd love it," I said. "Thank you for including me."

"My dear girl, you hadn't a prayer of not being included," said Mark. "Helen's been looking for a suitable mate for Eric for months."

"Did you know that Caro's really engaged to a rich elderly sardine tycoon back in Limerock?" said Eric.

"When I get Mark home I'm going to beat him up," Helen said. "Silent for twenty-three hours out of twenty four, and then when he does speak he comes out with gems. It's a wonder he has any friends. It's a wonder he has a *wife*."

"Heck, honey, his unpredictability is his charm," said Eric. "As long as it doesn't extend to the way he puts up prescriptions, why worry?"

We said goodnight by the MG in the club parking lot, and the Websters went off arm in arm. "I like them," I said. "I guess I said it before, but I mean it." I opened the car door and got in, then put my hand out to him. "Thank you for a wonderful day."

"Thank *you*." He held on to my hand. "Any chance of seeing you before next Wednesday?"

"I'm afraid not," I said.

"Can I call?"

"Well—" I couldn't come right out and say I didn't want him to call. Fortunately he took my hesitation for another sort of doubt.

"Do you have strong feelings about keeping your job and your own time separate?"

"That's it," I said with relief.

"Then I won't call. Unless," he warned me, "it's a matter of life and death, and of course I can't tell how often that'll come up." We both laughed, he released my hand, and I started the car.

At least I went through the motions, but nothing happened; there was only the empty whir of the starter.

"Let me try," Eric said, and I moved over. He fiddled in the way of men with recalcitrant engines, but still nothing happened. "Got a flashlight aboard?" There was one in the glove compartment. He opened the hood and looked in, fiddled some more.

"Your battery must be down," he said finally.

"It can't be!" I objected.

"That's what women always say," said Eric. "Well, there's a garage in town I can vouch for. Let's lock her up, I'll take you home, and tomorrow I'll see about her."

"That's an imposition."

"Look, I have a lot more free time than you have."

"That was only a token objection. I have to say something to salve my conscience. I'd be glad of a ride home."

He went faster on the winding country road than I would have dared. We met a few cars, saw lighted windows here and there, a white horse ghostly at a fence, and soon the headlights shone on the red brick of the Bellwood wall, and we came to the gates.

I showed him where the button was and he got out and pressed it. In a few minutes the gates swung wide and we drove in.

"Enter the Haunted Forest," said Eric as the woods closed in on either side of us. "What does he harbor in there? Survivals of prehistoric beasts?"

"Now that may be it," I said. "Maybe that's what I heard screaming instead of a bobcat. Though wouldn't you expect one of those things to *roar?*"

Suddenly we came out in the open again, to the front door standing open and the lights streaming out across the lawn. When we stopped Eric came around to open the door for me, but I was already halfway out. Tristan ran from the shadows to meet me, his plume straight up. I leaned down to pat him and when I stood up, Rees had appeared in the doorway.

"Well, Caro," he said pleasantly, "what's happened?"

"The car wouldn't start, so Eric brought me home, and—" Was I talking too fast?

"Hello, Mr. Morgan," said Eric.

"Hello, Eric." They shook hands. "This is awfully good of you."

"Oh, it was a pleasure," said Eric, beaming. "Well, I'll see about the car, Caro."

"Thank you very much. And thank you again for a lovely day."

"It was that for me too. I'll see you next week," he promised. "Goodnight, Mr. Morgan."

Rees and I stood on the wide brick step while he backed around and drove away. Then, as if with one movement, we turned to each other.

"Look at you, Caro!" Rees exclaimed. "Windburned, windblown, and the sea in your eyes. I can fairly smell it. Come in, come in!"

Inside, Jason pressed the button to open the gates for Eric. "Even Jason's missed you today," said Rees. "He's been to me five times in the last hour, wanting me to call the Coast Guard." Jason looked shocked, and Rees and I both laughed. "Oh, go to bed, Jason," said Rees.

Jason said goodnight and went away on soundless feet, and I yawned hugely. "I was going to ask you to have a nightcap," said Rees, "but if you're that sleepy—"

"I'd love a nightcap," I said, as if I were in the habit of drinking them.

We went into the living room where a small fire flickered in its last minutes of life. I sat on the sofa facing it, and Rees fixed drinks and sat down beside me. "*Now*," he said, "so you had a wonderful day. You don't know how happy that makes me. It means you won't be lonely here."

Fatigue and the day's exhilaration made my tongue easy. "I don't think I would be anyway. I love this house, and Tim. But they're a nice crowd, so that's a plus."

"What are you doing next week?"

"Oh, someone's having a birthday clambake." Tris jumped up beside me and began to wash.

"I thought you and young Allenby might be doing something alone together."

"He'll be there, of course." I sipped my drink and gazed at the dying fire, aware that he was watching me. I wanted to tell him I wasn't interested in Eric, but at least I had enough sense to hold that back.

"We'll have to be sure the car is in perfect order," he said. "We don't want you left without transportation and having to depend too often on Good Samaritans." He got up and went over to the mantel, taking hold of it with both hands and looking down at the fire. "I suppose you don't mind if young Allenby's the Samaritan, and I can't blame you. But I'd rather there was no precedent set."

I felt myself blushing all over. Instantly I remembered Phyllis Partridge's complaints, and how superior I'd felt to her; now I was being told the same thing. In a very courteous way, of course.

"I didn't intend to let a precedent be set," I said coldly. "If this should happen to the car again, I can call Jason. But if you're away from home at the time, he couldn't leave Tim."

He turned swiftly to me and said, "You're quietly furious, aren't you? You feel reproved, and unjustly. Well, you aren't being reproved." Above his head Valerie watched us from the shadows. "It's just—oh, bear with me, Caro! I'm eccentric, but it's the eccentricity of a maimed man."

He came back across the hearth rug and dropped down on the sofa beside me. One hand began nervously

84

stroking the cat between us. "I've tried to create a little oasis of sanity and peace and beauty in an ugly world. Not that the countryside is ugly here, or the people. But one has to set one's boundaries somewhere, and I've set mine around my hundred acres. God willing, Tim will never know anything else but the safety of his own private universe."

"I understand," I said shakily, my eyes on his. I had to set down my glass and lace my fingers together to keep from seizing that hand caressing the cat and holding it tight against my breast. Liquor and fatigue together were a dangerous combination. "I'd like to make an exception in the case of Eric Allenby," he went on. "But, as I said earlier, the line has to be drawn somewhere, and wherever it is, someone is bound to be kept out who shouldn't be."

"Eric doesn't have to come here. I never expected that. I'm not—"

I got no farther. He took my face in both hands and kissed my mouth. The touch was gentle and undemanding, but firm. I shut my eyes and went spinning dangerously through space, but still in some curious way I was held—all of me—suspended yet safe between those two hands. He moved his mouth away from mine but still held my face, and I opened my heavy eyes and looked at him. "Caro," he said in a low voice. "That was not premeditated. But you shouldn't gaze at a man with such solemn dedication."

"I didn't know how I was gazing," I said huskily. He took his hands away and smiled at me. "Forgive me."

"No," I said. "There's nothing to forgive." Some small but piercing voice of common sense told me to get up and head for the stairs while I could keep my face and voice steady. He got up too. I couldn't resist a swift upward glance at Valerie. Then I said, "Goodnight," and went toward the hall. Tris reached the stairs first, and flowed swiftly up over them in a tawny streak toward Tim's door.

Neither Rees nor I spoke at the foot of the stairs. When I reached the top I looked down and he was still standing there. Without smiling he lifted his hand, then turned away, picked up a sports jacket dropped over a chair and walked out of the house.

Upstairs I checked on Tim, put a package of modeling clay by his lamp, and went into my own room. I hadn't finished my nightcap, and it hadn't been strong. But I felt a delicious golden giddiness.

[9]

I woke up to thick fog—and to sanity. If I'd had any incoherent idea in my golden giddiness that Rees Morgan had fallen in love with me, it was gone by foggy morning. He'd been moved out of himself for a moment because he'd lived a monastic life for so long, or else it had been a gesture of genuine affection. But it wasn't love. It couldn't be. Men like Rees Morgan didn't fall in love with women like me. And I wondered painfully what sort of whimsical, original, and irresistible woman Valerie had been.

I'd always been moderately contented with myself beyond the usual whims and yearnings that assail the female from time to time. But now, lying in my silent room in the silent house, I felt the bitterness of my imperfections. *Mediocrity*. That was the word.

And to know it was far worse than to be it without knowing.

I heard a small giggle. I opened my eyes and saw an elf peering around my bathroom door. An elf with a crest of auburn hair. It came across the room and onto my bed with a healthy thud.

"Tim!" I said. "What are you doing out of bed?"

"I put on my robe and slippers, and I washed my face."

"And you aren't supposed to walk around without your braces."

He tried to look repentant, but failed. "Look what I made."

It was a lop-sided but recognizable cat made of yellow-tinted plasticine.

"It's Tris," I said. "I'd know him anywhere."

"He's for you," said Tim. He set Tris beside my lamp. "I couldn't make him standing."

"I like him sitting. He's thinking, you can tell."

"Tris thinks all the time," said Tim proudly. "Thank you for the present."

"Thank *you* for mine." I began to feel better, at least a little more pulled together. After all, Tim was my job here, and nothing else should concern me.

"Well, we'd better get up, hadn't we?" I said.

He snuggled down with his head on my other pillow. "In a minute," he said dreamily.

"Are you still sleepy?"

"No . . . I'm thinking." His eyes grew glazed under his long lashes. "I'm trying to remember," he mumbled. "I did this before once."

"With Mrs. Partridge?"

"*No!*" The lashes dropped lower. His thumb went into his mouth. He pulled up his knees and curled small.

"Wake up, Tim," I said. "Or do you want to go back to bed for another nap?"

He didn't answer and I wondered if I could slip quietly out of bed, cover him over, and leave him there for a while. I glanced down at his small face and saw tears at the outer corners of his closed eyelids. I felt as if he'd punched me in the stomach without warning.

"Tim," I said softly, taking him into the curve of my arm. "What's the matter? Tell Caro."

"I don't know," he said.

"Do you have a pain in your legs? In your back?" He shook his head.

"Do you have funny feelings in here?" I patted his belly.

He shook his head again and burrowed against me.

"Then let's get up and have breakfast. We'll have to stay in this morning, so we can play with the trains." They were set up in what had been the ballroom of this house in its prime as a wealthy quarry-owner's mansion. "Maybe Jason will play with us, if he isn't too busy."

His eyes flew open, wet and brilliant. He took his thumb out of his mouth. "Now you go back into your room while I get dressed, or do you want me to carry you?"

"Nope." He slid off the bed.

As I got dressed I wondered if he could possibly remember cuddling with his mother when he was a baby of two. His mute sadness had shaken me.

Going downstairs was always a long process, as Tim didn't want any help, but swung himself and braces capably from step to step by hanging to the banister with both hands. When we reached the hall I walked ahead of him toward the dining porch, and he called after me, "Caro, I'll show you my go-cart!" He had gone around the stairs and was wrestling with a doorknob. "It's in here," he exclaimed excitedly. His face got red in his struggles. "That ol' doorknob!" I never helped unless I was asked, but he had to ask finally, and I opened the door—it was sticking slightly in the dampness—and there in the average understair closet with raincoats, boots, and so forth was a folding stroller. "Look!" he said triumphantly. "You can take me out on the road in *that*."

"Maybe some day we can go," I conceded.

"*Today*."

"Tim, we have to ask your father, and he's probably working down in his study. Let's go to breakfast."

He came, arguing. "We can ask Jason."

"Good morning, Miss Brewster. Good morning, Tim." Jason lifted Tim into his raised chair.

"Jason, Caro can ride me in my cart, can't she? So I can see the cars on the road?"

"There won't be many stirring in this thick fog, Tim. Will you be having hot cereal, Miss Brewster?"

"Yes, please, Jason." I poured some coffee to revive me.

"Jason, why *can't* we go out on the road?" There was a fiery determination in Tim. "I *never* go on the road!"

"You do when you go to Boston." Jason left. Tim narrowed his eyes at me. "That hardly ever happens," he told me grimly.

When Jason came back with the cereal, Tim said, "I want to go on the road in my cart. I want to go *today*. I don't want to play with trains."

He sat back, folded his arms, and pushed out his lower lip.

"If Miss Brewster wishes," said Jason, "she can push you as far as the gates. Not outside, Tim." To me he said, "You understand, Miss. I couldn't take the responsibility."

"Of course, Jason." I smiled at Tim. "It would be dangerous out on the road too, with the fog so thick. A car might run into us. We'll go down to the gates, and maybe we'll see a rabbit, or a porcupine, or even a deer."

"The repairman's coming to fix the washer," Jason said helpfully. "You might be there when the truck comes." Tim relented and began to eat.

After breakfast we put on our raincoats, and Tim was settled in the stroller. We set off down the drive in a warm, hushed fog. Except for the soft shush of the stroller's rubber tires moving over the gravel, the only sounds were the distant foghorns, the patter of moisture falling from the leaves, and the birdsong strong and sweet. Soon the house was out of sight and we were alone in a damp, green, aromatic universe. Tristan, looking rather wet, paced alongside like a lion unaware that he was a miniature. Suddenly a red squirrel chirred angrily from a limb, and we stopped to watch him. At another turn we got a good view of two young raccoons before their striped tails disappeared into the underbrush. Tim was enraptured, then wistful.

"I wish I could go where they go," he said. "I could crawl around on my hands and knees." He tried to squirm around in the stroller to look at me. "Why can't I just do that anyway? I hate these old braces."

"Some day you won't need them and you can skip, or creep, or go any way you want."

"I wish I was a rabbit. I wish I was Tris."

His longings hurt me. He wanted things so *hard,* and

weren't most of them as impossible as turning into a swift rabbit or a free soul like Tris? I hoped passionately that there'd be a burst of traffic by the gates when we reached them, but it was very unlikely that even the repairman would come while we were there.

I lifted him out so he could get close to the iron railings and look through. The little figure in yellow slicker standing pressed against the gates, holding on and peering through, almost broke my heart. Why couldn't I take him for a ride now and then to see the boats in some quiet harbor, or a pasture full of cows, or the ponies I'd seen the other day? If we met and talked with no other people, how could this be the same as intrusions into Bellwood from a cruel outside world?

Tris sat on the drive and groomed his wet fur. From far off along the road we heard the sound of an approaching vehicle, magnified in the fog. Maybe it was the repairman! My heart beat hard for Tim as he pressed his face between two railings, tense with expectation. Louder and louder the sound grew, and then, from the wrong direction for the repairman, a car showed through the thinning mist, slowing down, until before Tim's enchanted eyes it came to a complete stop just to the left of the gate.

"Hi! Hi!" Tim piped eagerly, waving. A man got out on the driver's side and came around to the gate. He was a very big man with bare white hair, trim and erect. He looked down at Tim with a smile. "You're a friendly little soul on a foggy day. Hi yourself."

Tim grinned bashfully. The man looked past him at me and I expected him to ask directions. I smiled encouragingly.

"Would you be"—his hesitation was oddly delicate— "Mrs. Morgan?"

"Oh, no!" A superstitious chill ran over me as if he'd said something blasphemous. "Mrs. Morgan is—" I glanced down at Timmy's head, and the man said, "I thought Rees might have remarried."

"I look after Tim."

"What is it, Henry?" A thin voice called from the car. "Has he moved away?"

"No, dear, it's all right," the man called back. "Is Mr. Morgan home?" he asked me. His warmth had been for Tim. He was courteous to me, but there was a bleakness about him. "If he isn't, well—" He began to turn away, and I thought, He *hopes* Rees isn't here.

But the frail but determined voice called from the car. "Find out when we can see him, Henry."

"My father's home!" Tim sang out.

The car door opened, and the elderly woman began to get out. He reached her in three strides. "Esther, please," he protested.

"We've come all this distance to see Rees Morgan, and I'm not going to be put off by this young woman."

"This young woman hasn't said a word, Esther." He held her arm as she came toward the gate.

"Then *you're* putting me off, Henry," she said. "You didn't want to come, you've told me time and again that my dreams mean nothing, that my intuition's a sick fancy. You might just as well have come out and called me senile." Her dark eyes burned into mine; deep-lidded eyes that must have been splendid in her youth and were still impressive. Color flushed her pale cheeks. "Do *you* think I'm senile, young woman? Never mind, don't answer. It doesn't matter to me."

Tim had been staring up at her, entranced. She looked down at him and a faint smile pulled at her colorless mouth. "Do you think I'm Old Lady Witch, little boy?"

"What's that?" said Tim. She laughed suddenly and said, "Children, they're God's wonders until they turn into adults. . . . I am going to see Rees Morgan," she said, and pressed the button in the gate post.

"Come quickly, Tim," I said, "out of the way." He let me swing him back where the wide-open gates wouldn't reach. Jason was expecting the repairman, so he'd open the gates without coming down in the MG or on his bicycle to see who was there. In all the time I'd been at Bellwood none of the few persons who had driven through those gates had been unexpected, except for Eric last night.

As the gates began to open the old woman laughed a-loud, a cracked but vital sound. "You drive the car through, Henry. I'll walk across the sacred threshold." She did, so slowly and unsteadily that I went to help her. She didn't refuse my aid, saying fiercely, "It's this arthritis. I used to be swift as that cat there."

"Would you like to ride up to the house?" Henry asked me. "We could put the stroller in the trunk."

I was going to refuse, for some reason not wanting to be at the meeting in spite of my curiosity. But Tim said, "Yes, yes! Oh, can we, Caro?"

I couldn't arrange for him to turn into a rabbit or a cat, as he desired, but I could say yes to *this*. So he and I sat in the back seat and he didn't miss a detail of the interior, gazing, feeling, even sniffing at the upholstery. There was a tense silence in the front seat, and I wished I'd overridden Tim's wishes. By the time we'd arrived to the house at our slow progress—and I could have made it even slower—the elderly couple would either be making an innocuous call, or they'd be leaving because Jason would have smoothly and ever so politely kept them from seeing Rees.

I tried to think of reasons for the atmosphere of strain. Maybe Rees in his pain had shut off old friends, and these people had tried once to break through to him and were now trying again. "Esther" might even be an aunt, or a dear friend of his mother's. There were any number of safe, reasonable explanations. But my nervous stomach didn't believe any of them.

When the car stopped before the front door I got Tim rapidly out of the back seat, saying, "I'll call Jason." I hoped to be out in the kitchen wing with Tim, getting our midmorning snack, before there were any encounters in the hall. But Henry was already out and taking the stroller from the trunk, and Esther was getting carefully but resolutely out on her side. And Tim was not being whisked. He wanted to watch Henry. Swooping up a child with braces and rushing him off is not easily done.

I heard the big front door open behind us. Well, Jason would handle it. . . . Only it was Rees who came out and down to the car.

"Mrs. Faraday," Rees said softly. He took both her hands, then looked past her at Henry. "Mr. Faraday. Out of the past."

"It was more like two years ago than two hundred," said Mrs. Faraday tartly, "so don't sound as if we're a couple of reincarnations."

Rees laughed, and reached out to shake hands with Henry. The big man looked embarrassed and a little pale. "I didn't want to break in on you, Rees. I know you can't help us."

"He came to shut me up," said Esther. "Because I've never given up. A mother knows. What I wouldn't admit in my waking hours comes to me in my dreams."

Rees's blue eyes moved to me, not quite smiling but tender.

"We were expecting the repairman," I said.

"I know. It's all right, Caro."

"Come on, Tim," I said. "Let's see what Jason's got for us."

He came along, reluctantly. As we went down the passage I heard Rees saying, "Come into the library, to the fire. You'll have coffee, won't you? It's a good morning for it."

In the kitchen Jason took our raincoats and hung them in the laundry room. "So it wasn't the repairman."

"The Faradays," I said. "Old friends, I guess."

His bony face was uncommunicative. "Will you be having a cup of coffee, Miss? There's fresh cookies."

"I *smell* them." I breathed deeply. Tim imitated me, pushing out his small chest, and then giggled. The bell from the library rang and I said, "I can wait on myself and Tim, if you don't mind, Jason."

"Not at all, Miss." He left, putting on his white jacket as he went. He was back before I'd got Tim's milk out of the refrigerator. "Mr. Morgan asks will you join them. Tim can stay here with me."

I didn't want to join them. I wanted to drink my coffee at the kitchen table, with the smell of baking still in the air and Tim sitting opposite me wearing a milk mustache. And I could think about Rees, and my first meeting with him since last night; I tried to analyze the way he had looked at me, if his eyes had meant to remind me of last night. Surely he could have made them impersonal, to let me know that nothing of any significance had happened between us.

When I went into the library, Rees and Henry both rose, and Rees made formal introductions. Henry and I made the usual facetious remarks about having already met. I could feel Esther's splendid eyes going over me as if she suspected me of being a mistress in disguise. I felt a nervous, foolish mirth trembling in my chest like a trapped bird. The arrival of Jason with a tray saved me.

I poured the coffee and Rees carried the cups to the older people. "I'm glad you came," he told them, "even if I can't help you. We don't see many people here. For the most part our isolation is from choice. But that doesn't, and shouldn't, apply to old friends."

"Are we in that class?" Esther asked dryly. "Henry wanted to call from Ellsworth, but I wouldn't let him. I said you'd put us off, or that man of yours would."

"Esther," Henry reproved her.

Rees shook his head at him. "Don't stop her. We might have done just that. I'm inclined to sink into myself, as Miss Brewster knows. She doesn't see me for days at a time around here. But when I'm taken by surprise, like this morning, well—" He spread out his hands and laughed. "It's good for me. It's good for anybody. *Now.*" He turned abruptly serious. "You've still found nothing, no trace at all."

"Not the slightest," said Henry. His face seemed to grow more gaunt before my eyes, his eyes distant and sad. "We've had leads. Three amnesia victims, two of whom were pathetic, wanting very much to know who they were and to find a family. The third was a fraud. He'd done a lot of homework, I'll say that for him. He tried to convince us he'd been smashed up in an accident and had had enough plastic surgery to change his looks entirely."

"But I knew he wasn't my son," said Esther. "A mother knows."

"We all knew," said Henry wearily. "Stephen's brother and sister knew. His dog did." With bitter humor he added, "At least Stephen's dog *liked* the other two. He growled at this one. We've also investigated the deaths of a few dozen unidentified strangers in hospitals. But it's a big country, Rees. People die by the thousands, by hit-and-run, accidents, hold-up murders on the highways. They're thrown into bushes or buried in shallow graves and aren't discovered for years, or they're never discovered. We've faced the possibility that Stephen is one of those."

"I have *not*." Esther's cup danced in its saucer as she set it down. "I know he's alive. I dream of him constantly. He doesn't want to be forsaken."

"You dream because you want him to be alive," said Henry. "You're a Christian woman, Esther, or you say you are. Can't you give him up to God, and be content?" Then his strong face flushed, and he gave an oddly appealing look. "Excuse me. I shouldn't have spoken like that."

"Don't apologize, Mr. Faraday," Rees said. "God knows the two of you have suffered enough not to owe excuses to anyone. I just wish I could help."

"He hired a car at the airport in Bangor," said Henry, "on the nineteenth of April. The car's never been found. It could be sunk in a quarry, it could be—" He stopped.

Esther was staring at the fire, her arthritic hands clasped around each other.

"He came here in that car," said Rees. "And left in it. Jason knew that much. He might have said something about his plans to my wife. That we'll never know." Something about his tone made me turn swiftly toward him. His face was like a mask made of skin drawn tightly over bones. I could have sworn his eyes saw nothing; or else they saw through the wall of the house and the fog toward the cliff's edge.

"Would anyone like more coffee?" I asked desperately.

Suddenly Henry Faraday sprang up. "Good God, this is inexcusable!" he blurted out. "For us to come here tormenting you, with what that day means to you! I promise you, it's the last time. Come along, Esther." He stood over her, lifting her gently to her feet.

Rees was up too. "Don't go like this. We're all united, in a manner of speaking."

"No, we'll go," said Henry. "You've been decent about it, but we've no right to impose on you, and it won't happen again."

I expected a protest from his wife. But with impeccable dignity she said, "Perhaps Henry is right. We should not come here again. But I will not believe my son is dead until I see his—" She broke off and hobbled toward the door, refusing anyone's arm.

They both shook hands with me, and then Rees went out to the car with them. I was putting the cups back on the tray when Rees came into the library, shut the door behind him and stood against it. He closed his eyes. He looked white.

I didn't know what to say. I'd been shaken by the

whole scene; I felt in the way, a trespasser. My hands trembled as I handled the delicate china cups.

"Caro," Rees said. I looked around and he held out his arms.

I went to them and into them, my face in his shoulder, my eyes squeezed shut. He folded his arms tightly around me and I felt his jaw pressing hard along my temple, his breath faintly stirring my hair. "Oh God," he groaned. *"Oh God."* I put my arms around him then and held him.

I don't know how long we stood like that, until Tim's voice sounded in the hall. Then reluctantly we separated, but he still held on to me. I felt lightheaded, exhausted; he looked bemused as if he weren't quite sure who I was, his eyes searching my face for an identity. Then he smiled and gave my ribs a hard little squeeze.

"Bless you, Caro," he muttered. "I need you." He let me go, and without planning it out I went over to the fireplace, moved the screen, and knelt down on the hearth to add a small birch log to the fire. I was there when Rees opened the door to Jason and Tim.

"I made a gingerbread man!" Tim shouted.

[10]

The repairman came after lunch. He brought word that the car was ready (his brother was the mechanic), and a technically involved description of the small thing that was wrong. I didn't understand it, but the men did, and Jason rode back to town with him to get the car.

I planned to spend Tim's nap time in my own room, trying to straighten my mind out after this morning. It hadn't been *We need you* this time, but *I need you*. I was glad he was not even in the house when Tim and I ate lunch; I think that even if he were rooms away from me, with all doors locked between, it would have been the same for me as if he had been in the room. Conversely I was comforted to know he was on the property, down in the little stone house at the end of that dark, dripping path.

I had just settled Tim and left him when Rees spoke in a low voice outside my door. I opened it and he smiled at my expression. "You look as if you're expecting a ghost," he said. "One doesn't go with the house, I'm sorry to say. Come on downstairs, will you?"

No time to glance at hair, nose, or lipstick. I went

with him. If he had said, Come to the end of the world with me, I would have gone as quickly.

We didn't go into the library, with its sad stormy echoes of this morning's scene, or into the living room, but into a little room I hadn't known existed, between the library and the dining room. It had white walls and bookshelves, sea-blue curtains, a chair and sofa covered in flowery chintz. It would have had a sea view if the fog hadn't lain thick against the windows. "This was my wife's sitting room, office, studio," he explained quietly. "She wrote, and very well too. I think she would have been recognized as an important American poet, eventually. We had a play yard for Tim just outside here, and she could keep an eye on him as she worked."

A poet. That hateful word *mediocrity* clanged in my brain.

"At that time I worked next door in the library," Rees was saying. "Though the stone house was here then—it was part of the original property when we bought it. There was a rather grim story attached to it."

"What was it?"

"Oh, the son of the house was supposed to have gone mad through his excesses, in the best Victorian tradition. Rather than put him in an institution, they institutionalized him on home ground, so to speak, with a faithful but muscular attendant. I always had a feeling he wasn't so much insane as inconvenient. A genius perhaps. Certainly a nonconformist and a rebel."

"If he wasn't really insane, or at least if he knew what was going on, that must have really driven him over the edge. So how can you say this place hasn't a ghost?"

Rees said, "You grow so intense, you burn like a candle flame. You're burning now for that poor soul.

But he can't be the ghost, because he didn't die here. He outlived his parents and ended his days as a cheerful, witty old man with the freedom of the grounds of the State Hospital in Bangor."

"I don't know if that makes it any better. Who knows what the world lost in him?"

"And perhaps," said Rees, "he really wasn't much good. A charming drunk who had regular attacks of the D.T.'s, and his parents did their best for him. Anyway, he wasn't what I meant to discuss right now." He waved me to a chair. "We'll keep the door open in case Tim calls."

I tried to look more at ease than I felt in Valerie's room. Rees settled in another chair and began to fill his pipe. "The Faradays," he said. "What did you think of them?"

"They're tragic."

He sighed and looked past me at the foggy windows, his eyes narrowed as if in pain. "Stephen's disappearance and Valerie's death are so entwined for me, because one followed so quickly on the other, that just to see them this morning was . . . quietly hideous." Then, as if he had made up his mind to something, he sat forward and spoke in a cool brisk tone. "Esther and my mother were friends, and Henry was always kind to me, including me on expeditions with his own boys. My father died when I was seven. Stephen and his brother Richard and I grew up together, in a manner of speaking; we were familiars but not best friends, we only came together when Henry Faraday brought us together, but we got along well enough. We went to different schools, had our own circles of activities."

He smiled as if at amusing memories. "I was a puzzle to Henry sometimes, I guess. I must have really tried his soul with my repulsiveness. I was such an impossibly egotistical, arrogant kid."

"But aren't most of us egotistical, as kids, and arrogant in different degrees? Isn't it part of growing?"

"You didn't know *me*. Even my mother found me hard to take at times. Of course nobody knew how I despised myself under that hard shell, which wasn't hard at all. It was just a disguise. I was like one of the people actually born without the tough outer coat of skin. I was stabbed, slashed, bruised, a dozen times a day. Still, I did plenty of it back. And I got through college and graduate school, and various fellowships— safe within the academic womb, you see—without anyone ever realizing just what I really was."

I was trying so hard to live it through with him that I ached; I had to force myself to sit back on the sofa, to loosen my hands.

"I even served in Korea; the Army was another kind of womb, you see. I got along well. I was an officer. No doubt if I'd been a GI, living in the bosom of my buddies, I wouldn't have had a buddy. I wasn't the most popular officer, but we weren't there to conduct a popularity contest. . . . That's where I met Jason, by the way. He was in my company. A tough little infantryman, if you can believe it."

His pipe had gone out. He lit it again, and I went to the door and listened for Tim. There was no sound in the fog-bound house but the ticking of the grandfather clock.

"My Korean experiences are of no account," he said. "I threw them in out of vanity. I came back, I went to visit my mother and spent some time thinking what I was to do next; go back to my safe, solitary studies? Or accept one of the openings offered to me in publishing or university teaching? Stephen and Richard came home too, and for once we had something in common. War." He gave me an ironic glance. "I liked Stephen. I knew he was a good doctor and I respected him for his skill and learning. I liked many of the people I met around him, and for the first time in my life I began to question my role as a solitary. I began to move around more. One year I went to Wales to look up my grandfather's birthplace, and in London I met Valerie."

Her name brought her into the room, or had she been there all the time? She had died here; she could be the ghost. There was a thud and a shape against one of the windows; I rose up staring, my heart pounding, and saw a wet Tris standing on the sill and looking in at us. Rees laughed and went to open the window. The cat jumped in, spoke to us, and sat down on the rug to groom himself. His bubbling purr was loud in the little room.

He had also broken some mood, and I didn't know if I was glad or sorry. Rees walked around, his pipe in his mouth, looking at books, moving objects on the desk as he talked. "She was Stephen's friend. In all innocence he told me to look her up. She was studying at Oxford. But what was between her and Stephen didn't matter to either of us. The impact of our meeting was so powerful that she was frightened by it, and it took three years before she was ready to commit herself to me. By than she was working in New York, and I'd taken an editorial job so I could be near her. Stephen's practice was growing fast and he was devoted to it, but he tried to keep in touch with her constantly. Between the two of us she spent a pretty rugged three years. There were times when she was ready to run away to the other side of the world, at least to the other side of the country," he added dryly.

I found myself tight again, practically rigid. He's talking about his love, I thought. He's reliving it behind those sparse words. He hears her voice, sees the way her eyes changed color and her mouth quirked, the way she moved, the way she cried sometimes out of frustration, not wanting to release herself to anyone yet. . . . A poet, loving, giving love, moved by love, and terrified as it began like a great wave to sweep her out of her depth. A petrifying bliss. *I knew.*

"She was afraid," I heard myself saying. "Of something in you. A dark side."

"Why do you say that?" He stood above me, staring into my upturned face.

"You admitted it yourself. It's what made you a solitary for so long. You said it wasn't a happy, contented solitude. . . . But Stephen, the doctor, his life given over to other people, would be like day to your night. Maybe there wouldn't be any great soaring heights, but not any terrifying depths, either."

"How do you know all this?" Then he shook his head. "It's because you're a woman, I suppose. And you've had your own griefs."

"Nothing like what you've had. I wasn't deeply in love with Paul, so even that business is as mediocre as the rest of me," I said.

"Mediocre? *You?*" He laughed. "Never you, Caro." He sat down beside me. "Everything's there, as it should be. But in your own way you've been living as insulated a life as I led before Korea."

"I don't want to discuss me," I said. I got up to listen for Tim again. "It's Valerie." I had to say her name, it was like challenging her to her face. "After three years, she married you."

"Yes, and we planned out an idyllic existence, with no interruptions from the outside; only our work and our love, in as perfect a setting as we could manage. This was the one we loved at first sight, even though we didn't see it in summer but in November. Jason was with us almost from the start. He saw an account of my mother's funeral in a Philadelphia paper, and traced me through it. He showed up here asking for any kind of job. He had an idea he needed sea air to survive."

He got up and went away from me, stood looking out into the fog. "Valerie and I had four perfect years. Two without Tim, and then two with him. Stephen had kept in touch—at least she answered his letters, out of kindness, pity, for auld lang syne. He preferred to pretend I didn't exist, and I couldn't blame him for that. We both wanted him to find someone for himself who would make him at least half as happy as we were, then he'd be off our consciences." He turned his head and gave me a wry grin.

"Then one day he showed up here—that was when anyone could open the gates and drive in. I was off taking a long hike along the shore, trying to get some work organized in my mind. She told me later, and Jason did too, that he looked like a man helpless in the grip of an obsession. If I'd been here he might have flown at my throat."

He pressed his lips together and blew hard through his nostrils. "She talked with him a long time. She convinced him that she hadn't been hypnotized into marrying me, she hadn't been carried away and locked up, she loved me and I loved her, and our son was the proof of it. He left then. She said the defeat in him broke her heart, but perhaps now he would begin to live."

Rees had gone pale as he talked, his dark healthy color turned grayish. I wanted to stop him then, but I couldn't. "It was the nineteenth of April. After she told me about Stephen's visit, she took Tim out of his play yard for a walk around the lawn. She always liked to stand on the edge of the cliff, she had no fear of heights and space . . . Still, she wasn't too close when I called her back, and she turned to look at me, laughing at me for my fears. Then she leaned down and picked Tim up. . . . We hadn't realized how the edge of the lawn had rotted away underneath when the frost went. It sagged before my eyes—I couldn't reach her—I heard her cry—" His voice broke off. He stood silent, his hands over his face. I was on my feet and going to him, taking him in my arms as if he were Tim.

He turned and grasped me. For an instant I saw his face, blind and contorted, before he pressed it down into my hair. I could hardly breathe within his grip, but I didn't want to. My own words came back to me. *A petrifying bliss.*

"Don't *you* leave me, Caro," he was saying. "Don't ever leave me."

"I won't, I won't," I breathed.

Tim could have shouted the house down and we wouldn't have heard. We separated after a few moments, Rees holding me off and seeking something in my face. There was a fine moisture on his forehead, and I gave him a weak, wet-eyed smile. I was shaking so that if he hadn't held me I would have sagged into the nearest chair.

"But you must think this over," he said urgently. "Don't promise anything yet. I've taken an unfair advantage, I've appealed to your compassion. That may be what you are feeling, nothing more."

"No, no!" I objected. "I know the difference. I've been pitying people for one thing or another all my life. I used to cry for the ones in concentration camps, and I wanted to die rather than live in a world where such things could happen. Once I broke off with God because He allowed children to be murdered and animals to be abused. But what I feel now—"

He burst out laughing. "I can see you breaking off with God. Very stern and unrelenting. 'All right, God, if this is the way You're going to do things, I've had it. I'm through. And don't try to get me back!' " He looked much younger all at once. "What do you think of God now, Caro?"

"Some things I can't forgive or accept," I said stubbornly. "But I'll give Him credit where it's due. And that's for beauty . . . and for love."

This time our embrace was not that of a drowning couple, but of lovers.

Then Tim called.

[11]

In spite of my fervent assurances that I knew the real thing when I met it, Rees was determined to give me plenty of time and breathing space. For the most part I was grateful; sometimes I woke at night, hearing the surf building up on the shore or thinking again a cry had wakened me, and full consciousness was like the moment when the poor swimmer realizes he can no longer touch even a toe to bottom and the currents are against him. And I would think, shivering, it's only because he's been so lonely that he's reaching out to me.

But when I next met him I would feel myself changing, blooming, becoming more of a woman with every moment under his eyes and within reach of his voice.

Now we had dinner together almost every evening. Once we went out to eat, to a place far from Somerset, an elegantly simple inn on a secluded cove. I felt like a beauty walking into the dining room with him, and when the other women's eyes moved from me to him with a furtive casualness, I knew what they were thinking, and it added to my poise.

Sometimes we sat all evening in the living room, talking, and we never ran out of things to talk about. He wanted to know everything about me, from my first memories; he made me feel that it was all unique and important, like my quarrel with God. Little by little I was ceasing to regard myself as a mediocrity.

Somethimes we didn't talk. We didn't need to. The best times here were when Rees played. Chopin waltzes, curiously enough, saddened me. There were several that I asked him not to play again, and I couldn't explain why.

"Valerie felt that way about the waltzes too," he said absently. We both looked at her over the mantel.

"What would she think about us?" I asked in a low voice, as if she could hear.

"She would be happy for me and for Tim," he assured me. Then he drew me down onto the piano bench beside him. "Let me hear that spiritual, poignant version of *To a Wild Rose.*"

"No," I said. "Poor MacDowell came to me in a dream one night and said he was *so* tired from turning over and over in his grave, and would I please never assassinate his music again. So I promised."

He smiled and put his arms around me and kissed me. Our love-making was kept to a minimum, which was one of the hardest things about that week. I always hated to leave his arms after we had said goodnight, but in the cold sanity of those later wakings I was glad of his restraint.

He usually went down to his study to work into the morning hours; I would be lulled to sleep by a combination of those leisurely English mystery stories and whatever drinks we had had.

Jason must have guessed something when Rees

began having dinner with me every night. I'm sure it bloomed all over me, but he was always the same and I never surprised any change of expression. I wondered if he would resent me when Rees and I got married. He might still be devoted to Valerie; he might be possessive about the house which he had run alone for three years. On the other hand, he seemed to appreciate what I did for Tim, and he might appreciate the change in Rees, which was already evident.

Suddenly it was my day off again, and I hated the idea, much as I'd liked it last week. But I was not the same woman I'd been then. My life had changed so completely that it was a burden even to think of the outside world. Still, I wasn't actively fighting against it until Eric called that morning. Rees wasn't there. He had left early in the morning to do some research reading at the University of Maine, at Orono. After Jason told me Mr. Allenby was calling, he went to hang out the laundry, and Tim followed him. So I was alone in the house when Eric told me the cook-out was off.

"Mark Webster's father was taken to the hospital last night with a stroke, and he and Helen are all shook up," he said.

"Oh, Eric!" I exclaimed. "I'm sorry!" I was, too; it had come back to me in a flash of pain and nausea just what I'd felt at twelve when my father was taken away in an ambulance. I'd never seen him alive again. Mark was a man grown, but to lose a parent was like losing a part of yourself, no matter what your age.

"They won't know for a few days yet just what the story is, it could go one way or the other. And there's nothing I can do for them right now—Nancy's baby-sitting, but . . . Well, I'd like to pick you up early this afternoon and we'll go to Mt. Desert, or poke around the Blue Hill peninsula, or just take any back road that appeals to us, and then have dinner somewhere. How does that sound to you?"

My mind was blank except for the word *No.* "Under ordinary circumstances I'd love it, Eric," I said warmly. "But . . ." Now my mind was fully awake, slipping and dodging like a squirrel. "I was going to call Helen to tell her Tim's a little off-color today. . . ." *I* was off-color; I could feel myself blushing. "He gets anxious when he's like that, and since his father's gone for the day I think I'd better stay with him, and take another afternoon off."

"Then will you go with me on *that* day?" The Unsinkable Allenby indeed!

"I don't know just when it will be. He may be coming down with something."

"Poor little cuss. I hope it's nothing serious. Look," he persisted, "will you call me as soon as he's in the clear and you can take some time off? No, wait a minute. I'll call *you*, tomorrow, and check. Any time best?"

No time is best, better, or even good, I told him silently. I've got no time for you at all. "Well, during Tim's nap," I said. "From about one to three."

"Good!" He added in a softer tone, "Goodbye, Caro."

I felt a needle-stab of regret as I hung up, remembering how we'd had fun together. He'd also been useful in my reassuring letters to Mindy and Elliot. And I remembered the sense of ease and comfort I'd had with him. But that would be gone now; all my ease and comfort, like all my tears and sorrow, were in the keeping of Rees Morgan.

Now that I had lied, I felt shaky and excited. The

canceled party gave me a legitimate excuse not to leave Bellwood today, but I would still have to take one afternoon off this week. Rees had been very firm about that. I didn't want to spend it alone with Eric, feeling deceitful all the time. So I would go out this afternoon anyway, since Tim and Jason were prepared for it. I would say nothing about the called-off party, but spend the day alone in the woods as I'd been wanting to do ever since I came here. No one needed to know—no one would be harmed. And when Eric called again I'd have thought of another good reason to put him off.

Tim and I ate our lunch together under the birches by the ledges and the little pool, where his boats went back and forth in the slightest puff of breeze, and where we had erected a tiny village on its shore. He was yawning, as usual, before we finished; he'd had a long, busy morning. For one thing he'd learned five new letters by heart. He had been so anxious to commit them that I couldn't force myself to divert him without feeling false, and I had the uncanny sensation that Tim would know I was false. Maybe Rees underestimated his son's capacity; I was positive that Tim would be able to do some simple reading, and it could be a great pleasure to him as the years went on.

I shut my mind to the picture of a tall Tim, physically a man, reading over and over the adventures of Peter Rabbit in Mr. MacGregor's garden.

Once Tim was in bed for his nap, Tris hypnotizing him into sleep with his purr and his drowsy golden gaze, I changed into denim slacks, a jersey, and sneakers. I put a sweater into my beach bag, my book, the knitting I'd brought from home and hadn't looked at,

114

some of the English biscuits wrapped in a tissue, and a large, perfect, early peach which Jason had put in my room last night. The last thing was the compass I'd bought for Tim in the five-and-ten last week when I got the modeling clay. It was to be this week's gift.

Then I went downstairs. Jason was parking the car outside the front door. "She sounds like Tris purring," he said. "They did a good job on her. Have a nice afternoon, Miss Brewster."

"Thank you, Jason."

"The Websters have one of the really old places in Somerset. Their gardens are quite famous locally." He looked around him with an expression I couldn't read. "Mrs. Morgan had great plans for creating gardens here over the years."

"I'm sorry she didn't live to see them through," I said. "And you have so much lawn to mow, too."

He gave me a one-sided grin. "I'd rather do it than having an outsider poking around, Miss. We have a very good system worked out for running the place."

"I've noticed that." I got into the car, wondering if he'd been reaffirming his loyalty to Valerie and warning me not to intrude. But I could tell nothing from his face. "See you later, Jason!" I called breezily, and drove away.

When I had passed the outermost corner of the wall I slowed down. The overgrown wood road was hardly more than a crease in the line of hardwood and spruces. I turned cautiously into it. To my relief it was passable. Ferns brushed the bottom of the car, but the ruts were dry and not too deep. In a little while a curve hid me from the black road. I shut off the engine, and I was alone in a green world of summer silence. I was very happy; I hadn't been alone in any woods for a long time.

I could see a bit of the wall through a gap where some trees had blown down, and I reached it in a few minutes, by climbing over and ducking under the blow-downs. The wall was much lower here, along the side, and I wondered how Rees kept people off the property. There were no signs at intervals saying NO TRESPASSING, NO HUNTING, and so forth. I came to the conclusion that he was using psychology. To a certain mentality, signs are to be defied; a high wall is to be climbed over, an electric fence to be short-circuited. By not posting his land Rees hadn't antagonized anybody, and apparently the local population respected both his privacy and his tragedy.

I climbed a thick, many-limbed old spruce next to the wall, and stepped from it onto the wide brick top. When I dropped down onto a thick rug of spruce spills I was back in Bellwood, and the very birds sounded different.

I smiled at Rees's fear of my getting lost; I had a good sense of direction, I remembered marks, I could guide myself by the sun, and I had the little compass I was going to give Tim. "And there's always the Brewster nose," I said aloud.

I planned to find a place where I could knit and read through the afternoon, and I set off in search of it now, on a southwesterly course by the compass. I loved the hot resinous scent of a stand of spruce in the summer sun, and the stir and whisper of the wind in the tops. I crossed clearings carpeted in green and silver moss, and swampy spots damp and ferny and alive with birds.

Deer hooves printed the soft ground around flat ledges.

I found several places that recalled my hours of arranging playhouses under sweeping branches, of spill floors swept clean, and rooms marked off with clean round stones brought up from the beach. And others where, as a dreaming teen-ager, in love with all the frightening and ecstatic world of being grown-up, I'd taken poetry in great indiscriminate gulps, like Cokes and hamburgers. Love in those days was a marvelous shimmering thing, a Christmas tree ball, a mobile of stars and singing birds.

I walked along, sniffing, seeing, remembering, loving the woods as I always had . . . Then I stopped. Through the silvery tremble of poplar leaves I saw the stone house.

I had come farther than I'd intended, and I was as abashed as if I'd been caught. Still, I *hadn't* been caught; no one was around. I looked through the quivering leaves at the soft subtle colors of the fieldstone walls. It was a one-story cottage with a low-pitched slate roof and it would have been charming except that the deep-set windows were barred. Gooseflesh rose on my arms, and I took my sweater out of my bag and put it on. But surely Rees's books and manuscripts and his long hours of study had exorcised any ghosts. I wondered if Valerie had ever been invited into the study, then remembered he said he hadn't used it until after she died. It must have been a refuge for him, a place where she had never been.

I should go back, I thought. Yet I didn't move, and I couldn't understand the extraordinary power it had over me. I thought it must be because it was so much a part of his life. I stood there asking myself if I was one of those people who have to challenge NO TRESPASSING signs. No, I wasn't. If he wanted to keep this place absolutely his own, like an extension of the most private places of his mind, I would not violate it. Perhaps he'd never been allowed that much privacy as a child. Perhaps this was the way all true scholars were. . . . I'd never known such a man before, and he loved me. I hugged myself against gooseflesh for a new and rapturous reason. *He loved me.*

I turned to go, and as I did I heard a voice calling. With a feeling like doom in my stomach, I looked back. I expected to see Rees. But everything looked exactly the same, warblers flitted unalarmed through the poplars, shadows of the waving boughs moved over the fieldstone walls and slate roof. The pulse beating hard in my ears made it almost impossible to hear anything, but I tried. Then I heard crows arguing somewhere out of sight and I thought with relief, *It was a crow, that hoarse shout.*

But still I was shaken, and I ran back the way I had come, scrambling over blow-downs or squirming under them like a recruit in a commando course being fired at with live ammunition. I didn't slow down until I was at the wall. What if Rees *had* come home unexpectedly and seen me? My stomach began roiling again. What if that wasn't really a crow? Hadn't it sounded, though unintelligibly, like words? Or was it unintelligible only because I'd been so frantic with guilt?

When I reached the car I was astonished at the ferocity of my relief. I felt as if I'd got into my castle and lowered the portcullis just in time. "The Brewster nose really did you in this time, old girl," I muttered. I got out my knitting, a sweater for my niece, and worked on

it until it calmed me. Then I read, and after a while
fatigue swamped me as if I hadn't really rested for days
now, and I curled up in the back seat with my knees
practically under my chin, and went to sleep to the soft
rainlike patter of poplar leaves.

[12]

When I woke up I was cold and the woods were in shadow. I uncoiled myself, groaning, got out and walked around and stretched. I was very thirsty, so I ate my peach, sitting on a stump in a little clearing where late sunshine showered me with welcome heat. Then I combed my hair and put on fresh lipstick and backed all the way out to the main road. It was almost seven o'clock.

"Oh, damn it," I said aloud defiantly. "I'm going home even if it *is* early!"

When I pressed the button at the gates, I expected Jason to come down to check on my identity. But after a minute or so the gates opened, and the green woods of Bellwood closed around me. I experienced a sense of happy homecoming such as I remembered from my childhood, when both my parents were alive. The stone house and its atmosphere of bright nightmare were driven from my mind.

I drove past the front door to the carriage house and went in through the kitchen. Jason was washing dishes and Tim was wiping the silver. They looked at me in astonishment, and then Tim shouted happily, "Hi, Caro!"

"I thought it was Mr. Morgan driving in, Miss," Jason said. "He's late getting back."

"Well, I'm early," I said glibly. "Mr. Webster senior was taken ill, so the party broke up."

"I'm sorry to hear that, Miss Brewster." It could have been an ambivalent answer, I thought. "Have you had anything to eat at all?"

"Just some fruit. Look, Jason, if you and Tim have plans, I can sit here and have some tea and bread and butter, and you can forget all about me."

"I swam a little!" Tim burst out. "Didn't I, Jason?"

"Well, in a manner of speaking." For some reason Jason's bony face went red and he became busy emptying the dishpan. "With me holding him."

"I think that's wonderful," I said sincerely. "Swimming should be very good for him."

Jason cleared his throat. "Well, I don't know about that, Miss. I mean, Mr. Morgan . . . But he begged so hard . . . Well, if you wouldn't mind—"

I'd never seen him so uncomfortable, and after an instant I guessed why. "You mean Mr. Morgan prefers to take charge of anything like that, in case of accident?"

"Yes, that's it," said Jason with relief. He pulled out a handkerchief and patted his forehead. I felt sorry for him, but thought he was unnecessarily anxious.

"Don't worry, Jason," I said. "I wasn't here, you know. But somebody else was."

"But by tomorrow morning, little memories being short . . ." He patted his forehead again. Tim was looking from one to the other of us, the small terrier again.

"Are you going to read to me tonight, Caro?" he demanded.

"I'm sure Miss Brewster will," said Jason. "I'll just get her a bite to eat, and then you and I'll attend to your bath."

There was no use protesting I could get my own tea.

I went off to wash my hands and when I came back my place was set with a linen mat and napkin, and the simple Staffordshire china we used at lunch. Tea was brewing under a cosy. There was the thin Hovis bread I liked, cheese, butter, a little pot of wild strawberry jam.

"Thank you both," I said happily and sat down to eat.

Jason hovered. "You're sure you wouldn't like something else?"

"No, this is perfect."

"Then I'll just get Tim into the tub."

"I'm going to swim in the tub," Tim said as they went off.

Poor Jason! He'd allowed Tim to plead, as Tim pleaded with me; he'd given in, and now he was nervous. How well I knew what it was like. Yet Rees was no monster, and his protectiveness where Tim was concerned was perfectly understandable after all he'd been through. I decided not to ask him about taking Tim out in the car; he'd be sure we'd have an accident. But sometime . . . later . . . I didn't quite dare think *After we were married* . . . perhaps I could get him to take Tim out with us both.

Tim was delighted with his compass. We played with it for a little while, and when I was reading to him he'd break in at intervals to point to one corner of the room and say "North! That's north!"

"Yes, and I'll show you the North Star one night," I promised. I would expand Tim's horizons in as many small ways as I could, I swore to myself. It was true that he was surrounded with beauty and by protective love, but already he had longed for the companionship of other children. Even if he could have that contact for only a few hours out of each weekday, it would still make his world wider and infinitely richer. There should be a special class in the local school administrative district for mentally and physically handicapped children. But even before attending that, Tim should have some short trips away from Bellwood to get little glimpses of what lay outside the gates. I knew better than to argue the issue now with Rees, but I was positive that he would be receptive to the idea eventually, as his despairing loneliness was relieved and the cruel memories dulled.

Tim's day caught up with him all at once, and he fell asleep in the middle of the story. I tucked him in and left him. He had the compass in his hand, the needle quivering toward north as he slept like a living and watchful entity.

I took a leisurely bath and settled down in pajamas and robe to write to Mindy and Elliot. But I couldn't think of anything to say tonight. My mind still ran on Rees and Tim. I put out the lamp and lay down on my bed. The dusk was scented with new-mown grass and spruce woods heated all day by a strong summer sun. I wondered if Rees was driving home now from Orono along quiet roads, seeing the bright eyes of animals like tiny lamps along the verge, and thinking of Bellwood with a difference, because now there was a living woman there, listening for the sound of his car.

I saw clearly how in his torment he could not let Tim out of his sight, and how, when he had to leave him because of his work, he must know that the child was safe behind the gates of Bellwood and constantly under Jason's eyes or mine. But even *we* were not to be trusted to take Tim in a car or to teach him to swim, for fear of the sudden catastrophe—freakish, entirely undreamed-of, like the cliff breaking away under Valerie's feet.

I could understand, I could sympathize. But when Rees was living a more normal emotional and physical life, and there were other children, he should no longer be so obsessed.

Other children. For the first time I faced that. Until now I'd barely faced the word *marriage,* but tonight, teaching Tim the use of a compass, I'd made a leap past the wonder of it all, past the first night together, toward marriage as a day-to-day condition and all that it implied. Would I be expected to run the house, or would Jason? Would I go on trips with Rees or stay at home? Would I have women friends, like Helen Webster? Would Rees's isolation be less as his outlook changed, so that sometimes we would entertain? And would Tim get to know Elliot's children? ... And how much of a mother's part would I be able to take with Tim?

And then to be, literally, a mother. I laid my hands flat on my belly and thought of Rees's child growing there, not of a boy or a girl but of a *life*, and I trembled in awe at taking part with Rees in creating a miracle. I felt tears in my eyes and shut them tightly.

"Oh, my darling," I whispered shakily, and I didn't know if I was speaking to Rees or to the child.

Through the fragrant dusk my mind moved toward Mindy and Elliot and their children, to friends of mine whose babies I had taken for granted, expecting calmly that I would have my own in time. And though my mother had been dead for fourteen years, I knew her all at once in that dusk-filled room with a fresh and poignant intimacy, because she too had experienced this awe.

Valerie had, too. Her miracle incarnate slept in the next room, entrusted to me.

Downstairs the grandfather clock struck, and I counted the long deep strokes. Ten. Was Rees really on his way home, or had he stayed on at the University for dinner and an evening with friends? The idea startled me; I'd grown used to thinking of him as an introvert. But there would be people there who shared his interests and with whom he enjoyed talking. I knew absolutely nothing of his work, which gave me a frustrating sense of great gaps in our relationship. Why do you want to know? I inquired somewhat acidly. You've got enough now. Nothing should matter to you except the fact that Rees needs you.

Oh, I don't know, I airily answered myself. It must be the Brewster nose again.

It was also the fact that Valerie must have known all about his studies, and understood them, and discussed his work with him over dinner. She was an intellectual. I wasn't. Would I be in the end a shattering disappointment to him, as any woman must be after Valerie?

For the first time I was jealous of her, even knowing that if there had been no Valerie I wouldn't be here at Bellwood now.

One portentous stroke of the clock sent ring upon

ring of echoes circling out into the dark house. Where *was* Rees? I got up and tiptoed out into the hall. There was no sign of Jason stirring; Rees had a key to unlock the gates if he came home very late, so Jason could go to bed. Apparently Jason wasn't alarmed about anything now. I went back to bed, intending to lie awake till the car came, but like Tim I was taken unawares by sleep.

I woke sweetly to music floating up from below like the night scents, drifting about me so that I didn't know at first if I was awake or dreaming. Then foggily I recognized one of the Chopin nocturnes, a velvety evocation of the very words *summer night*.

Rees was back. I stretched happily in the bed. To imagine him down there as I listened was better than being there, because I didn't have to worry about those attacks of self-consciousness which still came over me sometimes when I was with him.

There were soft little steps in the room. Tristan had come through from Tim's, and was polishing all the furniture legs and purring loudly. He jumped up on my desk, and I was afraid he'd start knocking things over with his ardent head, especially a small bowl of violas and alyssum Tim had picked for me. So my dreamy mood was disturbed and I got up without putting on my light, took him off the desk, and sat down by the window with him in my lap. As I listened I looked out at the stars over the woods. The Dipper was outlined in diamonds. I found the North Star, and thought of Tim. Against the dark pool of the lawn and the shrubbery other stars flickered—fireflies. And like a river flowing under the stars, the nocturne went on and on, as if there'd never be morning, and who wanted it . . . ?

Another light appeared and disappeared, small, white, uneven in motion, casting a ghostly beam against the trunks of trees along the path to the stone house. I couldn't tell whether it was coming from there or going to it, the spot of light moving in the darkness deceived my sense of perspective, but it was *there*, and Rees was playing the piano below me. I sat up so straight I startled Tris, and he jumped down. It could be Jason out there, doing an errand for Rees, maybe putting some books away. But I'd never seen Jason going there, except occasionally with a covered basket of food when Rees didn't want to interrupt his work. . . . I saw the stone house as it had been in the afternoon, in sunshine, and my skin tightened at the thought of it in the dark. Rees's story of the madman was responsible . . . but just the same, supposing it *wasn't* Jason, but somebody who'd come over the wall?

I went out into the hall and listened over the banister. The music was clearer now. I ran down the stars in my bare feet. I had been in the dark so long I didn't need a light. As I went into the living room I headed toward the floor-to-ceiling bay window where the piano stood against the pale area of glass.

With a hideous start I saw there was no one at the bench.

In the next instant I realized the music was coming from the record player. I don't know why the fact turned me cold. I remember I wanted light, as if that would warm me. And *protect.* With the music playing I couldn't hear anything else, and my ancient childhood fear of things stalking me through the dark attacked me now. I turned on the nearest lamp with fumbling fingers. Then it was almost worse. I had the sensation, also from my childhood, that the furniture had just settled back into its various places, and was slyly watching me with hidden eyes. I stood there shivering, wishing I had the courage to cross to the record player and turn it off.

Suddenly I sensed motion behind me. As I spun around, Rees said softly, "Who's up?"

I ran for him. I don't know if I said anything or not, but I clung to him and he held me hard, murmuring comforting things against my temple, kissing me. I couldn't stop shivering and he said, "You're like ice. What's going on here? Come in to the fire."

He pulled the sofa closer to the hearth, settled me on it with his jacket over my legs and feet, and lit the fire. He went and turned off the music, then came back and stood gazing down at me. I'd never seen him look so well. There was color in his cheeks like windburn, and his eyes were brilliant.

"Now, my darling," he said, "what's wrong?"

"I woke up and heard the music and thought it was you. Then I saw a flashlight on the path to the study, and thought it was a prowler. . . . I came down to tell you, and—" A new attack of shivers hit me. He sat down beside me and gathered me in his arms.

"And what?"

"The music was a record, and the place was dark. . . . I don't know why it upset me so. . . . You must think I'm a neurotic female, but when I was little I had these fears and bad dreams, and tonight it was as if they'd all come true. As if I'd waked *into* one of them instead of out of one."

It was warm in his arms. "Why was it like a nightmare?" he murmured. "Analyze it and it'll be gone forever. Did you see something else beside the light? Did you hear something else beside the music?" More sharply he asked, "You haven't been out, by any chance?"

"No, no, I've only been downstairs a few minutes. I don't know why it was like a nightmare, Rees. Why should it be, here in this place that I love? It has to be an association of ideas. Maybe sometime when I was very small I woke up and went downstairs into an empty room, and the radio was playing but everybody was gone. I was never left alone that I *know* of, but if this really happened, they might have just gone next-door to a neighbor's for a few minutes. Maybe in the next instant my terror ended, because they came. But all I have left of the experience is the memory of terror. Maybe it's that."

"It's very likely that," said Rees. "Do you feel better now? You're not so cold."

I was almost blissful in his arms. "I'm all right now, and ashamed too."

"I don't want you to be upset," he said, "but there *was* a flashlight out there, and it wasn't mine. I was sitting here in the dark listening to Rubinstein when I saw it, and went out. Someone ran off through the woods like a panicky deer through the underbrush."

"I wasn't afraid when I thought it was a prowler," I said. "I just thought you ought to know, because it might have been someone looking for a chance to break in."

"Well, he wasn't a very experienced burglar or he'd have turned off his light and stayed quiet in the woods when he knew I was out there. And in the first place he wouldn't have allowed his light to be seen from the

house. I imagine it was an adventurous kid on a dare."
He laughed. "He must have used a compass to find his
way around." I thought uncomfortably of the compass I
had given Tim, and how I had used it that afternoon.

The clock in the hall struck twelve. We listened,
wrapped closely together. At the end of the bronze pro-
cession of notes he slowly released me and I reluctantly
allowed it. "We'll have a little sherry and then you'd
better get back to bed. My son's an early riser, or hadn't
you noticed?"

We sipped slowly, gazing at the fire. Or rather he
gazed; I tried to watch him without being caught at it,
loving the rugged beauty of his features, marveling at
the eye's spark of fire beneath the protecting bone, the
fine arch of nostril, the curve of lip against lip. I longed
for the courage to run my finger along the line of jaw
from chin to ear. At the thought of passing my palm
down over the back of his head I felt a little dizzy, but I
blamed that on the wine on an almost empty stomach.

I got up suddenly. I felt if we embraced again I
would not want to leave, and neither would he. We
would be on that sofa until dawn. And that wasn't how
I wanted it to be. But in another moment I might have
no authority over myself.

"Where are you going?" Rees asked.

"To my room." I set down my glass, swaying slightly.

Rees stood up and slid his arm around my waist and
held me. "Are you afraid?"

"Not of nightmares."

"Of me?"

I felt gay and invincible. "Never! But I'm trying to be
wise before the event, not after."

"*Caro*," he said in a husky voice and went to kiss me, but I turned my face, and his mouth went onto my throat. I looked up at Valerie and for the first time I felt neither embarrassment nor inadequacy under her eyes, but triumph.

[13]

In a few minutes we went upstairs, lights out behind us, arm in arm like a husband and wife after a successful party, and like parents we went in to look at Tim. As I straightened his bedclothes I didn't see the compass, and realized he'd put it under his pillow. Tris rolled over on his back and stretched and blinked.

Out in the hall again we kissed goodnight by my door.

"You weren't upset by that prowler around your study?" I whispered. He shook his head.

"He won't be back. There's an old yarn hereabouts that the stone cottage is haunted, probably an unrecognizable vestige of the lunatic story. And that youngster is probably sure of it now. *You* aren't going to be apprehensive, are you?"

"Never about flesh and blood wanderers. . . . No, I think my time for nightmares is past. You've driven them away, Rees."

He said, "That makes me happy. Because you've exorcised some of my demons, too. Look, would you like to drive out somewhere for dinner tomorrow night? Perhaps to the Inn again?"

I hesitated and he said, "Tell me."

"I enjoyed going to the Inn with you," I said, "but our evenings here mean more. It's like being alone on our private planet."

He was pleased. "You've caught it too. I'm glad."

We kissed again and I went happily and groggily into my room and fell into bed.

I'd completely forgotten Eric Allenby until Jason came to my door the next day after Tim had begun his nap. "Mr. Allenby would like to speak to you, Miss Brewster."

"Thanks, Jason." I wondered if he had been safely asleep last night while Rees and I were wandering around at midnight. But I'd never be able to tell anything from his face. I went to the upstairs telephone, picked it up, and watched Jason's sedate back as he descended the stairs. "Hello, Eric," I said.

"Hi, Carol!" His energy charged along the wires. What was I going to say to him? I'd forgotten to think up a fresh excuse. But I couldn't let him go on thinking that something could evolve between us.

"How's Tim today?" he asked.

"Oh, fine," I said warily, wondering where Jason was.

"I'm hanging up, Miss," he said from the kitchen, and did so.

"I'm glad the boy's all right," said Eric. "When are you taking your day off?"

I hated all this lying, but he was driving me to it. "I've decided not to take a day at all this week. That way I can have an extra day on my weekend at home."

He was quiet for a moment. Then he said with that

unquenchable good humor, "That's a great idea. I don't blame you. But won't I see you at all before that weekend? It's been a heck of a long time since a week ago yesterday."

"Well . . ." I wouldn't dare fake another afternoon off as I'd done yesterday. "I'll be coming to town next Wednesday, my regular day. Then I'll be going home that weekend."

"All right then," he said decisively. "So you're spending next Wednesday with me, before you take off on that weekend. Don't ask me *how*, because I haven't decided yet, but you'll like it, I promise you."

"I'm sure I will." I laughed convincingly. "Where shall I meet you? I can't come to your house; your mother will think I'm much too forward."

"You may meet her before the day's out, but why don't you come to the yacht club and I'll pick you up there?"

"All right. Until next Wednesday."

He held on. "Even if it rains, thunders, snows, or hails."

"I'll be there."

Next Wednesday was a week away. A lot could happen. I went back to my room, thinking that there wasn't anything else I could have done but agree to meet him. He was very persistent. But it shouldn't be for too much longer. Rees and I hadn't discussed anything beyond my being sure of my feelings for him; everything seemed to rest on how I felt after I'd been completely free of his actual influence for three or four days.

I was sure how I'd feel. So anxious to get back to

Bellwood I'd hardly need a vehicle. So, only one more date with Eric. I felt a faint regret, because he was so nice, and if he'd come along when I was going through my black period I'd have appreciated him with my whole heart.

Jason never took a whole day off, and I thought at first that he was saving up time to make it really worthwhile. Then I began to wonder if he simply didn't want to leave the place. He went marketing in Somerset, and to a local farm for eggs, but otherwise he seemed as deeply rooted in Bellwood as the big trees around the lawn. So when he announced one night that he had a dental appointment in Bangor the next day, and would take the occasion to do some shopping for himself, I was as astonished as if a tree had suddenly begun to walk toward the gates.

"Where did you work before you came here, Jason?" I asked him on the morning of the great day. He was setting the porch table for lunch, and Tim was laying the silver. I began putting the napkins around. "Were you a city person to begin with, or did you grow up in the country?"

He gave my activities a disapproving look. "You don't need to do that, Miss."

"I know I needn't," I said. "But can't I help? I know you're anxious to get started."

"It's very kind of you," he said primly. He didn't sound as if he really thought so. "I've made a seafood casserole for lunch, and it needs only to be warmed up; slowly, at three hundred and fifty degrees, if you don't mind, Miss. It's really foolproof if you take a little care."

"Thank you," I said, and refrained from telling him I'd done my first cooking when I wasn't much older than Tim.

"The salad needs only to be tossed with the dressing, and I've mixed the exact amount you'll need. Please be sure to shake it well first."

"Oh, I *will!*" I promised with overdone enthusiasm.

"The rolls—"

I protested at last. "I've warmed dozens of rolls in my life, Jason. In fact," I added with a triumph I couldn't resist, "I've *made* them by the dozens from scratch. I have my grandmother's recipe, and it's delicious."

"Oh?" He set a majolica bowl of fresh fruit on the table as a centerpiece. "Perhaps you might let me have the recipe, Miss. I'd like to try it."

"I'll write it out," I said, and with a small formal nod Jason left the room. I had not found out where he used to work, or whether he was born a city sparrow or a countryman. I must remember to tell Eric that Jason could sink the Unsinkable without a trace.

When he was ready to go, dapper and solemn in well-tailored slacks and sports jacket, Tim and I saw him off with proper ceremony. Tim was to press the button to open the gates.

"I'll call from Somerset on my way home, Miss," Jason told me. "So you'll know just about when to expect my signal." I wondered why he didn't have his own key, but not for long.

"I'll open the gates for you then too, Jason," Tim promised importantly. Then his lustre dulled. "When can *I* go to the dentist?"

Jason said grimly, "Your time will come, never fear."

I wished him good luck and he gave me an eloquent glance and started the car.

The instant the MG had gone out of sight I felt a sudden soaring happiness, as if I were a balloon just set free into the blue summer air. It was the first time we three had been alone at Bellwood. Of course Rees was in his study and might not appear for lunch. But I didn't have to see him to be conscious of him.

"Time, Caro? Time?" Tim was demanding, his arm stretched up, his finger poised.

"Yes, it's time." He pressed the button and stood back with an engrossed expression, as if he were actually watching the gates opening. Then with a sigh of accomplishment he turned to me. "Now let's study."

With only a slight qualm I could divert him this morning; at least he wasn't thrusting a book or a slate under my nose and demanding information. "I thought we might add more to our village. We can get some little sticks at the edge of the woods and build a log cabin."

"The way you did when you were little? All right!" He started off for the edge of the woods as fast as he could. Jason's gardening didn't extend to keeping the nearest woodland manicured to insipidity. It was left strictly to itself, and we rummaged around finding bits of branches broken off in the spring storms, and carried them back to the pool. We had to select the straightest pieces, which took some time, and carefully build up our walls. Then there was a trip to the workshop in the carriage house to find a thin piece of wood for a roof. It was all very engrossing, and by the time we had finished our miniature cabin, and admired its reflection in the pool, it was time for my midmorning cup of coffee and Tim's fruit juice.

We were in the kitchen when the bell rang. It was as unexpected as a sudden shriek, and it seemed to go on forever, while Tim and I stared at each other. After a moment he cried in delight, "Somebody wants to come in!" and went for the button, but I called sharply, "No, Tim!" The peal stopped as if the mysterious caller had heard me, and I said, "We don't know who it is, Tim."

My heart pounded ludicrously; I don't know why terror brushed me like damp and unseen wings. He looked from me to the button, obviously dying to push it. "It's Jason," he said.

"He won't be back till tonight. Anyway, he'd call first." I wondered why Rees didn't have a telephone connection between here and the gate. Anyway, whoever it was had gone along. Perhaps it had been a roving salesman, selling combination windows or home freezers.

Suddenly the bell began again. It was as impossible to ignore as a stubbornly ringing telephone, which always sounds like the voice of disaster even when you're sure it isn't.

"Let's go outdoors," I said to Tim. I put our drinks on the tray and we went out the back door. We had to go slow because of Tim's braces, and it seemed as if we would never get out of reach of that bell. Even out at the pool we could still hear it through the open windows, as persistent as an air raid siren.

The last time someone had come unexpectedly it had been the Faradays. For that reason, perhaps, the name *Stephen* kept going through my mind; I thought with a sickening flash, What if it's Stephen ringing? Back from wherever he's been. *Back from the dead.*

I was beginning to sweat. I said abruptly, "Tim, would you sit right here and promise not to move while I go tell your your father about the bell?"

He stared solemnly at me and I repeated, "Will you promise? Don't move even to sail your boat."

"I promise," he said at last.

"Just drink your juice. Don't do anything else."

"Can I breathe?"

I looked at him sharply. This was one of the times when Tim could bring me up with a round turn, as my grandfather would put it.

"By all means, breathe," I said with a grin. "I'll be right back." I ran across the sunny lawn, scattering the birds, toward the wall of shade; after the brilliance outside, the woods seemed to have a burning blackness that blinded me. Then I adjusted and ran down the path to the cottage. The door faced me, painted a soft green, and on either side was a window set deep in a green-painted frame. They were open inside the bars, and I heard conversation inside. I was out of breath from my fast run, my ears were pounding; I knew only there were voices.

I didn't hear *words*, only Rees's voice, calm and thoughtful, which I would recognize through a hurricane, and another one that was simply male, uneven, jerky as if breathless. . . . What with that bell still echoing in my head, my rapid heartbeat, and the unreasonable terror that had brushed me back in the kitchen, I was not now struck with wonder at hearing two voices. It was all part of this general craziness. I pounded on the door, crying, "Rees! Rees!"

Inside a door slammed shut, and something was violently moved—a chair? The heavy outside door was wrenched open and Rees came out, pulling it shut behind him. The look in his eyes was like a blow to my stomach, I could have doubled up from it.

"What is it? Has something happened to Tim?"

"No, he's all right—" My tongue could hardly move in my dry mouth. He's furious, I kept thinking. He was almost white in his rage, and his eyes looked black. "It's the bell from the gate. Someone's been ringing it for a long time. . . ." I stepped backward down onto the path, wanting to run and cry somewhere in shame and disappointment, as if I had just done something incredibly stupid that had probably ruined my life. But I knew I didn't deserve it, and this knowledge saved my poise.

"What was I to do?" I asked coldly. "We can't get away from it. Tim's all agog to answer it . . . And it may be something dreadfully important."

"It isn't important." His pale lips hardly moved. "What's important is that you left Tim alone." He came down the steps. "He's never to be left alone, didn't you understand that? Didn't I make it clear?" He began to run. Following him, I cried, "He promised not to move!"

"What's a promise, from a child that young? Good God!"

"I believe him," I said stubbornly, but he was too far ahead by that time.

I forgave him his panic and his rage, he had a right to it where Tim was concerned; but I wasn't surprised to look across the lawn and see Tim on the ledge in the sun, stroking Tris.

Rees stopped abruptly and I caught up with him.

With more color in his face, he murmured, "It seems you know my son better than I do. Forgive me, Caro, I'm not quite sane where Tim's concerned."

"I wouldn't have left him for more than a few minutes," I said, "and then only because the way that bell went on and on. It could have been for some awful emergency." I listened. It had stopped now, we heard only the birds. A goldfinch sang a long canticle of thanks after a drink. "What if there'd been a bad accident out there and someone was bleeding to death?"

"I didn't know you could be so dramatic, Caro," he said with a smile. His eyes had become blue again. "It was no doubt some enterprising youth selling brushes."

"I did think first of salesmen," I admitted. "But usually it doesn't take so long to convince them nobody's home. This went on and on, and it sounded so frantic."

"Don't you think any signal or summons does that, the longer it goes on?" He took my hand and drew it through his arm, and started walking me across the lawn. "Now that I'm up here I'll have a cup of coffee with you, and mend my fences. You must have thought you were meeting the original mad scientist."

I remembered Eric's remark about the mad scientist, and my mouth wanted to turn up. Some day when I knew Rees better I'd tell him.

"I know you were angry," I said.

"Not so much angry as disoriented. I was so completely lost in what I was doing. The shock of interruption is always so great that I have my strict rules to save me."

"I don't blame you," I said humbly, "and I'm sorry. Next time I'll—"

"Next time you can turn off the bell," he said. "I'll show you how. Anyone with legitimate business here knows enough to call first."

"I didn't move, Carol!" Tim shouted at us. "I only breathed! And I patted Tris."

"You're a good boy," I said. I picked up my cold cup of coffee and the tray and said to Rees, "I'll bring out hot coffee for us."

"All right, dear," he said absently, as Tim began talking to him.

I had the blissfully exhausted sensation of having reached shore after nearly drowning as we sipped our coffee by the pool. Tim talked to himself while he played, and the big golden cat watched the boats float on the water and lashed his tail.

"You must have been startled to hear voices down there," Rees said. "Did you think I had guests who'd come by tunnel somewhere? Or outer space?"

Light dawned. "It was a tape recorder!"

He smiled. "I'd taped a rather interesting and revealing interview at the state hospital when I was last in Bangor. To put it simply, my work consists of compiling case histories of criminals of low intelligence, and of their families, in an effort to trace the hereditary aspects of their behavior. Now this young man has recently wiped out wife, sister, father, and mother in one fell swoop."

I winced, and glanced quickly to see if Tim noticed my reaction, but he was too absorbed in his play.

"He's been committed for observation," Rees continued, filling his pipe. "He's more confused about his acts than ashamed or afraid, and he feels he had reason but he's not quite sure what it is. He's certainly not articulate enough to express it. After I left the hospital I drove back into the country to see the farm where the murders occurred. Even now, in the richness of summer, the place looks barren . . . devastated . . . as if the soil had given up years ago producing anything but rocks. God alone knows what hell has been going on there and for how many years."

The compassion in his voice impressed me. I said, "Will you try to find out about the family?"

"Oh, yes. I'll make contact with relatives and friends, such as they are, at the trial. They're almost always willing to answer questions, and they'll even volunteer information if they think it's for a good reason. If I'm very lucky, and very persistent, I may find out when the family tree began to warp."

"To use an overworked word, it sounds fascinating," I said. "Grim, but absorbing."

"Not grim when you think what it may someday help to accomplish," said Rees. "When I'm not outside on my research, I'm putting my records of the last year in order, writing up notes, clothing the whole thing in some sort of readable prose."

"I'll never interrupt you at your work again," I said, trying not to sound as fervent as I felt. "But supposing something happened here, an accident to Jason, or to Tim when Jason wasn't here with us. How can I get in touch with you?"

"I'll show you. You should have been informed before."

It was in the wall panel beside the gate-button, behind a little door; a small phone and another button which sounded a buzzer in the stone cottage. "Tim doesn't know about it because it would be too much temptation to him," he said. "He'd have a hard time getting up on a chair to reach it, but he's a stubborn little imp and he'd try it, braces and all, and probably get a bad fall out of it."

Then he showed me how to silence the gate bell in case of another persistent caller. "Now I'm back to work," he said. He put his arm around me and tipped my face up to his and kissed me as if I had been Tim. I gazed at him solemnly and then for no discernible reason we both laughed. We walked across the hall to the front door, still laughing softly at each other. It was one of those moments that bathe you in a sort of miraculous sunshine.

In the doorway we looked out like parents at Tim. And I said on an impulse, "You know, when that thing kept ringing and ringing I remembered that the last unexpected people had been the Faradays. . . . And then I thought all at once, *Stephen Faraday*. Supposing it's Stephen Faraday."

The arm around me sprung tight like the jaws of a trap. "Why did you think that?"

"The connection, I suppose." His grip hurt. "And I'm always intrigued by mysterious disappearances."

"Don't be intrigued by that one." His voice was rough, but he did loosen his arm. "It's a tragedy that doesn't bear thinking about. Stephen was a doctor, and a dedicated one. He wouldn't wilfully walk away from his patients any more than from his parents." He went out onto the step. Looking back through the screen door he said with a slight smile, "Certainly not for unrequited love. Stephen was a realist as well as a humanitarian. No, I'm positive Stephen's as dead as—as my wife is."

He went back across the lawn, straight, vigorous, black head high in the sunshine. " 'Bye, Daddy," Tim called after him and Rees waved without looking around. I stood watching him go, conscious of the loud hum of bees in the roses, and of something else: that Valerie might not have gone over the cliff. She might have gone away with Stephen Faraday.

[14]

Once I got this into my mind, I was obsessed by it. It would mean of course that the whole story of Valerie's death was false, and that he had lied to the elderly Faradays. But I would only love him more for the desperate attempt he had made to wipe the whole thing from his mind, this lonely brilliant man who had found a whole world in one woman only to lose her. I knew how I would feel if I should lose him now, and I'd known him only about a month. He had had Valerie for four years. However he lost her, it had been a brutal blow, and if it was by betrayal, that was worse than by accidental death. I was all the more passionately determined to make it up to him.

Jason came home with a sore jaw. In the morning he felt better and gave Tim a dump truck he had bought. It meant we had to go down to the beach at once, to make roads in the damp sand. Rees had started off early somewhere; perhaps, I thought, back to try another interview with the mentally defective murderer in the state hospital. I had made up my mind not to think any more about Valerie. However she'd left Bellwood, she was not here, and I was, and I would not even admit the possibility that someday she might come back to see her son, if not her husband.

"A boat, a boat!" Tim was shouting. "Caro, look!"

She was skimming into the cove, a slim small sailboat heeling far over in the light wind; we could hear the wash of the bow wave. Then she came about with a loud slatting of the sail, and I saw Eric Allenby at the tiller. He grinned and waved, and Tim waved back wildly, laughing aloud in his rapture, so excited I thought he was going to cry. When the boat was almost ashore, the sail came down, an anchor splashed overboard, and then Eric dropped over the side too, in bare feet and shorts, and waded to the beach. Tim sat gazing up at him as if he were a god suddenly descended from a cloud.

"Hello, Tim," Eric said.

Tim went speechless. Eric looked over at me, who was practically speechless for another reason. I could imagine Jason watching from the top of the cliff.

"Well, whaddya know?" Eric said cheerfully. "I just happened to be sailing by, and—no, I didn't just happen to, I came out this way on purpose."

"What's happened to *Kingfisher?*" I asked.

"She's fine, thanks. I borrowed this one because she's a little handier for dropping in on people. Hey, that's some dump truck you've got there, Tim," he said. "I never saw one like that before."

"Look," said Tim proudly, and turned the crank to make the back tilt up and dump its load of sand. Eric whistled. Tim became practically luminous, and Eric reached down and lightly touched the auburn head. Then he sat down beside me.

"I don't think you like to be dropped in on," he said.

"I'm not supposed to have what they call 'followers' in Victorian novels." I tried to sound amused, but I was unreasonably nervous, and not only because of Jason's probable and disapproving surveillance.

"I didn't come over the wall, or get in through the sacred portals under false colors," said Eric. "I didn't come to the door twisting my hat in my hand or digging my toe in the turf. I just happened to be sailing by. Owen Glendower, or whatever his name is, owns the beach only to low-water mark, well beyond which I dropped the killick."

"And then walked up *past* the low-water line," I pointed out, getting into the spirit of it. "So you're trespassing."

"Would he deprive a passing sailor of fresh water?" Eric wheezed, clutching at his throat. Tim looked up in alarm, and Eric winked at him. Tim tried to wink back and blinked both eyes frantically.

"No matter how you came, you came. I can't help it, Eric," I said. "I'm uncomfortable." I was annoyed too, because behind his bland, ingenuous smile he was laughing at me; I was sure of it. I wanted to explode at him, but I thought that was what he was waiting for. He lounged on one elbow watching me. I tried to concentrate on my mending, but I felt his eyes, and heat ran up my throat. *Why don't you go?* I wanted to shout into his face.

"You're uncomfortable because you're so conscientious," he said. "Now I'm very comfortable, and so's Tim. Aren't you, Tim?"

"Yes," said Tim. "Will you help me make a castle?"

"He can't help you today, Tim," I said. "He has to go home."

"I get the impression you're trying to get rid of me," said Eric. "I thought that even if you gave me the bum's rush you'd at least show a little spontaneous joy at the first sight of me." His manner was mildly mocking, but not his eyes, which looked soberly into mine as if he actually did hope to find something else there. "You do like me, don't you?"

"*I* like you!" Tim piped.

"Thanks, old man," said Eric, resting his big hand for a moment on Tim's skinny, sandy shoulder. Then he looked back at me, and I said crossly, "Of course I like you, Eric. But if they only ask this one thing of me here, and everything else is for my comfort, I don't want to look as if I'm ignoring the house rules. I despise people like that. It's a form of cheating, as far as I'm concerned." His eyes never left my face. Neither did Tim's. Both males looked absolutely fascinated, and my cheeks grew redder. "There are no restrictions on my free time, and no objections to your calling me. But don't you see, this could look like a *date?*"

"An assignation!" He struck his brow. "Dear God in heaven, Jane Eyre is up to no good."

"Oh, Eric Allenby!" I burst out in exasperation and laughter, and he grinned and got up.

"All right. Now that I've proved I can get through to you, I'll leave before the palace guard surrounds me with pikes at the ready. Hey, how'd my head look stuck on a pike at the gates as a dreadful warning, huh?"

"Positively Cromwellian," I said.

"I'll call you tomorrow, through the grace and favor of 'is Lordship."

I wanted to say *Don't*. But this was just one of the things I had to go through until Rees and I took a definite step. I was still in Never-Never Land half the time, sure in my half-dreaming states that it would never happen, and yet so positive at other times that I was an entirely different woman, walking tranquilly and competently toward her destiny.... And in between I was this one, nervously mending Tim's jersey while the thread caught my agitation and snarled itself impossibly, and I was so hot that my eyes felt half-scalded.

And this Eric standing over us, with Tim gazing up at him as if his yellow head brushed the clouds; Eric, looking down at my nape as if he could read its very defenselessness ... surely no neck ever looked more helpless to a black-masked headsman, because this in-between woman *was* without defense.

Why didn't he go away? Then she could go too, and be replaced by the serene and affirmative one again, she who was to be Tim's mother.

"*Can* I call you, Caro?" Eric asked in a low voice, and I realized I had not answered him. I tipped back my head and smiled.

"Of course."

Tim held up his arms. "Will you help me swim?"

Eric reached down to pick him up, and I said, "Mr. Morgan doesn't let anyone do that but himself."

"Listen," Eric protested, "all through college I was a counsellor at a camp for youngsters a lot worse off than this one. I know how to handle them."

"I know you do," I said, "and I hate to say no to either of you, but he's very nervous about accidents ever since—" I regret to say that in the midst of my uneasiness that morning the Brewster nose asserted itself. My curiosity was as exasperating as Eric was. "Were you here when it happened, or were you in Vietnam?"

"Yes, I was overseas, but a friend of mind in the state police told me about it afterwards. He'd just finished his training and been assigned here. It was almost his first call, and when he saw what was at the foot of the cliff he wanted to turn and run. He thought he was going to disgrace himself either by heaving up his breakfast or bursting into tears." Eric's voice was carefully devoid of any emotion that could communicate itself to Tim, who crouched over his truck again. Eric gazed down at him thoughtfully. "Then Ted saw the baby move. He swears that's when he became a trooper, not when he graduated from the academy."

"What baby?" Tim's head came up alertly. "Where was it?"

"Oh, it was a baby I knew a long time ago, Tim," Eric said. "He fell down and broke his leg."

"Did he have to wear braces?"

"As a matter of fact he did, for a while. But he's all grown up now, and he can swim, play baseball, ride a bike—"

"*I'm* going to have a bike. Jason's got one, too."

"Good for him. So long, Tim. See you again sometime." He looked back at me. "Between one and three tomorrow, right?"

"Right," I repeated. "I'll be expecting it."

"Now that's the second positive note I've heard today. I'm glad I came." For Tim's benefit he made a big splash wading out to the sailboat and getting aboard. He pretended the anchor was heavy, grunted and groaned while Tim laughed out loud in ecstatic suspense. We both clapped and cheered when he finally got it aboard, and he took a bow. As the sail went up, with a slatting and rattling in the light breeze, Tim said wistfully, "Will he take me sometime maybe?"

"I don't know, Tim, but maybe your father will get a sailboat when you're older and you can help him sail it."

"After I get rid of these old braces, like that boy."

"Yes," I said. We watched the small boat cut away across the whitecaps, heeling far over as the wind filled her sail. Eric's yellow head and tanned face showed against the creamy canvas. He swung his arm in an energetic farewell and we waved back, Tim with all his might.

I looked away before the boat disappeared past the long point of rock around which she'd come. I had grown up with the salt-water superstition that to watch a vessel out of sight brought bad luck to her.

But I was hardly thinking about Eric. The sparse account of his friend's experience was still with me; the only relief from it—if you could call my reaction relief —was knowing that Valerie had indeed died as Rees had said. She hadn't run away, and she had probably been laughing at him with love when the turf gave way.

At intervals all day the story came back to me, depressing and disturbing. In between I was conscience-stricken for not telling Eric the truth straight out, that everyone else was a shadow beside Rees.

But when Rees came home that night and we walked on that same shore in the long gull-haunted hour when sunset darkened into dusk, all the rest went away. There were neither ghosts nor shadows, just Bellwood and the four of us within it—five, including Tris.

Eric called me the next day. He told me that the clambake was on again, because Mr. Webster was very much better. Once more they were having the party on a Wednesday because of me. "Helen doesn't give up easy," he told me. "For some reason she doesn't believe in that rich elderly character back in Limerock."

"Well, for some reason I don't believe in him either," I said. "But I'd like to think they all liked me for my own sake rather than as a safe choice for you."

"They do, they do," he assured me. "This match-making business is just a reflex action. They like you and want you around. If you were a woman the others didn't like, you wouldn't stand a chance. You ought to know that, being a woman."

"Well," I said, sounding more dubious than I felt.

"And I wouldn't give a nickel," said Eric warmly, "for a woman that other women didn't like. They can tell, you know. It's the same with men."

He seemed set for a long discussion, taking advantage of the fact that there was no telephone ban. But, though Rees was down in his study, I was too conscious of Jason's presence in the house, even if I couldn't see him from the upstairs hall and I could tell he wasn't listening on the kitchen extension. He hadn't said anything yesterday to indicate he'd seen Eric on the shore, but I wasn't sure that he hadn't seen us.

"Where shall I meet you tomorrow?" I asked. "At the yacht club again?"

"Let me come and get you."

"I wanted to go in early enough to do some shopping, and you wouldn't want to come that early," I objected. I began to feel fenced in.

"Who says? I'll be waiting outside the gates for you —when?"

"Three o'clock," I said, defeated.

"All right. I'll be there. Bring your suitcase and we'll elope." He laughed. "Goodbye, Caro."

"Goodbye, Eric." I hung up and sighed. A motion at the far end of the hall caught my eye, and I saw Jason coming through the door that led to his quarters, the way to the third floor and attic and the back stairs to the kitchen. He walked down the hall toward me, carrying some of Rees's clothes that he'd been pressing, and we exchanged the courteous smiles of strangers passing on the deck of an ocean liner. Then he went across the landing at the head of the stairs toward Rees's room, and I went into my own.

The next morning I waked hoping for bad weather, but the day was relentlessly fine, and in spite of myself I began to look forward to the clambake. I'd always loved being on the shore and it came to me how much I'd missed having some occasional fun with a congenial crowd during the months when I'd gone around with Paul.

I walked to the gates that afternoon, instead of letting Jason drive me in the MG. Jason's expression said clearly that this was beyond him. "Don't you ever feel like getting out and walking, Jason?" I asked him.

He looked as if I'd said something improper. I laughed. "I guess you're a city slicker at heart," I said.

"If you don't mind my saying so, Miss, you'd better be away from the house before Tim wakes up. He'll be expecting you to be gone."

Sunk again. I departed, determined to find out about Jason in spite of himself. Rees would tell me.

The gates opened as I reached them, and there was Eric's old convertible parked on the verge. Telling him about Jason's snub the other day, and this new one, took care of the first few moments and, as always after I'd been with Eric a little while, I enjoyed him and stopped worrying.

After we parked on Main Street, I wanted to buy something for Tim first, and headed for the five-and-ten. I told Eric he could leave me on my own and I'd meet him somewhere, but he insisted on coming along, and before we finished we'd covered the whole store like tourists in Tijuana. He was especially fascinated by the kitchen gadgets, trying everything that had movable parts. He whistled at the parakeets and was so taken with one particular bird that he was going to ask his mother if she'd like it. He gave the framed reproductions of French impressionists as serious an examination as if they were the real thing.

"Are you expecting to find an original slipped in there by mistake?" I asked him. "Where's your glass to pop in your eye while you study the brush strokes? I know all about those things because I go to the right movies, you see."

"I was thinking of a heck of a good gimmick for a suspense story. Somebody steals a priceless collection and hides it out in the art department of the local five-and-ten."

155

"Yes, but how does he keep the Renoirs and Matisses from being sold off at"—I looked at the price tag—"three dollars and ninety-five cents?"

"Hey, wait a minute!" He snapped his fingers, and the only other person in our far corner, an obvious summer lady, swung her head around as if she'd just been accosted. He didn't even see her expression, which was at once indignant and excited, as if at last Something had happened in her dull life. "His girl already has the job, you see? That's how he gets the idea. She keeps people from buying them by saying they're samples— Not for sale, madam, but you can order one if you'd like." He pretended to scribble, tongue just showing between tight lips. "How was the name spelled? Is that with four o's or three? Oh, yours was the branch that came over with William the Conqueror! Isn't that *fabulous!*"

The summer lady had retreated behind a display of hideous imitation Toby jugs and was regarding us through them with horrified delight. "But how did they smuggle the paintings *in?*" I asked. "The manager would—that's it, *he's* the manager!"

"That's it!" Eric shook my hand violently, then stood off still holding my hand and said in a voice gruff with emotion, "Welcome to the firm—partner."

"You *mean*—" I put my free hand to my throat.

"I never meant anything more. Things haven't been right around here since old Scotty—went away." We both gulped. "But now I have a hunch that they're going to be right again for a good—long—time." He snapped me toward him like an apache dancer, and clamped his arm around my waist. I thought the summer lady was going to faint. "What we do now," said

Eric crisply, "is a soft-shoe down past the dishes and between the baby clothes and the stationery, then I swing you up onto the checkout counter, and pound out the beat for you on the cash register—"

"And the Legion band comes marching in through at the front doors for the fade-out," I finished.

"No, the Somerset Town Band, because they're worse," said Eric. "We have the garden club in majorette costumes, and this great big brassy finale of the theme song—"

"I Found a Million-dollar Painting in the Five-and-Ten-cent Store!" we sang together, and when I looked around the summer lady had disappeared from behind the imitation Toby jugs. "Cut!" called Eric, and marched me toward the doors. I never did go back to see if she was lying in a heap beyond the counter.

"Well, that wraps it up, baby," snapped Eric. "Let's get the film into the cans." We leaned on parking meters and laughed the way I'd forgotten I could laugh, till my midriff hurt and there was an ache under my ribs. There were few people out there at the moment and those who passed either smiled in sympathy or looked as if it was nothing out of the ordinary. . . . The last time I'd laughed like that I'd been with Paul. I couldn't remember why, but I remembered the place. It was outside the Wainwright Museum and we'd made it just in time.

I straightened up, wiped my eyes, and said, "And I never did get anything for Tim. I'll have to go back in again. And *you* stay here."

"All right, Mother," said Eric in a hearty Midwestern voice. "You go right ahead. I know you want to get some little souvenirs for the grandkiddies."

I went back in and bought Tim a paintbox and a large block of drawing paper. "Now," I said, when I came out, "I want to buy a birthday present for Mark, but I'm exhausted."

"How about a little pick-me-up at the hotel bar, Mother?" He winked excruciatingly. "The Ladies' Aid will never know."

"Lemon and lime," I said firmly. "I'm emotionally immature. . . . In Webster's Pharmacy," I added, seeing the sign at the next corner.

"I'm afraid you're far gone in decadence," said Eric. "Next thing you'll be sniffing glue. Come on." He took my package and pulled my arm through his, and as we headed for the corner we came face to face with Phyllis Partridge.

Eric beamed down at her. "Hello, Philly, m'dear!"

"Oh, you!" she said, poking him in the chest. "It's a good thing I don't take you seriously or I'd think I was engaged by now." She smiled at me. "How are you getting along out at Bellwood?"

"All right so far," I said. "Probably because you gave me that advice."

"Well, I'd hate to see you walk into that in all innocence. I'd never forgive myself. You don't look a bit tough."

"She is, though," said Eric. "Tougher than tripe. She knows karate."

"You're kidding!"

"No, I'm not. She splits all their fireplace wood out there with her bare hand." He looked respectfully at me. "Do you yell each time, Caro, the way they do on television?"

"I scream," I said. "Because it hurts. And then I go

like this." I flapped my hand as if in agony and blew on it. "I've only known Eric a couple of weeks and already I don't believe a thing he says, so why do you?"

"I shouldn't," she said, "but it's those eyes of his, so *honest*. I guess you shouldn't go by anybody's eyes." She stopped, frowning, her mouth moving as if she were saying words in silence, then she blurted out, "Rees Morgan's eyes. Don't you let them fool you."

"Aw, come on now, Philly," Eric patted her shoulder. "Forget it. It's all over and done with now."

"Not for her it isn't," said Phyllis defiantly.

"I won't let anybody fool me," I told her. "I did once, and that's how I learned all about it. Once bitten—" I shrugged.

"Well, just so long as you don't forget how the bite hurt. I've got to wag myself down to the Sail Loft fast. Sharon's alone, and these summer kids get in there and give her a hard time."

She hurried on past us. He called goodbye after her and she waved a hand without looking back. With the meeting something had been quenched, so that we walked along quickly to the drugstore without speaking. It had been like a fairy-tale encounter with the mysterious old woman whose presence at a fête throws the whole occasion into gloom. Yet Phyllis with her healthy coloring and her gift for baking good things certainly couldn't be likened to a wicked fairy or a witch. I told myself that the way I felt was the normal reaction after laughing so hard.

But why should anything quench Eric? I glanced up at him as we went into the drugstore. He looked preoccupied, which made him seem older.

We sat on stools at the soda fountain, where two women were treating their young to ice cream and having a social hour with the girl clerk. The small children ate their vanilla ice cream (with chocolate jimmies) with solemn dedication to the rite, dipping the spoons carefully and licking them off each time. Their youthful mothers, in brilliant shells and tight hip-huggers, talked of dances and booster shots in almost the same breath. They and the clerk called Eric by name, and glanced at me with candid and friendly curiosity. At the far end of the long narrow shop I caught a glimpse of Mark behind the prescription desk, explaining something to a man who looked like a lobsterman. The explanation must have been reassuring because the man was still smiling when he went out past us, carrying the small envelope with the name WEBSTER'S DRUGSTORE printed on it in blue. Mark turned to the next customer in the little cluster waiting with prescriptions.

"What shall I get him?" I asked Eric.

"How about the Philosopher's Stone? I always thought Mark looked like an alchemist back there, measuring and compounding."

"I'm sorry, I've already given it to my brother. That's why he's known as the Midas of Limerock."

It wasn't very good, but it was an effort in the right direction. We finished our drinks and went out, walking along and looking in the shop windows. The harder I tried to think, the more scatter-witted I became, and Eric said nothing at all, except for an infrequent monosyllable. Finally, after a dim session of staring at the window of the Somerset Bookshop, I said abruptly, "Look, Eric, if there's something else you'd rather be doing, why don't you go and do it, and I can meet you later? I can't collect my thoughts for thinking you're bored and annoyed and wishing you hadn't stuck your neck out."

"I'm not any of those things," he said, looking hurt.

"Then help me! I don't know a thing about Mark, but I'll be darned if I buy shaving lotion or a fifth of liquor."

He took me by the arm and swung me around and into the bookstore, past the gaggle of ladies brooding over the gift counters, and down to the pleasant isolation of the bookshelves. In less than five minutes he had located a new edition of *Tales of Land and Sea* by Joseph Conrad, and said, "Somebody borrowed his and never brought it back. He'll love you forever for this."

"I'll be sure to give you credit so I won't break up the marriage," I said. I bought a card and some paper, and wrapped the book up there.

[15]

It was close to six now, and we drove out of the town and onto one of the long points that made the harbor. The road wound through woods that were a mixture of hardwoods and spruces. Once we passed some children on horseback, now and then someone came along on a bicycle. Very infrequently there was another car. We passed gates, some hospitably open, some closed like Bellwood's.

The woods were lovely, the hour golden. Eric was giving me a commentary on a few of the rare characters tucked away in the unseen houses at the ends of the winding drives, but I hardly heard him, even though I tried to laugh in the right places. This was too much like Beauchamp Point in Camden, where Paul and I used to drive in early spring and late fall, when many of the places were closed for the winter. We'd walked up driveways that hadn't been closed off or had only a chain between posts, and had crackers and sardines and beer on the broad verandahs of huge old houses called cottages by their millionaire owners. If I shut my eyes now—and I willed myself not to—I could be back in a mild day in March when there had been only birds' voices around us, and still ice along the shores; and then a pale gilt day in November when the light on the Camden hills had a haze of sleepy sadness. We'd sat on the end of a dock, our feet dangling.

"What do you think, my dear," Paul asked, "of increasing the staff this year? A footman to help Maynard, perhaps? The old boy's getting on."

"But it would break his heart if we even mentioned it," I said, seeing at once a frail silver-haired old butler who had come into the family as a young footman himself before Master Paul was born. "Now I'm thinking of training Betsey to be my own maid; she's wasted dusting the Chippendale. It might be fun to take her to Paris and Rome. She'd adore it. But you're to keep your hands off the girl, my love. Her mother *trusts* her to us."

Paul twisted an imaginary mustache and tried to look lecherous, which was impossible with his delicate and boyish features.

"My darling, couldn't you for once forget the bourgeois moral code you were born with and entertain yourself at times with our robust young chauffeur while I—"

"Paul!" I exclaimed in my own voice. "Talk about bourgeois morals! You're positively immoral in *any* class if this is how your unconscious mind runs."

He burst out laughing at my expression, but the laughter had a harsh quality. "Okay, so it's wishful thinking, because I'll never get a chance to raise even the midlest hell. Even too many drinks on a weekend, if I take 'em in public, will shake people's confidence in the bank. The bank, the bank, my mother's pounded it into my brain ever since I could walk. It's like being destined for the church." He wasn't laughing any more, his voice had a strident edge, and his hand savagely clicked his lighter on and off. "God, if I'd only been born into money! And why the hell couldn't I have been? I used to drive myself half-mad with wondering what powers put me into the wrong place, and then took away my father so I couldn't even have *that* much to take the curse off it!"

He stared out to sea, his eyes squeezed up as if the light hurt them—or as if he were trying to hold back tears of frustration. I reached out and took the lighter away from him and held that nervous twisting hand in both of mine. "I'm sorry, Paul," I said. "At least I had a chance to know both my parents for a while, and I had Elliot and my grandparents."

He slatted his hand free of mine and folded his arms tightly across his chest, and still wouldn't look at me. "*Money*," he muttered. "Why couldn't I have had it? With money you can do anything. I could even put up with *her*."

It was the first I knew that Paul hated his mother. "*Carol!*"

"What?" I cried out, my heart jumping, and stared aghast at Eric. I felt a little sick to my stomach, as if I'd been violently wakened out of sleep. Eric glanced at me and then back at the road.

"Where were you?" he asked.

"I was listening to you," I objected, blushing. Was he offended?

"What was the last thing I said?"

Blushing even more, and enraged by my own panic, I fumbled. "The respectable old Philadelphia family with the son-in-law everybody thinks belongs to the Mafia."

"That," said Eric severely, "was at least ten minutes ago and I've been talking ever since. And you looked very worried and depressed. That isn't how I like my women to look when they're with me."

"I'm sorry, Eric," I said. "I guess it was bad manners on my part, but I remembered something unpleasant, that's all."

"Is it anything you could, or should, do something about?"

"Not a thing. It was all done long before I was born."

"Then forget it."

"Yes sir, Captain Allenby, *sir!*" I snapped out. This time it was easier to laugh, and as we turned into the drive by a mailbox marked WEBSTER I had shed the whole bad experience and was letting the Brewster nose take complete charge; I watched as alertly as Tim for my first glimpse of the house and the gardens Jason had told me about.

The low gray-shingled house branched off in all directions into ells and wings. The central section had a modestly elegant front door facing open sea; this, they told me, was the original house built by Israel Webster when he settled here as a young veteran of the Revolutionary War. He had owned the whole point then and farmed its rocky acres, much of which now had reverted to forest.

The thick cushiony turf, the flowers everywhere in billows of color, were familiar to me; everything dazzles in the New England seacoast summer, and many

things go on blazing to the first heavy frosts, sometimes to the first snowfall. But because of the uneven
terrain and the granite outcroppings, there were exquisite surprises at every turn. The children, Gordon,
seven, and Kim, six, took me to the edge of the woods
and showed me where in May daffodils and scilla
bloomed along an ancient stone wall, and around wild
apple trees hidden among the spruces. In the lee of the
house there were masses of the tall flowers the winds
could break down; at the edge of the lawn where it
sloped to the shore there was a low wide border that
glowed like the oriental carpets at Bellwood.

Helen had everything ready in the kitchen. Nancy
Allenby and another girl, a thin, spirited redhead
named Stephanie and called Steff, had been there most
of the afternoon to help. Steff's date, home on leave
from the Navy, and Peter Gillespie had dug the clams
and fetched the lobsters and had that part well under
way on the beach. Burr and Tamara would come out
with Mark, who would have gone to the hospital for a
short visit with his father after he left the drugstore
at six.

The evening was perfect; the new couple added no
false notes to the earlier combination, everybody was
hungry, and the food was like Kublai Khan's honey-
dew and the milk of paradise. Any food—even sardines
and crackers—eaten by the ocean tastes that way to
me. And tonight, because I was in love and because
Eric was right without knowing why when he told me
to forget something which I couldn't help, and because
I was young and healthy and liked good company, it
was all magnificent.

Mark liked my gift so much he kissed me on my

cheek and said, "Bless you, Caro." We drank a birth-day toast to him before we adjourned to the beach. The children enjoyed the clambake without being ob-noxious. The two older ones settled with their tin pie-plates, loaded, on a natural rock shelf with a lobster crate for a table; the baby, already in his pajamas, had had his supper earlier but he stood in his playpen, hanging to the rigging like a sailor in a hurricane, and chewed on lobster legs. The dogs were opportunists like all dogs, but polite about it; they were a Labrador retriever, and a whiskery mongrel Tim would have loved.

The baby was asleep, bundled in blankets, by the time the cake was brought down at dusk, and the candles lighted. The wind had died down; the little flames burned gallantly and across them I saw the faces of the two older children gilded by candlelight, their eyes shining. I felt like crying for Tim, missing this. We all sang "Happy birthday, dear Mark, happy birthday to you," which always makes me feel disgust-ingly sentimental anyway, and which I've noticed al-ways shakes up the recipient. Mark blew out the candles in one breath while everyone cheered, and we all ate some cake, stuffed as we were, as if this were some profoundly significant ritual, a kind of magic we were making for the year ahead.

The older children crawled into sleeping bags after that, to listen snugly to the singing around the fire. They soon fell asleep. Around ten we were sung out and yawning, and beginning to straggle toward the house with our hands full. Eric and the Navy man each flung a child-laden sleeping bag over his shoul-der and carried them up across the lawn in the moonlight. The children hardly woke, and sank back into deep sleep as soon as they were deposited on cots on a screened porch.

Burr and Tamara were going to stay to help clean up the kitchen. The rest of us headed back to town. This time, by moonlight, the road was not haunted. Eric didn't question my silence, guessing that it was a peaceful one.

When we came to where the road forked, one fork pointing to the town and the other around a moon-silvered cove toward the road that led by Bellwood, he took the village way. "You're certainly not going for something to eat!" I said.

"Nope. We're going around by my house. Don't worry, I'll have you home by midnight."

"What will your parents think, having you bring in a stranger at this hour?"

"That I'm being a good son," he said smugly. "Bringing my girls home for them to inspect."

"Do you have a different one for every night in the week?"

"Only on Wednesdays."

"I'm not anybody's girl, you know," I said.

"Were you ever?"

"If I hadn't been by my age, I'd have lived a pretty withdrawn existence, don't you think?"

"Which tells me exactly nothing," said Eric. "But I'm not interested in how many dates you've had since you were sixteen. What I want to know is—you know damn well what I want to know." He sighed loudly in exasperation and I tried to think how I would answer the next and inevitable question. But to my relieved surprise, he didn't say anything more—then.

The Allenby summer home lay along the side of a hill, and in the warm moonlight we sat out on the flagstone terrace which Eric and his father had laid. It overlooked the town, the harbor, and the great bay where the black islands looked like sleeping whales. We drank very hot black coffee, and talked. Eric's mother was a slight graying woman with an unexpectedly firm handclasp, and a way of looking searchingly into my eyes. I liked her at once, apart from her position as Eric's mother, a position which might have made me rather self-conscious if I'd actually been Eric's girl.

His father was the big man I'd seen Eric with at the public landing. He smoked his pipe in silence, now and then delivering an opinion in a leisurely rumble that received everyone's attention.

I loved it there and I liked them; it was like a return to something dear and familiar, so that now it was Bellwood that seemed remote, dimmed by more than physical distance when I tried to summon up details like the nocturnes and the bronze strokes of the clock, the gleam of polished wood and the noiseless fall of flower petals upon it, the turn of the banister and the ruby glow of the old carpets. Then I thought, quite deliberately, *Rees,* and it was as sharp as a knife wound. He was here, conjured up by that silent saying of his name, and suddenly I felt displaced and alien with these people. It was true, you can't go home again. It is never home again, because you are never the same *you* who left it.

"I must go," I said. "Tim's an early riser."

"That reminds me," Eric said. "I've got something for Tim." He disappeared into the house.

"Eric's spoken several times of that youngster," said Mrs. Allenby.

"Tim's very appealing. It was love at first sight for me."

"And probably vice versa," said Mr. Allenby gallantly.

"Doesn't he say nice things?" asked his wife. "That's one of the reasons I married him."

Eric came out with a tied-up shoebox under his arm. "I've found an heir to my miniature cars."

"I thought this day would never come," said his mother. "Once I wrote to Eric in college, suggesting that he distribute some of his ancient toys to various children in the family, and he objected so strenuously—I might almost say *passionately*—that I thought he was a case of arrested emotional development."

"Most of the kids in our clan have too much of everything," said Eric. "These cars wouldn't mean anything to them."

"They'll mean a lot to Tim," I said. "Because they were yours, and also because he's very attached to his things. Perhaps it's because his world is so limited."

"It will be so nice for him when he goes to school," said Mrs. Allenby. I agreed, not thinking it necessary to say that Rees wouldn't let him go to school. After all, I had my own hopes for Tim along that line. I told the Allenbys how much I'd enjoyed meeting them, and they said they liked me; I was to come again, for dinner when I could. Mrs. Allenby would call me next week.

Eric pulled off to the side before we reached the gates, and parked in the shadow of the wall and the tall trees leaning over it. The road moved away from us like a narrow canal of moonlight. The spruce woods on the other side looked black and silent; you have to have been in the woods at night to know how alive they really are.

"I suppose Cerberus is lurking behind the gate waiting for you," Eric said.

"Not till I ring."

"When do you start your weekend?"

"Early Friday morning, and I'll be back here sometime before Monday night."

"Will you call me when you get back?" Eric asked. "I want to do something away from people next week. We've been with the gang, and you've met my parents, and that's enough for the time being."

I thought it was more than enough. I didn't want to talk about next week; the weekend was bad enough, looming up before me like Everest. I was already aching for it to be over and for me to be back. I ached now to be entering the front door of Bellwood, where Rees would be waiting for me.

Without thinking I reached for the door handle, but Eric drew me back against him, turned my face up to his, and kissed me. It wasn't a long kiss or an insistent one, but it was firm and knew its own mind, like its perpetrator.

Suddenly an early cricket began to chirp close to the car, and Eric lifted his head and said over his shoulder, "No comments called for, chum." Then he leaned over me again, his face close to mine. There were glints in his eyes like the gleams on quietly moving water. He had become mysterious, suddenly, as any human being must surely be once we realize how little we know of him. I knew again that Eric couldn't possibly be the sunlit, uncomplicated, extroverted soul he appeared on the surface.

"That's just to show you I mean business, Caro," he said. "I knew from the first. It may take you longer. I don't want to rush you, but I do want a chance. Give me a chance, Caro, give life a chance. Whatever happened to you before you came here, it couldn't possibly be worth shutting life outside those gates."

Outside those gates. No, he wasn't simple. In fact, he might be uncomfortably complex.

"Why do you think something happened, Eric?" I asked.

"A feeling, hunch, intuition. And then you said something to Philly today."

"What?" I asked in honest bewilderment. I'd completely forgotten the encounter with her.

"You said you'd been fooled once, and you started to say 'Once bitten, twice shy.'"

"Oh, that!" I hoped my chuckle and shrug were convincing. "We were talking about jobs, weren't we? Didn't you ever work for someone or have a certain teacher, or even a superior officer, whom you thought was wonderful, and then you found out with a great shock that he *wasn't?*"

"You," said Eric, "are about as transparent as that windshield. More so, because the windshield's dusty. All right, Caro. It's your business and I've got no right to ask." His arm tightened around me again. "But if I barge in where I've no right, it's because we've got so many years to catch up on."

"Don't forget, at our first picnic we decided we had at least a year and a half behind us."

"Now I feel as if we'd just met. Today," he said. "Everything else has been a false start. Caro, I hate like hell to let you go in there tonight!"

"But *why?*" I straightened up and tried to move naturally away from him. "It's simply the place where I work, it's home for the time being. You might be letting me off at a hotel, or a boarding place, or my own flat."

"I wish to God it was any one of those places." Then he tried to throw off his grimness, but the effort was obvious, and disturbing; I wanted Eric to stay the same as he had been at the first, I *needed* him to stay the same. "Oh, I guess it's just a reaction to the wall and those locked gates," he said. "Maybe I've got a dormant claustrophobia."

"Oh, do they make nice pets? I've always wondered."

"They're all right if you keep their claws clipped and the fleas off."

The effort improved. We exchanged rather sad smiles, as if each were acknowledging each other's weakness and his own. I said impulsively, "I like you, Eric. I hope we can be friends. But that's as far as I can go tonight." I hoped he would remember those words later, and realize that I'd been as truthful as I could be.

"That's a start," he said, sounding as optimistic as ever. He got out of the car and came around to open my door, and take out the box of cars for Tim. We walked the short distance to the gate together. By illusion the shadow was cool and the moonlight warm. No cars came along, there was not even the sound of one in the distance, and except for my eagerness to return to Rees I felt as if I could have walked miles in this pure mild light cast over a sleeping countryside.

Eric pressed the button, then put his arm around me as we stood waiting. "Caro by moonlight, Caro by sun," he said. "Are they two separate persons, or really one?"

"Eric, I didn't know you were such a poet!"

"Oh, that's just one of my many gifts. I'm a throwback to a Viking ancestor who prided himself on his poetry as well as his raids."

I stood off to look at him. "Yes, I can see you swinging a broad-axe, burning down houses, flinging captive women over your shoulder and lugging them off, and then sitting down to compose an ode about it. . . . The winged helmet is very attractive, too. Twelfth-century Mod."

"You're lucky if I don't revert and lug *you* off." Then we heard the car coming, and the gates began to open. "Open Sesame," Eric intoned. "In five minutes my girl turns into a pumpkin."

The lights appeared through the trees and we stood back as the MG came around a bend, through the gate, turned expertly in a small area, and stopped facing back along the drive.

"Don't get out, Jason," I said, and then saw that it was Rees.

[16]

"Young Allenby seems fairly ardent," Rees said when we came into the house.

"Whatever gave you that idea?" It sounded artificial to me. Worse, it sounded arch.

"Oh, just an atmosphere around him. It takes one to know one."

"One what?"

"One lover." He took me into his arms. I shut my eyes and leaned my forehead against his shoulder. He said, "Are you hiding your face? What's the trouble, Caro? What's happened tonight? Second thoughts?"

I snapped my head back. "No! It's just that I'm so glad to be home. It seems like a month since noon."

"It's seemed longer for us. You don't know what you've become in this house, Caro. Its heart, perhaps . . . . Even Jason misses you."

"Now that really sets me up. I've been trying to please Jason most of all, you know." We laughed and went into the living room, where the fire, drinks, and sometimes music composed our late-evening ritual.

I did not want to take my weekend. Though I knew

I should go, though I wanted to see Mindy and Elliot and the children, I still didn't want to leave Bellwood; it was as if I'd already grown roots in the place, that to loosen myself to travel as far as Limerock would be to leave myself a bruised and dying plant.

In Rees's arms on Thursday night, whispering good-nights outside my door, I said, "Rees, I needn't go this weekend. I can put it off."

"Till when?"

"Never," I said, and then laughed. "Not really *never*. But more and more my whole life seems centered here. And I have this—oh, an almost superstitious feeling about going away for these few days, as if it hasn't been real after all and it'll all disappear behind my back."

"I assure you, this is very real." The way he kissed me weakened my legs.

"I don't want to leave *you*," I said, feeling deliciously clinging and dependent.

"By Monday evening we'll all be together again. Including your secret love Jason. This will be a good time for us all to get some things done. So this evening I called Tim's doctor in Boston and made an appointment for Saturday, and we'll be flying from Bangor late Friday afternoon. And I'm sending Jason off to see his sister for a couple of days." He held me off and studied me humorously. "You don't believe Jason has a sister? Well, he has, and she runs a millionaire's household at Bar Harbor with an iron hand, according to Jason. He says that his lifelong acquaintance with his sister has put him off marriage.... So now you see why *you* must go and see your brother. We're all doing our duty this weekend."

"Who'll look after Tris?"

"Tris will be left with food and water for three days, and the run of the house from cellar to attic. He carries on the mouse patrol."

"Nobody needs me," I said. "Not even the cat."

"All your men need you, Caro. Believe me, the weekend will crawl for every one of us."

I left at sunrise on Friday morning, my reluctance tempered slightly by the use of the car. It was a tie with Bellwood, it was registered in Rees's name. Tim was awake to see me off, with a tight hug that I fervently returned. He had his new collection of cars around him in bed.

"Have a good weekend, Miss Brewster," Jason said. Rees and I had already said goodbye, in privacy.

The roads were practically empty at that hour, and it was a beautiful ride around pale blue silk coves, past dewy pastures and aromatic woods. The small towns woke slowly under their elms. It was the time of roses in Maine, and they bloomed everywhere, on old-fashioned untidy bushes by farmhouses, on glowing hedges around the sea captains' mansions, and the wild roses shone like pink stars along the stone walls.

In three hours I was driving into Limerock, a city that I had known all my life but which was now seen with new eyes, as if I had become a new person. And I had. I felt like breaking into song to relieve and express the exquisite tension I felt. Now if only I didn't burst out with the whole story almost the minute I met my family; turning into Elliot's driveway I was wishing for a mild tranquillizer.

I waved to Nora next door, who was out doing some

early work in her garden, and said that I loved my job, thanks. Elliot's shaggy mongrel, Scott, came galloping to meet me, uttering little cries of rapture and trying to jump up, but he was too short-legged to reach above my knees. I loved him even though as usual he smelled richly of all the things he found to roll in. With him bouncing and panting beside me I went up the steps to the back door, and walked in, calling joyously, "Where is everyone? Not in bed at this indecent hour, I hope—"

Mindy sat alone at the table, a cup of coffee before her, her head in her hands. She snapped up straight. "Carol!" she cried and started to get up, then stopped. "No, I'd better not touch you, darn it. I may be coming down with it."

"With *what?*" I exclaimed. "Where are the kids?"

"Oh, they've got some darned intestinal virus. They were miserable all day yesterday, and all night, and I never got any sleep. Now *they* feel better, and they're sleeping like logs, but I—" She yawned enormously. "Darn it, what are you doing here at nine-fifteen Friday morning? We didn't expect you till tonight at the earliest, and I was going to call up today and tell you about the kids—" She yawned again. "I didn't think you'd want to stay here, on account of maybe carrying it to Tim."

I wouldn't want to take any chances, but . . . Oh, *damn it,* there!" After I'd got on the road I'd begun looking forward more and more to my weekend. "Look, if all I do is just sit down and have something to eat right now, I don't think I'll catch anything, do you? Then we can decide what to do. . . . You sit there, I'll wait on

178

myself." I put bread in the toaster and got out a cup and saucer.

"You could stay with just about anyone," Mindy said. "They'd all be pleased."

"Mrs. Rideout," I suggested, and Mindy giggled and said, "Oh, that's mean of me. But Paul may not have to do a year, so she's feeling a little better." She yawned again. She looked worn out, and I couldn't even tell her to go crawl into bed while I tidied the place, waited on the children, and got the meals. I couldn't take a chance on catching the virus or taking it back to Tim.

"Mindy," I said suddenly. "I think I'll go back, and take another weekend when the kids are all right. I don't want to stay with anybody else, I want to be here with my family."

Mindy brightened. "That's what *we* want, Caro. It would be awful to know you were in town and not be able to get together at all. But you'll have that long drive twice in one day."

"I don't mind. Driving's practically ecstasy in that car."

"I've got to see it." Mindy went to the door to look and to marvel. A little later she stood on the lawn while I backed out, and we blew kisses at each other past the maples. Scott barked me away.

Then I drove downtown and parked, and bought a bagful of little books, puzzles, and miniature toys to amuse the children while they were convalescing, and took the collection up to Elliot's office.

He hugged me violently, to the amusement of his secretary, (with whom I'd gone to school); then we

179

went into his office and talked for a few minutes. He argued about my driving straight back, but I said that was the way I wanted to do it, not adding that I had to get back before the house was locked up for the weekend. I rushed into enthusiastic accounts of Tim's charm, Jason's housekeeping, Rees's absorbing work, and the people at Somerset, with a heavy accent on Eric. It gave me a queasy sensation to make use of Eric like this, as if his feelings for me were simply a lucky accident I could put to my own use. I tried to compromise with my conscience by saying he was good fun. I couldn't tell them about Rees and me, at least not all at once. They'd have to be prepared for it, and I didn't know how to attempt even the slightest hint. Besides, how do you hint slightly at something like that? Either a man is interested or he is not; either you reciprocate his interest or you do not.

So I decided to be brazen about my small deception, and carry it off with *élan*.

At last I was on my way again, and I actually burst into song once I was out of Limerock and on the open road.

At half-past twelve I stopped in the village west of Bellwood and called the house. No one answered, and I had expected they'd be having lunch. At least Tim and Jason should be eating, even if Rees were still busy in his study. I was disappointed, but not worried; maybe Tim had begged Jason to eat lunch outdoors. Or he could be already having his nap, early today because of the plane trip this afternoon, and Jason might be out cutting the grass with the power mower.

I drove happily on, imagining my reception. Taken by surprise, Rees would have to leave me there. I'd promise not to leave the place or to let anyone in; I'd lock everything tight at night and Tris and I would hold the fort. Eric wouldn't know I was back; no one would know that the men had gone and I was alone there. I could convince Rees I would be perfectly safe and as happy as it was possible to be without him.

There were the warm red bricks of the wall with the shadows moving over them in the summer wind. When I got out of the car I heard the thrushes and white-throats of Bellwood like chimes and flutes. I listened to them for a moment, and then pressed the button and got back into the car. "Open Sesame," I said aloud, as Eric had done.

They hadn't opened within the proper time limit, and I got out and rang again, looking through at the drive disappearing into the rustling green woods. When they didn't open this time I said, "Oh, damn!" No one would answer the bell at the house if no one was expected, and they certainly weren't expecting *me*. "Why couldn't you have been in to answer the telephone, Jason?" I inquired crossly. "And why don't they have some communication between here and the house anyway?"

Maybe Rees would have something installed if I really wanted it, I thought. The vision of someone bleeding to death outside the gates still returned to me now and then.

Well, I knew a way in. I drove on past the end of the wall, into the wood road, and parked where I had on that other afternoon. I found my convenient ladder-tree and again blessed my early climbing talents as I got myself to the top of the wall. I had left my bag in the locked car, just in case I did find a closed house and had to come back to the car and go find a motel. But I was positive Rees was still there. His plane didn't take off from Bangor until four o'clock.

I didn't have a compass this time, but I have a good sense of direction, and I knew where the sun was supposed to be at this hour of the day in relation to the house. So I set off through the woods, recognizing landmarks from that other time; a distinctive ledge, a rotting stump growing a moss-and-mushroom garden, a brook bed all ferns and boulders, a wild apple tree.

And then, at last, the stone cottage gleamed through the branches.

This time I wasn't stopped short but went boldly toward it, intending to cut around the side and take the path to the house. The two barred windows in the back wall were open, but I didn't look toward them as I approached. All my curiosity about the place had vanished along with the distaste its story had aroused.

What did stop me was a sound from inside, and I froze instinctively, thinking Rees was in there and would see me. For the first time I felt a little nervous about my explanations, which had seemed so reasonable until now. Rees *shouldn't* be displeased, especially when he heard about the virus, but still . . .

Perhaps I'd better go back into the woods a little distance, and find my way to the shore and approach from *that side*. As I teetered indecisively, from behind the windows a voice said distinctly, "Out there. Who's out there?" It was slurred, as if the speaker were either very drunk or very weak. The tape-recorder, I thought. The words weren't addressed to me, they were pure coincidence. I turned to hurry away.

"Oh God." It was a groan. "Answer me. Who's out there?"

Sweat trickled down my spine. The voice became stronger, as if the speaker were making a desperate effort. "Listen, whoever you are . . . get the police . . ."

There was a thump, a scrabbling, a moan. As if he'd fallen and couldn't get up. *He.* A man. Not a tape-recorder.

A reflex for self-survival sent me plunging back into the woods, otherwise I'd have stood there frozen indefinitely. A nightmare fantasy danced through my head; the insane son hadn't really died in Bangor, but still lived in his stone prison and had been passed along with the deed to the property. . . . Local young adventurers thought the place was haunted; what had someone heard on a nighttime exploration that sent him crashing back to the wall, never to return?

Rees was coming. Through my green screen I saw him on the path for an instant, then the angle of the cottage hid him and the rest of the path from me. Sweat running into my eyes and making me blink, I set off in the direction of the salty wind that set the tops of the tall spruces to swaying.

At this point I felt a little sick, but not terrified. I was not afraid of Rees, I just didn't want to meet him when I was still dizzy with the shock of the voice from the windows, and when I was not expected to be on the premises at all. There had to be a legitimate reason for the man behind the bars, and soon I would know what it was. In the meantime I was a victim of my own purely female imagination.

I came out to the shore at last, gulping the cool

strong wind from the sea. The water was a choppy blue-green, the tide half gone and splashing noisily on the rocks. The cliff wasn't as high here as it was directly in front of the house, but it was steep enough, and I had to go along the edge, away from the house, over descending ground till I found a place where I could go down to the beach. I kept cautiously back from the outer edge, remembering how Valerie had fallen. My dress was already decorated with pitch, spruce needles stuck to the pitch, and smears of black dirt where I'd skidded on damp moss. There were twigs and spills in my hair and down my neck, making my damp skin itch. When I sat and slid down the bank to the shore, I added grass stains to my dress, wild rose scratches to my legs and arms, and dry dirt inside my sneakers. I sat down and shook that out, then started along the shore back in the direction of Bellwood.

It was probably not even half a mile, but I felt as if I had been walking over and under obstacles for most of my life. The sea breeze was cool and invigorating, and I needed all the vigor I could get. I crossed ledges, and steep beaches where sea-rounded rocks rolled under my feet, and all the time I kept hearing that voice imploring for help from behind the windows, and my throat would clamp shut, closing off my breath; my chest would begin to ache until, with a great effort, I would force air into my lungs and try to keep them working naturally.

I came to the beach at last, a short empty stretch of sand dazzlingly bright in the early afternoon sun, the blue-green waves breaking with a thump into scallops of white lace. Gulls paddled together a little way off-shore. There were sails toward the horizon, and I wondered if one set belonged to the *Kingfisher*. I sat down at the foot of the cliff path to collect myself. It was all right to appear tired and untidy, but not like a fugitive from a nightmare.

As I sat there the nightmare grew less and less real. Suddenly I knew who the man was in the stone cottage. It involved deception on Rees's part but a reasonable one; he'd wanted me well away from Bellwood this weekend because he was having one of his research subjects here for extensive interviewing. He might have sent Tim away with Jason for overnight, too, so that neither the child nor I might accidently glimpse someone both sordid and pathetic, as these tragic cases all must be.

He'd pay the man well for his time, and let him have all the liquor he wanted. . . . He'd sounded drunk, hadn't he? Very drunk. Maybe he'd been left alone for a while, had fallen asleep, and when he woke up he couldn't remember how he'd got there, and the barred windows had confused and frightened him. But by now Rees would have reassured him, and they might be already talking, with the tape-recorder turning silently out of sight.

He could have told me the truth; I was nothing fragile, I hadn't been cushioned from life. I smiled tenderly at his rather Victorian way of protecting the little woman. Well, I would go along with it. Sighing, I looked back the way I had come. If I had to spend the weekend in a motel, so be it. It would all be in the cause of love.

But I couldn't even begin that hot trek back to the

car without a drink of water first, and if Rees was in the study, and the house otherwise empty, he needn't know that I'd ever been there.

I climbed the path. At the top the rose hedge gave off its perfume in the sea wind. It was loud with bees. The lawn, not freshly cut today as I had imagined, was empty. I crossed it, feeling rather strange and somehow like a trespasser. Tris met me cordially in the kitchen and streaked up the back stairs ahead of me; I got my drink in my bathroom rather than leave any traces of just-run water in the kitchen or the downstairs bathroom. I was hungry enough to feel faint in my stomach too, and that was another reason why I went up. With Tris languishing around my ankles and purring like a drunken bumblebee I put a handful of English biscuits in my pocket and went out into the hall, and paused.

I heard the slight whish of the front screen door opening. Rees came into the lower hall. I stood without breathing, expecting him to look up. But he didn't. Whistling softly, he went into the library.

I backed into my room, almost falling over Tris. The clock struck half-past one, and I managed to shut my door at precisely the same instant, so that no faint click would be heard. With one ear against the door and the other covered against Tris's purring, I tried to guess at Rees's movements. I heard his voice distinctly and decided he was talking on the telephone. Possibly he was reporting to someone on the condition of his guest. Then I heard a goodbye and then nothing more. Praying that he wouldn't come upstairs for anything, I retreated to my chair by the window to wait. If he went out the front door again, I could see him from here.

He didn't appear, and I began to feel extremely uncomfortable. I was humiliated and angered by my own foolishness in dashing back to Bellwood like a love-sick teenager. If I was caught here, such idiocy would be hard for a man to forgive. On the other hand, I argued defensively, he shouldn't treat me in this overprotective nineteenth-century fashion.

Tris jumped onto the wide windowsill, and pressed his forehead against the screen, trying to look down. I expected it was a bird or a butterfly until I heard the soft swish of tires on the crushed gravel. It was Rees's car going out.

Past Tris's ears I watched the car pass around the edge of the lawn. As it disappeared into the drive, I sprang up and ran downstairs. If I ever get to that motel, I thought, *any* motel no matter how shabby, I'll say prayers of thanksgiving from now until Monday morning.

Tris ran down behind me, and followed me out to the kitchen. He had plenty of food and water in his dishes, and the door was propped open to the cellar. That was where I thought he'd gone; but as I reached the outside door he shot past me and around the corner of the house toward the front. I took off after him. Rees might not have noticed whether Tris had been in the house or not when he left. But then he might have been sure he'd last seen the cat in the kitchen, or sprawled out on the desk in the library; to come home and find Tris waiting on the doorstep for him would be disturbing.

"Tris, come back here," I called in exasperation. But he, so moderate and reasonable most of the time, skittered across the lawn on cotton-ball feet, his plume crooked sidewise. I knelt down and tried the melting tone that usually brought him, but all I got was a fey look, and he scampered off down the study path. He was a flash of moving sunshine as he went from light to shadow and back again. Tris's sense of humor was usually a delight, but not today. He became a part of the bad dream, and made it all the worse because of his innocence. We were playing a game, and he was very happy about it.

When he went around the corner of the stone cottage, I was ready to give up and take a chance on Rees's ignoring the situation. "All right for you, Tris," I said, and at once he sat down and began cleaning very thoroughly the pink pads of one forepaw.

Who was I to turn this chance down? I walked along by the wall of the study. Tris blinked affably up at me and I picked him up and slung him over my shoulder; he went back to cleaning his paw. "*Now,* you little devil!" I said.

"Please listen to me," said a voice over my head. I had forgotten, and my scalp grew tight. Tris stopped his washing and stared up at the window. The voice was clearer and stronger now. He's sobering up, I thought.

"You out there," he said. "You're human still, it's in your voice. Help me. If you're not entirely lost, help me."

"How can I?" I asked, looking up like Tris at the bars, and the sunlight on the ceiling beyond. I was deeply moved by the cry from a sick soul. "Are you afraid to be alone? Mr. Morgan should be back soon. He's very kind. He only wants to talk to you."

"Oh, dear God," he groaned. "What's he told you? What do you believe about me?"

"He hasn't told me anything except about his research with—" I didn't want to say *mental defectives* or *the criminally insane*, even to one of them. "I mean, I don't know anything about *you*," I tried to explain. "Except that he must have brought you here today to interview."

There was something profound and aching about the silence that answered me.

"Listen," the voice came at last. Slow, utterly weary, but patient. "Go to the police. And call Richard Faraday in Salem, Massachusetts, and tell him . . . " He seemed to be running down, as if he'd used all his strength in the last few moments. "Tell him Stephen is alive. Or was, at whatever time it was that you talked with me. You'll have time if you hurry. He's gone to her grave. He always does after a session with me. It's unspeakable . . . It's obscene."

I tried to speak but couldn't. My skin seemed to be drawing unmercifully taut, numbing my whole body. After an instant I got the words out. "He found you, then! Or did you come back here?"

"I never left."

I stood there staring upward, stammering, "But—but—" and there was no answer. It was as if there had been a voice from space and now there was no voice, there was nothing. I must have squeezed Tris because he squirmed suddenly, and I put him down. Then I came out of my trance and ran for the house.

It was like running in a dream, when you sob with

the anguish of your effort but still make no headway. Ahead of me the goldfinches flew up from a birdbath, and the faded red brick was gilded by summer sunshine. Leaf shadows danced on grass that added a green fragrance to the smell of the sea. And horror sucked at my feet like quicksand, dragged at my arms, and clogged my throat so I could hardly breathe.

[17]

Rees hadn't locked the front door—apparently he didn't expect to be gone long. *Rees!* The name rocked me. I couldn't comprehend anything; my mind wanted to explode. In the library I sagged on the side of the desk and lifted the telephone with a shaking hand and dialled for the operator. My throat was dry from my running and when at last she answered I couldn't speak at once. She kept saying, "Operator . . . Operator," like a machine. Then she must have heard my harsh breathing, because suddenly she said, "What is it, are you sick? Take your time, but try to answer—"

Rees's car went by the window, toward the carriage house.

I slammed down the telephone and ran for the front stairs. I don't know where the strength came from. I thought I could escape down the back stairs as soon as he returned to the study. After I got back to the car I'd stop at the first possible place and telephone the police.

I got into my room and shut the door. In my mirror I saw myself, disheveled and wild-eyed, my face very flushed after the chill. I went into the bathroom, wet a washcloth under the cold faucet and sponged my face and neck, and cleaned my hands as best as I could without running the water strongly. I felt a little refreshed and went back to the window again to watch for Rees.

I didn't know how I felt about him. I was conscious only of having a mission to perform, and I didn't dare think of what that might mean; explosion threatened again in my brain whenever my thoughts moved toward any possible explanation.

So I felt quite calm—call it numb—as I stood there brushing the twigs and spills out of my hair and watching the empty lawn below.

There was a sound at my door.

Still in this curious, almost entranced, calm I waited. The knob turned and the door opened slowly. Rees looked into the room. I felt neither love nor fear, only a lack of surprise. I thought, *I might have known.* The nightmare begun at the stone house moved into a new phase.

"I was crossing the hall and I heard something," he said politely. "I thought the cat had knocked something over. What are you doing here, Caro?"

It wasn't quite like the time I'd gone down to the study to get him. And now I knew why he'd looked the way he had then. This time he was courteous, almost preoccupied. He seemed no more surprised than I, unless his shock went too deep to show.

"I came straight back," I said timidly. "I hope you're not angry. But Elliot's children are both sick with a virus and I wouldn't stay there and take a chance on catching it, or bringing it back to Tim."

He nodded absently. "Logical," he said. "And considerate. Go on."

"I called here to say I was coming, but no one answered." With relief I heard my voice strengthening. "I didn't expect everyone to be gone until well past lunch, so I came straight along. . . . I thought you'd let me stay here alone, but if you don't want me to," I offered eagerly, "I'll go into Somerset."

"How did you get onto the grounds?"

"Well, I rang and rang at the gate but nobody answered. So I parked on that old wood road outside the wall, and walked to the shore, and came over the rocks and then up the cliff. Look at me!" I said with a nervous laugh that wasn't acting. "I'm all stuck up with pitch, scraped, bruised—"

Suddenly Rees smiled. "You look just right to me, after fighting your way back to me through savage jungle and along brutal shores." He put his hands on my shoulders and kissed me on the forehead, the nose, and finally on my mouth.

It was the sort of gesture that had always made me stand motionless in a kind of silent bliss. That was what his touch had always done to me. His touch and his voice.

Now I stood motionless beneath his hands, my eyes closed, and not in bliss. I knew now what I felt about him. I was afraid.

I've always *felt* guilty even when I wasn't. In school, if anything happened when the teacher was out of the room, she was sure to single out my flushed face and blinking eyes; I'd even had to fight undeserved sensations of guilt in Paul's case. Now I was sure that my feelings were as obvious as a shout, that in another instant Rees would accuse me of lying, and have the whole story out of me. Instead he held me off, still smiling, and said, "Have you had lunch?"

"No, I drove right back without stopping to eat. And I'm starved."

"Well, I haven't eaten yet, and Jason left something prepared. I'll go down and heat things up and make some coffee, and we'll take trays outside and look out to sea as we eat. How will that be?"

"Marvelous," I said. "I'll clean up. My case is back in the car but I've got plenty here to do with."

He brushed my cheek with his finger and went out. I began to tremble. I hope never again to experience the panic I knew then, and was to know constantly over a weekend that lasted for an eternity. The fact of Stephen Faraday's existence and imprisonment hammered like a mallet against my temple. Whatever Rees's reason for his actions, this sensitive and intellectual man was as warped as any of his mentally defective murderers.

I had to get away from Bellwood as soon as I could and reach the police. And at the moment I couldn't use the back stairs as a way of escape, with Rees in the kitchen. The only thing was to wait until he'd gone back to the stone house again. I breathed deeply five times, saying to myself, "Be calm. Be calm." Then I took off my clothes and got under a tepid shower, as a form of hydrotherapy.

Dressed, brushed, wearing fresh make-up and cologne, I had a rather feverish brightness about the eyes that could pass for excitement at being alone with a lover. At least I hoped so. Every time I thought of

Stephen Faraday waiting behind bars for three years and now so sure he was to be freed, my heart jumped and a pulse beat in my throat. I thought I could see it, and wondered morbidly if Rees would think that was love also. I had no time to contemplate the ruin of what had seemed a perfect love affair, and my mindless ecstasy about the whole thing; I had time only to contemplate my next step, whatever it was.

I couldn't stay upstairs forever. I went down to the kitchen, where Rees was setting two trays. We exchanged smiles and I went to the stove and looked into the teakettle to see if it had started to steam. I didn't care if it never boiled, but I had to do something to keep from making a dash for the back door. Rees came behind me and put his arms around me and kissed the back of my neck.

"You haven't asked me yet where Tim is," he murmured.

"He's out with Jason somewhere, isn't he?" I asked. "When will you be leaving for Boston?"

"We aren't. The great man's secretary called just after you left and said he was down with a strep throat this morning. She gave us an appointment for two weeks from now." How smoothly he lied, I thought with envy; if I could do so well, it might save my life. And Stephen Faraday's; now I was positive that Rees had cleared us out this weekend so he could get rid of his prisoner once and for all. "And—" he tightened his arms and kissed my neck again. "You're going with us. We'll take you on the swan boats, and to the Museum of Fine Arts, and you and I will see a show. . . . This time Tim was absolutely sunk with disappointment, so

195

I told Jason he could have his weekend as he planned if he'd take Tim along with him. The gardener has children. It will be a great experience for Tim."

Considering that he wanted to keep Tim completely insulated from the outside world, he was remarkably casual about him now. "Oh, he'll be in seventh heaven," I said, trying not to overdo my vivacity. "But under the circumstances I'd better stay at the Harbor-view Motel, hadn't I?"

"Why?" He sounded amused. He lifted the steaming kettle and began to turn boiling water into the top of the drip pot. "For propriety's sake? Who knows you're here? Or rather, who knows that we're both here, without our two chaperones?"

He looked around at me, his eyes narrow with laughter. "Are you afraid to be alone with me?"

"*No!* It's only that you didn't count on my being here, and—"

"So I've been pleasantly surprised." Then his eyebrows came together and he said bitingly, "Have you by any chance made a date with Eric Allenby for this weekend? Did you call him as soon as you got into the house, or from some place along the road?"

"Of course not!" I could say that in honest indignation. "I never even thought of such a thing!"

He laughed. "Forgive me. Let's eat."

We got through the meal somehow. I remember it as lasting for hours, but it couldn't have. Thank goodness we were out of doors, and there was an impromptu sailing race going on. I never talked so hard about sailing in my life. I saw the *Kingfisher*, and with the binoculars I thought I could pick out Eric's yellow head. My eyes blurred, and I went weak. *Eric, Eric, come somehow, do something!* I shouted silently.

"What's the matter, Caro?" Rees asked me, and I jumped. He leaned toward me in apparently genuine concern.

I rubbed my hand across the back of my neck and said listlessly, "Oh, it's this headache. It starts at the base of my skull and works up; it bothers my eyes and makes my bones ache, and if I keep fighting it I feel worse and worse. I'm sorry, Rees," I said plaintively, which wasn't hard, "I don't have it very often, but when I do it's horrible."

"Did something upset you today, to start it, or is it fatigue?"

"Both, perhaps. Going home I thought about Paul, and then Mindy and I discussed him. I should have known better. He's been on my mind ever since."

"But why? You certainly weren't responsible for his actions."

"But perhaps I was without knowing it," I argued. This was a safe subject. "There may be a grain of truth in his mother's accusations. Anyway, there were times when Paul was good fun. I enjoyed his company, and now he's behind bars and I'm—I'm—" My voice had trembled on the word *bars*, but not with sympathy for Paul.

"You're a foolish girl and I love you," said Rees. "I love your compassion and your sensitivity. But stop tormenting yourself about Paul and think about us and our future. . . . Now what do you do for that headache?"

"Give in to it," I said weakly.

"Then give in to it, so you'll be free of it by to-night."

I had a sudden chill that raised gooseflesh on my arms and I hoped he hadn't seen it. I began to pick up my tray, but he put his hand on my arm. "No. Go to your room and lie down. You're very cold. Are you having chills? Shall I find you a heating pad?"

I shook my head, remembered to wince at the motion, and escaped. In my room I didn't dare lock the door, but I arranged myself in the chair by the window, with my head on a pillow and my feet up on another chair, ready to close my eyes and look ghastly if he should come in to check. In the meantime I could watch for him to go down to the stone house. With any luck I'd be well out of sight along the shore, perhaps even to the car, before he got back to the main house. Another chill shook me; what if he killed the helpless man in that interval? And why had I told him where I'd left the car? He was likely to meet me there, demanding the reason for my frantic behavior.

I'd better call the state police as soon as he left the house, and tell them too that they'd have to come over the wall; *then* I'd escape. No, first I'd push the button so the gates would be open when they got there. *Then* I'd run. Rees, immersed in his dreadful business in his "study," wouldn't know anything about it.

So I watched and I waited, cold one moment and bundling into sweaters, then too hot. I didn't dare leave the window, but meanwhile there was no sign of life in the house around me. He could be reading or writing in the library, he could be walking on the lawn overlooking the sea. He certainly hadn't gone out again in the car.

Tris came through the bathroom from Tim's room, and chirped at me. If he hadn't run toward the stone house I'd have gone away believing the man down there was one of Rees's case histories; and that when he'd been removed he'd simply been taken home or back to an institution. What if I had never known about Stephen Faraday? What if, in all other ways, Rees was the man I believed him to be? If Stephen Faraday had lived and died in that stone house without my ever knowing, would Rees and I have gone on to a rich future? Was his hatred of Stephen the only disease in him? And when that was resolved, would he be like a man totally recovered from cancer or madness, or would the seeds have been still there, to blossom again in another way?

It was a question to start up the headache I'd lied about. I was glad I knew the truth, if *glad* was a word to be used in any context right now, when it would take practically nothing to turn me abject with terror. Still, I tried to be objective as I watched the lawn, and Tris watched me with blinking golden eyes.

Why had Rees done this to Stephen Faraday, anyway? What had happened on the day Valerie died? How had he been able to face the old people's grief, and . . . There I went, being emotional again. I got up and tiptoed to the door, opened it like a burglar, and listened. I heard nothing. Yet I was afraid to take a chance; he could be anywhere.

That afternoon lasted a year; I'm sure of it. Never had hours of sunshine been so endless and hateful. And never in all those hours did Rees go past the front of the house, either in the car or across the lawn to the path. I tried not to think what Stephen Faraday must be going through, wondering if I'd got away, expecting help at any moment. Just about the time when I was beginning to feel like making an insane bolt for it out a window somewhere, or openly calling up Eric and getting some message across to him in a code he'd be brilliantly intuitive enough to catch, Tris's ears pricked, and I went stiff. I shut my eyes in an ardent prayer that Rees would go by the room, that he would leave the house, that—

Rees spoke my name softly. I didn't answer, but Tris jumped down and went across to the door. After a moment of silence the knob turned noiselessly, and Rees looked around the door. His eyes widened slightly at the sight of the empty bed, and then he saw me. His smile was tender as he came into the room. "Feeling better, darling?"

"No." It was no effort to sound shaky as I gave a description of Grandmother Elliot's sick headache. "It hurts so much to lie down, as if my pillow were cement. And I'm so nauseated, it's worse than being seasick. I've only had it like this a few times in my life, and I had to have the doctor." I put my hand to the back of my neck and said even more feebly, "It bothers my vision too. I see things double and all quivery . . . Please, Rees, I think I'd better call somebody. I'm feeling worse every minute. Do you have a doctor around here, or do you go away for everything?"

"My dear girl, you're having a full-fledged migraine, which I should know, because I'm no stranger to them myself. And I have something you can take." He stood over me, affectionately shaking his head. "We're alone, and you develop this. I suspect its origins, my girl. I really do."

My stomach knotted. "What do you mean?" I remembered to squint my eyes as if the light hurt them.

He laughed. "Never mind. It's a long weekend, and Tim and Jason won't be back till Sunday. I'll get your capsule."

I looked malevolently at his back. He *would* have something on hand so that I couldn't have a doctor. Why hadn't I faked such an unbearable pain in my head that it had to be a brain tumor at the least? I should have rolled about in agony with it. Or I could have worked up a good imitation of acute appendicitis, remembering Elliot's attack.

It was weird to go from adoration to terror in a day; I felt as if I'd got lost somehow in the fourth dimension. I fought against it. Maybe the man *isn't* Stephen Faraday, I argued. Maybe it's exactly what you thought in the first place, but he's got hold of the name somehow.... That premise faded out of its own weakness. And Rees was back, getting a glass of water from the bathroom. He was soothingly matter-of-fact, treating me with a tenderly amused indulgence I would have loved . . . before now.

"Onto your bed now," he ordered. I felt like someone being marched to the wall as I obeyed. He knelt and untied my sneakers and slipped them off, then swung my feet up onto the bed, unfolded a light blanket from across the foot, and laid it over me.

"Now swallow this and when you wake up the headache will be gone," he said.

As if I were Tim, I thought, and all at once I was wretchedly homesick for the dazzle of happiness just past, for the things that had seemed sound and sweet and good. My eyes filling with tears, I took the capsule from his hand. I would only pretend to swallow it. But what with my fight against breaking down, and the way he watched me as he instructed me to place the capsule far back on my tongue, I couldn't manage to tuck it away between teeth and cheek. I had to swallow. But if he didn't wait too long, I could get it up before it dissolved.

"There," he said. "Now lie back, and I'll guarantee you that pillow will soon stop being a cement block. Poor Caro," he said at the sight of my tears. He leaned down and kissed me very gently. "You'll feel better tomorrow. Sleep well, my darling. I'll stay with you a little while."

He went over to the chair by the window, and I lay with my eyes shut and the helpless tears running out at the corners. I'd lost my chance, but not for want of watching for it. It just hadn't come. Tris jumped onto the bed and stretched out beside me. My arms and legs began to grow heavy, my thoughts dim and fragmented. I fought, but with a hopelessness that was both mental and physical. My last coherent phrase was, *Rees has murdered me. This is death creeping over me.*

It was both sad and funny. I know that much, as the cat went on purring, blissfully unaware that I was dying beside him, and across the room the chair by the window creaked slightly. The curtains flapped softly against the screen. Far away, back in life, the thrushes still sang at Bellwood. *Ironic,* I thought, no longer knowing why. And then I died.

[18]

And woke, shivering in the cold, dewy, silver light before sunrise. Dizzy, loose in my limbs, weakly rejoicing to be still alive, I got out of my clothes and into my pajamas, and huddled down under the bedclothes and went to sleep again. I was not used to strong drugs, and my brain was befuddled. I hardly knew what had happened except that I had not been murdered—yet.

When I woke later my head was clear, and I felt strong and rested. It was as if, having lived through yesterday, having survived when I expected to die, I could now live through anything. If Rees intended to kill me he could have done it as I slept, or even forced me to swallow enough capsules to do it. So he didn't suspect anything. Very well. It was up to me now to do the best I could for myself and Stephen Faraday. If he was already dead, at least the world should know what had happened to him.

It was now a little after seven. Anything could happen in the day ahead. If Rees didn't suspect anything he'd leave me alone sooner or later.

I washed and dressed and went downstairs. When I went into the kitchen Tris was waiting to be let out the back door. I opened it, and in the instant it took me to consider a run for it now, Rees said, "Good morning" behind me.

I turned, with my smile already formed.

"You do look better," he said in what seemed sincere pleasure. When he took me into his arms I behaved with a hypocrisy that at once appalled and pleased me. In fact I was so warm that he held me off and looked quizzically at me. "Caro, we'd better make plans," he said. "When will you marry me?"

This called for an even more blatant lie than my arms and my kiss, and it almost stopped me. I looked into his face, and it seemed as if all the times I had done this were blended into one, beginning with the evening in the Wainwright Hotel when I'd first met the dark blue eyes, with the black Celtic lashes, that were to blot out all the rest of the world for me, and make up for all the griefs and losses I'd ever suffered.

Thickly I said, "In a month. In two weeks." I slid my arms tight around him and put my face against his shoulder. I shut my eyes, I felt his heart beat, and I wished with passion that I had awakened this morning from nightmare into clear and shining truth.

"My dear," he said. "My very dear."

"The teakettle's boiling," I mumbled against his jacket.

He laughed, we separated, and I was cold. The chill had nothing to do with the room's temperature, but he insisted on lighting a fire in the Franklin stove in the porch, and we ate there. We got onto a conversation about Tim, which helped me a great deal. Deliberately

I provoked questions I'd stayed away from before, so as to keep off the subject of *me*. "Tim would love to go to school," I said. "Don't you think he could try it out? He could start out in the subprimary."

Rees went on eating scrambled eggs.

"And for later on," I continued, "there's a special class for youngsters with various problems—"

He put down his fork. "Have you been discussing Tim with any of your Somerset friends?" he asked coldly.

"Of course not! But don't forget, Mrs. Partridge lives in Somerset, so they know a little about him."

"I did forget for a moment. Will you forgive me, Caro?" He held out his hand across the table and I took it, gave him a quick smile, and returned to my own scrambled eggs. "Tim will go to none of those classes, splendid as they may be. It is impossible for most of these children to live in an environment tempered to their particular need. They have to live in a harsh world. But Tim will never need to know that he's different from others, that he's lacking in some things. He'll never suffer from comparisons."

"I know how you have planned it," I said, "but if Tim outlives you, what then?" I looked earnestly at him. "This isn't cold-blooded of me, Rees. You must know by now how much I love Tim." I was speaking the truth, but as I spoke it I realized how false had been my vision of my own children by Rees. He would never have allowed me to bear children to compete with Tim. They'd have been the enemy—even if he were their father.

"I know you love Tim," he said. "And I think both father and son fell in love with you simultaneously.

But Tim's future is assured, no matter what happens to me. Of course, this presupposes that my lawyers are going to do their damnedest to find the right person to maintain a home for Tim. If I go before you, my darling," he said lightly, "I expect you to be that person."

"I'll do my best." My throat clogged up. *Oh God, what was* to become of Tim? It was not a silent cry but a prayer.

I expected him to follow his usual practice and go to the stone house after breakfast, but today he didn't, and I felt sure that Faraday was dead. Perhaps he'd been dying when he spoke to me. Dying of *what?* Torture? A slow, meticulously charted starvation? Somehow this was worse to contemplate than a bullet or a deadly injection.

"Let's take a lunch and walk along the shore to the south of us," Rees suggested as I washed the breakfast dishes. "There's some pretty rugged territory along there, but the tide's down. We'll see some unusual rocks, shore birds, even an ancient Indian camp-ground."

"Do you suppose we'll meet any ancient Indians?" I asked.

"That was unworthy of you," he reproached me, and I managed a convincing little chuckle.

When I went upstairs to change into suitable cloth-ing, I wrote a note. There might not be many houses along this shore, but the study of birds, rocks, and Indian artifacts were three powerful addictions almost anywhere in Maine, and I was going to be ready to meet any possible addicts. Sitting by the window, so I could see if Rees made a trip to the stone house, I wrote, "Please call the State Police and ask them to investigate the stone cottage on the grounds of Bellwood. The gates will not be opened. Anyway, it will be better to come over the wall without any advance warning. Please hurry. This is literally a matter of life and death." I signed my name to it and put it in the snug hip pocket of my Bermuda shorts. Rees hadn't gone down to the stone house, in fact he was now calling from the stairs, asking me if I was ready. I was suddenly clammy all over. I took out the note and wrote an unsteady P.S. "And tell them to get me away from the place, no matter *what*."

I'd guessed wrong, as I'd been guessing from the first in this business; there were no addicts, unless we were too early for them. I ate my lunch in an oppressed silence which I hoped Rees would take for enchantment with the view and his company. Afterward we wandered in different directions. I was apparently as absorbed as he was in looking for arrowheads or rare fossils. But I didn't find what I was searching for. There were no other cliff paths up which I could conveniently disappear if Rees got any distance from me, which he didn't. I felt as if I'd been wandering for forty years in a wilderness whose very beauty made it all the more intolerable.

When we got back to the house (was it possible I'd ever fled back to it with joy?) I said, "Rees, I'm so saturated with fresh air, I'm going to take a shower and a nap."

"All right. I'll attend to our dinner." He sounded like an indulgent husband. He walked to the foot of the stairs with me, put his arm around me and kissed me slowly and fondly, then stood watching me go up. I turned to look back, drawn not in affection but unpleasant fascination, and expected to surprise the truth on his face, that he knew or at least suspected. But he smiled and said, "Rest well, and we'll have an evening to remember the rest of our lives."

I took a fast shower, and as I was dressing in my room I saw him cross the lawn. He walked very quickly and lightly, like a youth. Tris appeared out of the woods and ran across the grass to him. He leaned down and rubbed the cat's arched back, then went on toward the path. Tris sat down and watched him go. Upstairs I watched too, and as he turned down the path I ran to the upstairs extension.

But the line was dead. I pressed frantically on the button, I dialed for the operator. Nothing brought it to life. Suddenly my terror, held under strict control since morning, was full-blown. I wanted to shriek, cower, run, freeze—I didn't know what I wanted to do. Downstairs the grandfather clock struck four like a death-knell; as if it were the hour for my execution, or Stephen Faraday's. Or for us both.

I rushed back into my room and jammed my damp feet into my sneakers. The laces defied my cold and frantic fingers, and with strings dangling I raced down the hall to the back stairs. Once I was outside and around behind the carriage house I couldn't be seen from any window in the house; once down over the cliff, with Rees thinking I was asleep upstairs, I'd be safe. As I ran down the winding stairs I was thankful that Tim was far away from the scene; I had no time to think of what tomorrow would mean to him if I reached the police today.

I bolted into the kitchen, my eyes fixed on the door across the big room and freedom shimmering beyond its screen. When I reached it I could have laughed aloud in hysterical exaltation.

The impulse was rammed back down my throat. Rees knelt at the far side of the kitchen garden, cutting chives. If the man had met me on the threshold with a physical blow, I couldn't have been stopped more absolutely. I almost fell back against the door as if I *had* been struck. My breath was sickeningly gone and my wits too. Across the neat green rows of the garden Rees stood up and looked at me.

"Oh, it's *you!*" I gasped, and slid down onto the doorstep with what I hoped was a pantomime of acute relief.

"What's the matter?" He sounded half-concerned, half-amused.

I blew hard and pushed my hands through my hair, which hadn't been brushed since I came out of the shower. "I thought I heard a sound in the house that shouldn't have been." I panted a little, and gave him a weak but brave grin. "I'd seen you go down to the study, so I thought someone was prowling around, someone who'd come by boat maybe, and then up the cliff, to try to break in." I wiped my forehead. I was sweating all over, and my voice trembled as I fought to hold together. This was no act.

"So I rushed downstairs, and then beyond the screen door I saw a man's head—what a feeling!" I put my head back against the door and shut my eyes. Tris purred around my legs. When Rees spoke again he was so close I jumped; and looking up into his smiling face I knew all at once what it must have been like to be a sacrificial victim stretched on the altar of the Aztec priests.

"I didn't go to the study. I changed my mind," he said. Because there was no longer any need to go there? "I thought this was the girl who'd never be afraid of a flesh-and-blood prowler," he teased me, putting his finger on my nose.

"Big talk," I said weakly. "Today was the moment of truth—Rees, I just remembered the car!" I was out of breath with no faking; I *had* just remembered it. Even in making my escape plans upstairs I hadn't taken it into account, I had thought only of getting as far away along the shore as possible. Eventually I'd have come to someone else's beach, a house, sane people, a telephone. But I'd never remembered the car, and my set of keys was back in my room.

"Hadn't we better go and get it?" I asked now. "Poor little thing, left out all night in the dew, and probably hungry too." Somehow I'd manage to slip away, once outside the gates.

"She's sleeping peacefully in her stall now. I walked to the wood road and got her last night when you were asleep."

I was sick to think I'd actually been alone in the house for at least a half-hour last night. To hide my reactions I jabbered, "But how could you find it in the dark?"

"She whinnied when she heard me." He laughed. "You were asleep well before dark, my girl. I brought her back in the twilight."

"That was a pretty powerful dose you gave me," I said.

"But it worked, didn't it?" He sat down beside me.

"Thanks to the freezer and Jason's exotic choices we can eat elegantly, but I like to add my own touches. I do a magnificent salad."

"I'm beginning to think your talents are numberless."

"And you've only begun to know me. . . . Are you going back to your nap?"

"Oh, I couldn't sleep now. I'd better finish dressing, don't you think? I came out in a hurry."

"So I see," he murmured, looking at my untied sneakers. "You have marvelous ankles." He encircled one with his thumb and forefinger. It was all I could do not to stiffen like a wild animal in terror. "In fact," he said, "all things about you are marvelous, as far as I know up to this moment. I expect more delightful revelations in the future."

He put his arm around me and kissed me long and hard. It was a subtly yet increasingly passionate embrace, as if he were notifying me that he was tired of waiting. Ahead of me there was the night alone with him, and he would not believe another migraine—if he'd really believed the first one.

When he let me go I gave him a wavery smile and he said abruptly, "Caro, are you a virgin? Your answer won't put me off, no matter what it is. I'm simply curious to know if there's been anyone before me, that's all. You know about *me;* now what about you?"

"I've never slept with anyone," I said.

"Not even with Paul?"

"I told you how I felt about him. Even when I thought I was actually in love with him, I never wanted to go that far."

"You wouldn't make love simply for pleasure?"

"*No!*" I used my indignant reaction as an excuse to get up. "I'm probably a whole century behind the times, in fact I've been told so, but I want that experience for the first time with a man I'm deeply in love with, and who's deeply in love with me. And now, if you'll excuse me—" I went into the house.

Behind me he said, "Caro, I love you that deeply, and more."

My eyes filled with tears. I ran blindly up the back stairs. Was it possible that he did love me that much, and that the side of him which loved me, and loved Tim, was completely detached from the side that terrified me?

It could be possible; the only trouble was that I couldn't concentrate on one and ignore the other.

[19]

We had dinner by candlelight on the porch. Afterward there was music in the living room. I could be silent throughout that, because I always was. Alternately I tried to think and then not to think. My mind scurried in circles, getting nowhere. I gave up finally, in favor of believing blindly that Something would happen to keep him out of my room, or me out of his.

I wondered what he was thinking as he played. I wondered if on such summer nights the sound of the piano ever reached the man in the stone house like distant echoes from the earth. I wondered how Valerie had really died and why Stephen Faraday had been a prisoner for three years. It was as if I had reached a point beyond terror when, exhausted and without hope, I could consider the facts dispassionately.

Suddenly he rose from the piano and came over to me, where I half-lay in a corner of the sofa, and took my face in his hands. "You'd better go up," he said. "In a little while I'll come."

"All right," I said in a low voice. He leaned down

and kissed me. Then he pulled me to my feet and walked to the foot of the stairs with me, and waited while I went up.

I had got into my room and shut the door when the music began again, the nocturne which to me was one of the saddest melodies ever written. Listening, I couldn't see Rees as a sadist, but as a man warped by grief. I thought of Valerie and her death, and that brought me back to Faraday, as I wandered about the room, not quite sure what to do next. He must have been here when Valerie died; what if he were somehow responsible for her death, and Rees had taken his punishment into his own hands? What if Faraday had actually struck Valerie during an argument? I saw him coming there, trying to get her to come away with him or at least making violent love to her against her will. But if he'd caused her to fall, he deserved to be in the hands of the law, and by keeping him a prisoner—and perhaps killing him at last—Rees had himself become a criminal.

I wished I had known earlier about Faraday. I might have been able to talk to Rees about him, taking advantage of his growing love for me. Now I was afraid it was too late, that the murder had been committed. I saw this weekend as the time set for the killing, though Rees would call it an execution. He might have intended to keep his prisoner indefinitely, but then I had come to Bellwood, possibly forever, and it would be too much of a risk. How could he expect that a growing-up Tim would stay away from the stone house, or that *I* would? Some accidental happening could take one of us close to it, if not an irresistible curiosity. Maybe Rees suspected my Brewster nose, I thought with morbid humor.

Tris scratched delicately at my door and I let him in. He glimmered like a ghost cat as he padded about my room in the long summer dusk. Night fragrances and the night music came in at the windows. The Something I had blindly expected hadn't yet materialized. I was not so much afraid of being made love to as that I'd not be able to carry my part through, and yet I knew that to save my life I must make believe that I was as ardent and eager as I'd been on those nights when I could hardly bear to leave him.

Think of those clever female spies, I urged myself. You could do as much to save your life, couldn't you? But cynical humor was no help. Should I undress? Or should I tell him when he came that I was sorry, but I preferred to wait until we were married? That virginity of mine would be a complication a man couldn't dispute, unless—

The *unless* was the unknown quantity. And I was alone with him.

Like a dream of long-ago warmth and safety coming to a man adrift on an ice floe, my memory of Mindy's kitchen tortured me. I'd still had a choice as I sat there yesterday morning, drinking coffee, and I'd made the wrong one.

I lay face down across the bed, too weary and too far past hope to cry. My return had made no difference to the prisoner in the stone house except to give him a cruel hope. He must be dead by now, as Rees had planned for him to die. . . . And supposing I'd taken the choice, and stayed in Limerock this weekend. I would never have known about the darkness in Rees, the wilderness where no birds sang and no sunlight came. Or would I have known it sometime later, to my own sorrow?

Tris jumped onto the bed and stretched out against my side. He purred for a while as he always did, with exuberant, companionable pleasure, and then the sound grew fainter, and kept breaking off as he sank deeper into sleep.

I woke up cold, still lying on my stomach, my neck aching, my whole body so stiff I couldn't move at first. The dawn chorus outside was at its peak. Beside me Tris was vigorously cleaning up for the day.

I felt the same overjoyed astonishment that I'd felt yesterday morning at having survived another night. Wincing and groaning, I inched off the bed on my stomach, and then slid onto my knees on the rug. It seemed at first as if I'd have a permanently wry neck. But by the time I'd stood up I felt looser, though my neck still hurt. Shivering, I got out of the peach silk shantung I'd worn for dinner last night, and into slacks and sweater, socks and sneakers. Tris went to the door, and I opened it and listened. The house was silent in the gray light.

Now, I thought, and followed Tris down the stairs, thankful for the carpeting that made me as quiet as the cat. I had reached the foot, and Tris had already turned expectantly down the kitchen passage, when Rees spoke to me from the head of the stairs.

I wasn't surprised, it had happened too many times. I even managed to look up at him with a smile. "Good morning! Did I wake you?"

"No, I've been awake most of the night." He was dressed, and there was something odd about his face, even in this dim light. "If you're going for a walk, wait until after breakfast, and I'll go with you." He started down, and when he was halfway I saw that one side of his face was badly bruised, his mouth swollen, and there was an abrasion near his temple. His eyes looked very tired, a little sunken.

"What happened to you?" I exclaimed.

"Oh, I took a turn around the house last night to smoke a last pipe before I went upstairs, and when I was coming in I tripped on the front doorstep and hit my face." He gave me a one-sided smile. "I must have been too preoccupied with something else, don't you think?"

"What have you done for it?"

"I've let it alone. Oh, it's nothing serious, but it was so damned painful I couldn't sleep . . . and I was certainly in no mood for anything else." He pulled my hand through his arm. "I hope you'll forgive me, Caro."

"For what? For having an accident? I'm only thankful you didn't break a bone, or damage your eye, or hit your temple hard enough to kill you." If I sounded fervent it was because I wished fervently that he *had* been hurt enough to handicap him, if not kill him.

But at least the Something had happened; I'd gotten through another night.

He didn't want any breakfast, only coffee; he said it was too hard to move his mouth, even though I offered to boil some eggs for him.

He joked about his face and his reason for the misstep, but after that he seemed so absorbed with his own thoughts that when I offered him more coffee he didn't hear me. I'd never known him to be like this. The brightening light appeared to hurt his eyes, and I suggested that he might be able to get a nap now, but he said he couldn't sleep in the daytime.

"Let's go for a walk," he said abruptly. "In the opposite direction from yesterday."

"Shall I fix a lunch?"

"Oh no, we'll just take some fruit. Jason will be back with Tim by noon or soon after."

I didn't know whether to be relieved or not by this news. We went for our walk, prisoner and guard, though I didn't know if the guard knew that's what we were. When we sat down on a long spine of ledge to rest, he said, "I can't say our weekend together has been a conspicuous success, you with your migraine and I with my bashed-in face."

"It's all my fault," I said. "I shouldn't have come back. We weren't meant to have this weekend, you see. That's why nothing's gone right."

"Do you believe that things have to be meant?"

"Don't you?"

"I couldn't stand thinking that some vast, omniscient Intelligence had arranged portions of my life. I'd be like some character in the old myths, cursing God and condemned to suffer for it through eternity."

I pounced. "You believe in God then."

"I didn't say that," he said. "It was a figure of speech. No, I believe in nothing but myself."

"Am I a figure of speech too?"

He smiled crookedly with his sore mouth. "I used to think you were a figment of my imagination. That I'd dreamed you, out of longing. But now I know you exist, darling. I really do." He put his hand over mine on the rock between us.

My overstrained nerves couldn't take any more. Reality and fantasy had melted into one another like the sky and sea out there in the warm haze; as if neither Stephen Faraday nor my horror had existed except in a long nightmare, and as if I were just waking up, dazed and relieved. I wasn't trying to get away, my day off would come next Wednesday as usual and I'd go freely out the gates and come back as freely. We were going to get married.

Suspended in time, I dabbled my feet in a salt-water puddle, ate a plum, and didn't think. Rees lay back against the rock, smoked, gazed out to sea; handsome in spite of his bruises, not at all sinister.

The soap bubble remained unbroken as we walked back to the house. It was a curious interlude in that weekend, like an hallucination or waking dream experienced by someone forced to stay awake past his mind's capacity for coherence. And in its spell I must have rested enough so that all my energies could draw together in concentration on whatever came next.

Tim and Jason were in the kitchen. Tim glowed— no, he sparkled. He wanted to tell us everything at once. He wanted to hug his father violently and then me, he kept appealing to Jason to back him up in great statements not yet made. Finally, after this joyous confusion and Jason's more staid greetings, Tim thought of something else.

"We saw a *naxidunt!*" His eyes blazed. "The car was all smashed! A wrecker was hauling it away. We watched it pull it up—up—" His hands demonstrated.

"We didn't see it happen," Jason assured Rees. "It must have been sometime yesterday, but they were just getting the car out of the ravine today when we came by, and the telephone men were putting in a new pole. This line must have been out, then."

"I wouldn't have known," said Rees. "I didn't try to make any calls."

I remembered the dead telephone yesterday afternoon, and my sense of peril came back to me with all the impact of a crash through the ice.

"What's the matter, Caro?" Tim's small face puckered. "Have you got a pain?"

"No, I was hoping nobody was badly hurt."

"Daddy, I brought you something," said Tim, off on a new crest. "Come on, it's in the library." He pulled at Rees's hand and they went together, the man's pace timed to the small boy's brace-encumbered one. Neither looked back at me and I was relieved that they hadn't asked me to join them. For too long I'd been thinking of Tim as my own; now, to look into his eager, expressive face and bright eyes, to hear his voice saying my name, was almost unbearable. I wished I could seize him and run away and keep him safe forever.

Jason cleared his throat and I jumped. "Tim must have had a wonderful weekend," I said quickly.

"The other children were very good to him. But it's not hard to be good to Tim."

"I wish he could be with other children more," I said, "but then—" I shrugged, and went back to my room. As if sanity had returned with Jason and Tim, suddenly I thought of several escapes, so simple that I could hardly believe they would work. If my nerves held on till next Wednesday, I could simply *not* come back from my day off, but send the police out. (Don't think of leaving Tim, I kept warning myself. You can't spend your life a prisoner here, as much a prisoner as Stephen Faraday was.)

Or tomorrow morning I could write a letter to Elliot and Mindy, as I did every week, and tell Elliot to come and get me, and bring the police with him.

Or I could simply quit my job.

Then I thought of the alternatives to my ideas. There might be some perfectly unanswerable reason why I shouldn't take my day off. Rees might suggest that we spend it together, driving somewhere to eat. If I argued that I had errands, he could offer to take me to do them.

As for my letter, Jason always took the mail to the post office. Until now it hadn't occurred to me that my letters might be censored by Rees; but it wasn't impossible, given a man who had kept another man locked up for three years and was able to face that man's elderly parents without flinching.

And if I announced I was quitting—after apparently being deeply in love—I'd be cross-examined by an expert.

I slumped onto the bed, my mind frighteningly blank. Then I heard Tim in his own room, and after a few minutes he came through the bathroom and tapped politely on my door as I'd taught him.

"Come in!" I called.

He looked around the door, his face afire with pride. "I've got something for you too, Caro!" He set a shoebox on the bed. "You know what I brought Daddy? You'll see it, but I'll tell you. It's a great—big—horseshoe *crab!*"

"Really?" I looked properly astounded.

"It's only the *shell,* but it looks real as anything. He's going to keep it on his desk."

"It must be magnificent," I said.

"It *is,*" he assured me, and opened up the shoebox. It was half full of rocks, creased white whelk shells, small yellow and orange periwinkles, a few big purple mussel shells, some bits of frosty green and amethyst glass, worn smooth by the sea. He rummaged happily through it all and came up with one special rock.

"This is rose quartz," he told me solemnly. "It's for you. Tony says you can't hardly find rose quartz anywhere. And I found this all by myself."

"Who is Tony?"

"Oh, he's a big boy." His eyes shone. "He's ten. He knows everything."

I wonder, I thought, so cold that my skin was prickling, if Tony knows that you aren't any more retarded than he is. Aloud I said, "I'll keep this all my life, Tim. Thank you very much. It's simply beautiful." I laid it against my cheek and shut my eyes. But why—why—*why?* my mind was shouting. Stephen Faraday is one thing, but to do this to his own child!

"Listen to the ocean," Tim cried, and pressed the largest whelk shell against my ear. I had to fight to keep from taking him into my arms. What astonished me wasn't the sudden discovery of the truth, but the fact that it wasn't too sudden, after all. I remembered my doubts, my questions to Rees and his smiling obstinacy. I knew now that after the first few days with Tim I had begun unconsciously considering him as a perfectly normal five-year-old, I'd had to keep reminding myself that he had serious limitations even if they didn't show up now.

There was to be no school for Tim. "No competition." In other words, no freedom for a bright, ardent mind. It was to be deliberately warped and repressed; as the leg muscles would slowly lose their resilience in the heavy braces. He was to be kept, if not literally in his father's arms, always within reach, always dependent. In a few more years he wouldn't know how to think or move freely.

He would be imprisoned. Prisoners, all of us, for one reason or another. Hate, love ... And what kind of love deformed a child? Phyllis Partridge had a right to be afraid.

"You *have* got a pain, Caro," Tim accused me.

"Just a little one," I said. "It will go away."

"We can tell Jason. He has things for pains."

"It doesn't need a thing. It'll go away by itself."

"Not even orange aspirin?" Tim enticed me. I smiled and shook my head. *Jason.* Was he a prisoner too? It was certain he knew about Faraday—I'd seen him often taking food down there and I thought it was for Rees, so he wouldn't have to leave his work. I suspected he knew the truth about Tim, too. There'd been the time he let Tim swim, and then was so nervous for fear Rees should find out.

It was out of the question to appeal to him to help me now. He was clearly bound to Rees for one reason or another. "He thought he needed sea air to survive,"

Rees had said. Had Rees saved him from something, or was he too one of Rees's captives, without the volition to escape even when he had the chance?

"I have a new boat Tony made me," said Tim. "Let's go sail it in the pool."

A July Sunday at Bellwood. The chatter of goldfinches and catbirds around the birdbaths; the scent of new-mown grass and roses, carried on a breeze from the sea that glittered like blue diamonds past the birches and the three great old spruces. A pair of soaring gulls. The house, someone's late-Victorian vision frozen in brick; it must have been a monstrosity in its glaring newness, about eighty years later the bricks were faded, and tree shadows danced softly across them, ivy climbed the chimneys, and torrents of roses splashed from the walls.

I sat on a lawn chair under the birches and watched the boy playing with toy boats in the pool set cleverly in the fold of ancient gray ledges. Tris sprawled near us in the shade, gazing out into the sun with drowsy golden eyes, like a lion. Far off in the deep woods thrushes called, in the fine sweet chiming that had given the place its name. *Bellwood.* Everything was the same as it had been a week ago, except that now I was so frightened that as I sat there in the stillness perspiration sprang out on me, and a deathly faintness seized me. I fought it silently; wanting to give into it was like a compulsion to jump off a high place.

The boy talked to himself as he played, and I concentrated on him; for him I had to stop being afraid, or at least gain control of my terror. But all the time I could feel my head wanting to turn inexorably toward that opening, dark in the brilliant day, that shadowy leafy tunnel in which the thrushes sang, the way through the woods to the small stone house.

[20]

I had slept from drugs Friday night, from exhaustion on Saturday night. On Sunday night I lay awake in the dark listening to the clock downstairs striking the hours, and then I would compulsively check the time on my watch. "What good does that do you?" I scoffed. "You aren't going anywhere." I was so conditioned by now to having my escape attempts circumvented that I wouldn't make a new one, even though I could hear no human sound in the house and Rees had gone into his room and shut his door hours ago. Jason was safely tucked away in his wing . . . or was he?

When the darkness began to thin and the first bird voices were heard, I fell asleep, and dreamed. Tim must have been tired too, from excitement and no nap the day before, because he was still asleep when I got up a little past seven. I sat on my bed and held the chunk of rose quartz and tried to remember my dream in every detail. In it I had quarreled bitterly with Eric on a highly personal plane, as if we were lovers. Or at least very close; some of the dialogue could have been with Paul, in the charges and countercharges. I suppose Paul came into it because he was the only man with whom I'd ever deeply, hurtingly quarreled. Brother-sister rows between Elliot and me didn't count, you always know you will get over those.

I woke from the dream of a fight with Eric feeling rather bruised by what he had said and ashamed of what I had said. It was queer to be so moved by a dream, when my real life at this moment was so perilous.

Still the vivid sensations remained. I wish I'd apologized before I woke up, I thought, and then my hand sprang open and dropped the piece of quartz—onto the muffling bedside rug, fortunately. *Apologize!* That was more than the word, it was the clue, the direction, the command. My unconscious mind had done what my conscious one was too worn out with fear to do.

After I dressed I tiptoed in and looked at Tim. He was still sleeping, his new treasures laid out on his bedside table beside the dory and the compass. Then I went downstairs as silently as possible. The smell of coffee told me someone was up; I hoped for it to be Jason, and it was. He was sitting at the table drinking coffee and reading Rees's newspaper. He sprang up when he saw me, and I gave him a conspirator's grin.

"Sit down again. I didn't intend to interrupt you, but Tim's still asleep and I wanted to use the telephone while I had the chance."

"Help yourself, Miss Brewster," he said with a nod toward the kitchen extension. "Or you could go into the library if you want to be private."

"This is all right, if you don't mind my barging in on your peace and quiet." I was all ready to take the phone from the wall hook.

"Not at all, Miss. You go right head." He concentrated on his paper. I dialed the Allenby number, praying that Eric wouldn't already have gone out for a day's sailing but was up early just the same.

When he himself answered I almost blubbed out the whole thing then and there to him, and Jason be damned. But I controlled myself and said, "I'm so *glad* I got you before you went out! I've been putting in some terrible nights waiting for you to call up, but you didn't, and I don't blame you, but I can't wait *another* moment to apologize to you." I couldn't see Jason, but I hoped I sounded properly breathless and contrite.

"For what, for heaven's sake?" Thank goodness he spoke softly; the rest of the family must have been asleep still.

"*Please* don't be that way about it," I urged him. "At least give me a chance to take it back. It was a terrible way to act, and you didn't deserve it. I don't know what *possessed* me!" I could practically see my emotional italics. Such gasps of contrition sent Jason out onto the back doorstep. But I expected he'd still be listening.

Eric's laugh was bewildered, as if he were humoring a mental case. "I don't know what you're talking about. I don't think you're drunk, but maybe you've got me mixed up with somebody else. Look, I was going to call you tomorrow—"

"Oh, Eric, *please!*" I pleaded. "You were my first friend here and nothing can change it. I wish you'd— oh darn it, I *can't* wait till Wednesday. Look, can you drive out here today? No, I don't mean the house, but if you stopped outside the gate, oh, around ten, we could talk for a few minutes, couldn't we? *Please,* Eric?"

"I will be there because I like you, and because I can't wait to find out what this is all about." He wasn't laughing now. "Caro, are you all right?"

"Thank you," I said with dignity. "I'd appreciate it very much. Ten, then. I'll only take five minutes of your time." I hung up and went out to the back doorstep where Jason sat with his coffee and magazine, studiously pretending he hadn't heard my approach. He even jumped when I spoke his name, then got up.

"You may have gathered what that was all about," I said, trying to sound self-conscious, which wasn't hard. "I'm sure you've probably done the same thing in your life. Said things you'd give anything to take back."

"I'm sure everybody has, Miss." He gazed glassily past me.

"I don't believe there'd be any objection to my talking to him at the gate for five minutes, do you? After all, soon I won't be seeing him at all, and since he was nice to me when I was a stranger I'd like to end things on a friendly note."

"Of course, Miss. That's understandable."

I turned my head aside and nervously fingered a dewy leaf. "I hope it's also understandable why I ..." My blush was real, the heat of anxiety and fear. "Why I didn't want to mention it to Mr. Morgan." Like Tim's swimming, I wanted to say, only blackmail didn't come easy to me.

"Yes, Miss Brewster. Quite." His voice was without expression. Perhaps he thought the blackmail was implicit in my hint. Anyway, I went back upstairs to

Tim, convinced that if Rees wasn't around at ten I'd manage to see Eric all right.

Rees appeared while Tim and I were having breakfast outdoors, and kissed his son and then me, which made Tim giggle. He refused a cup of coffee, saying he'd had a quick breakfast in the kitchen and was now off to a morning's work.

"Now that Jason's back we can return to normal," he said. "I was never cut out to be a housewife."

"I'm back too," Tim clamored.

"And you make things very normal, you imp." Rees pretended to steal Tim's nose, gave me a fond smile, and strolled off, a looseleaf folder under his arm. It was like any other Monday morning I'd spent at Bellwood. Except that now I no longer saw the interior of the stone house as a scholar's quiet workroom. And Rees's smile terrified me, and his touch turned me as cold as Stephen Faraday must be by now ... wherever he lay.

"Why are you all gooseflesh, Caro?" Tim asked me, and I was glad his father was too far away now to hear the piping question. "Did somebody walk over your grave?" He grinned at my surprise. "That what Mrs. Partridge used to say when *she* got all gooseflesh."

"Well, *I* felt a little breeze, that's all."

"I don't feel any breeze. Where is it?" He was all normal five-year-old, bent on the maddening pursuit of detail.

"It came and went," I said.

Tim's weekend with the other children had stirred him up. He was full of it, swinging back and forth between what he had done and seen there and what he wanted to do here. Learn to read, go down to the beach, sail boats; Tony blowing bubbles in his punch, a whiskery dog named Skipper, going rowing with a real big boy, even bigger than Tony. Baby chicks. Hot dogs on the beach. "Why can't we have hot dogs on the beach, Caro? And toast marshmallows? They get all on fire and you wave them around." He laughed in gleeful memory. There was also a girl his age who was going to school in September. "Caro, am I going to school? I asked Jason and he said he didn't know. Am I? Why don't *you* know?"

Rees must have been desperate to let him go away from Bellwood for that weekend; it would be a long time before Tim forgot the world outside, teeming with other children who slapped each other and made up, played croquet, blew bubbles in their drinks, had convulsions of laughter, waved flaming marshmallows, climbed up and down the ladders in a big barn—he'd had to watch that, but you could see the longing in him; fished off a wharf (Tim tended by the masterful Tony who knew and could do everything)—and went to school.

I answered questions as best I could without lying, told him he'd have to take up some things with his father, and quieted him somewhat by letting him read. He loved that. Bonnie, whoever she was, had read to him and her little sister in the shade under a big tree, and he was all on fire to read more for himself. We'd progressed to sounding out a few simple words now, and he applied himself with fervor.

And now it was half-past nine, and we could make a leisurely walk of it down the drive. Jason was helpful, even cheerful when he got the stroller out. Naturally he didn't know that I didn't intend to come back from the gate. I was going to boost Tim up onto the wall where he could drop into Eric's arms, and then get myself up and over too. There were plenty of trees close to the wall near the gates, and I knew all about that method.

Nobody would call it kidnapping when they knew the truth, and Tim would be in a safe place when the police went to Bellwood, in case there was violence.

Tim chattered as we went along, more about his wonderful weekend interspersed with comments on everything he saw. I was almost lightheaded with confidence. This time I was going to make it! I didn't dare think ahead to the actual moment when we'd both be over the wall and driving away in Eric's car, but I was as positive that the moment would arrive as I was that I would draw my next breath.

The gates were in sight now, gleaming dully in the sunshine at the end of a rustling green arch of fresh summer leaves. A scarlet tanager sang somewhere out of sight, purple finches caroled their long bubbling songs from the tops of spruces.

A pick-up truck went by, and Tim said, "Hurry up, Caro! Maybe the next one'll wave to us!"

I hurried, though by my watch I had ten minutes before Eric appeared. Unless he came a little early . . . My heart beat faster, and I moved faster.

Rees came out of the woods by the gate, smiling at us. "Daddy!" Tim shrieked in surprise. "What a trick!"

Yes, what a trick. And I'd come to the end of invention. I looked stupidly at him. I knew I was white, by the coldness in my face and the emptiness in my head. He said gently, "I've come to walk back with you, Tim.

And a good thing too, because Caro isn't feeling very well."

Tim squirmed around to look up at me, frowning. "She said yesterday she had a pain."

"I'm sure she did have one," said Rees.

"I *told* her Jason has those orange aspirin."

"We'll see that she takes one, son." Rees put one hand on the stroller handle, the other over my wrist, and began turning the stroller around. My hand went limp in his grip, the fingers loosening on the bar. I could not look at him. His presence, so close, was taking my breath and my strength, and not with love.

"We were going to watch the cars!" Tim protested.

"Later," said Rees. His very quietness was deadening; the child was suddenly silent, trying no longer to look up into our faces.

The return took no more than fifteen minutes, but it was all my lifetime for me, because I knew I was walking to my death, and it was as if everything in my life up till now had been a preparation for this final walk. Everything had pointed, guided, and led me to this instant. There could have been no other ending. I had chosen it far back, before I'd ever heard of the existence of Rees Morgan. My experience with Paul had been the dress rehearsal; Rees had been waiting in the wings for the gala performance. And now in the deadly intimacy of our performance, his left arm tightly around my waist while he guided the stroller with his right hand, our only audience was a five-year-old child who was to be dulled into a state where he would never remember this day.

I didn't think all this in so many words, naturally. All

I realized was the inevitability of it, as one is hardly ever surprised by any great catastrophe that befalls him but thinks as it happens, *I should have known.*

At the house Jason was mowing the lawn. He looked toward us in perplexity, and shut off the machine. I knew by his expression he hadn't told Rees anything. I don't know what my expression showed him, but he glanced quickly away from me.

"Jason, will you take Tim down to the beach for a while?" Rees asked pleasantly.

Don't go! I shouted at Jason in silence, but if he received my frantic message he didn't blink.

"Of course, sir."

"Miss Brewster doesn't feel well. She's going to her room to lie down for a while." He released me. "Go along now, Caro. Do as I tell you."

I walked across the driveway and through the front door. Tris was sitting there and he rose in greeting, chirped, and went in with me. At the foot of the stairs I stopped and looked down the kitchen passage, measuring my strength or lack of it, but Rees was close behind me, calling back in his most reassuring voice, "I'll see that she has an aspirin, Tim. Stop worrying and go with Jason."

Suddenly the gate bell began to ring. *Eric.* Rees turned it off, and I ran up the stairs with the intention of locking myself in, but Rees caught up with me. He put his arm around me again and propelled me upward. I thought, When we reach the top will he push me down and hope the fall kills me? Or will he break my neck first and then pretend to discover me at the foot of the stairs? Or will he drop me out of my bedroom window? It would have to be an accident;

two mysterious disappearances from here would look odd. There were other Faradays to notice the circumstances besides the tired old parents. That was no consolation; they could do me no good now.

At the head of the stairs I said indignantly, "We were only going to watch for cars. Why do you act this way?"

Smiling at me, those smoky blue eyes narrowed behind the black lashes, he nodded toward the telephone. "'I don't think you're drunk,'" he repeated softly, "'but maybe you've got me mixed up with somebody else.'"

Eric's words.

"Pure coincidence, my darling," he mocked me. "I picked up the telephone to call my lawyer at his home and I heard a most interesting conversation." He urged me into my room and shut the door behind him and stood against it. "Now," he said. "What were you really going to say to that young man?"

"You heard me."

"I heard him too. He had no idea what you were talking about."

"He was being generous. He's far too kind. I'd been very unpleasant, and that's not natural to me." My desperation inspired me. "That's why I was so distracted all weekend. When something's on my conscience it taints everything."

The trouble was I still couldn't look at him, except in quick glances. "Rees," I plunged on. "I like him better than I thought. I haven't wanted to admit it, because, well, I know I'm crazy to prefer him to *you*, but—" I began to fall all over myself, which was all to the good, I thought. "You must think I'm a hopeless idiot, and if you want to fire me right now I don't blame you—"

"My dear Caro," he said, "you haven't been a guilty, conscience-stricken girl all this weekend. You've been a terrified girl. Tell me, when did you find out about Stephen?"

"Friday," I said. I sat down suddenly, not able to stand any longer. He came across the room to me and pulled another chair close to mine, and took my hands, leaning forward till his face was close to mine and I couldn't look away from it.

"Listen, Caro," he said in a soft, rapid voice. "When you know the truth you'll know that what I'm doing is right. That's not a man down there, it's a monster. You love me, no matter what you say, and so you'll accept what I've done. It's justice, it's due me. There was no way of proving before the law that he murdered my wife, and tried to murder my son. But *I* knew it."

I flinched and tried to free my hands, but couldn't. I stared into his face trying to find the truth. If this was a mental illness and he could be cured, would he then be *my* Rees?

"I sentenced him to life imprisonment, Caro," he went on in that hushed, urgent voice. "If he'd gotten that sentence from a judge he'd have been comfortably looked after, with everything possible to occupy his mind and help him pass the years. Then he would be paroled. With my sentence he has unlimited time to remember what he did, to dwell on it, and every day I help him . . . a little bit."

He tightened his grip on my hands till it hurt. "You see, Caro?"

"I do see." I tried to sound as reasonable as he did.

"You know how I feel about your wife dying like that, and about Tim being hurt, and it's even more horrible if this man is responsible. But Rees, haven't you had enough of it?"

Stephen was still alive, then. There was time for Rees to save him and himself both.

"I'll never have enough of it!" He laughed, and brought my hands to his mouth, kissing one and then the other.

"You say you love me," I protested. "You say I'm everything to you, I've changed your life. So why do you need to keep this up? Doesn't it sicken you now?"

"It will never sicken me," he said, and I recognized the way he'd looked when he'd come in some evenings, fresh color on his cheekbones, his eyes brilliant. Nausea rolled over me in one great drowning wave and I almost retched. I began to sweat. He got up and went into the bathroom and brought me back a glass of water, which I refused. He stood watching me while I fought the attack of sickness, thinking if he killed me now I wouldn't even care.

After a moment it went by. I looked up at him. "If he's still alive, Rees, let him go," I begged. "I'm sure he'd be so glad he wouldn't retaliate. He'd make up some story about amnesia and leave it at that." His expression told me nothing; he seemed bemused. "If you love me, Rees," I said, "you wouldn't want to carry this over into our life together."

"The two things are absolutely separate."

"No. I couldn't let you make love to me when you'd just come from . . . whatever you do down there. And as for Valerie, you're profaning her memory with this sadism."

One of his eyebrows went up. He gave me a contemptuous glance. "What do *you* know of sadism, an ignorant child like you? What do you suppose has kept me alive, given me a purpose in life?"

"I should think Tim would be purpose enough," I said angrily. "But you've already got him put away into his little cell. You're keeping him a prisoner here too, aren't you? As much as Stephen Faraday is, only with a different kind of torture. To grow up treated as a retarded child, uneducated, solitary, shut away! He can't even *walk* freely because you keep those braces on him that he doesn't need! When did you last see that specialist? A long time ago, wasn't it?" I would talk until he silenced me; at least I'd go out fighting. There was a kind of terrifying glory in it, like taking off on the most dangerous run at the Snow Bowl, that first icy swoop through blue space and not knowing what came next.

"There never was any appointment for Saturday, was there?" I said, standing up to him. "How do you manage to get the braces changed? You've even got somebody under your thumb for that, I suppose!"

He was like gray granite, except for the fiery life in his eyes. Even his lips hardly moved. "Tim's my son. He's all I have of Valerie. He'll always be mine, I'll see to that. He'll never betray me."

I had caught the faint emphasis on the *he'll*. "Did she?" I demanded. Now I wasn't afraid to look into his face; I knew I would never be afraid again in what short time was left to me and it gave me an intoxicating taste of what the one true freedom must be. "Is that it? Then you're not punishing Stephen for her death but for her love!"

The slap knocked me back into my chair, my head spinning, my eyes blurred out of focus for an instant. He stood over me saying very softly, "You must realize you can't ever go away from here again." He went out and locked the door. Then I heard him locking the door from Tim's room into the bathroom.

[21]

The slap knocked me out of the drunken recklessness into a bleak sanity that wasn't half as comfortable. Now I wasn't accepting my own murder as inevitable, but I was the only one who could prevent it, and that wasn't a sure thing.

I sat there till my head cleared and then I tried the doors, which were well and truly locked. The bathroom window and the two in my room didn't give on any handy drainpipes or tough vines.

Failing that means of escape I looked around for something to hit Rees with when he came again. If I could only take him by surprise from behind the door. Of course I would have to knock him out with the first blow, or it would be no good. I unplugged the lamp by my bed and hefted it. It had a substantial base of dark red glass, and it might work if I hit him in exactly the right place. And then Jason would be the unknown quantity; I'd find out just how loyal he was.

But waiting was going to be difficult. As I stood in the center of the room trying to rub some warmth into my cold hands, a movement outside caught my eye and I saw Rees crossing the lawn toward the path. I knew that I was really alone in the house at last, and the thing now was to get a door unlocked.

Just as my unconscious had helped through a dream (even if I had got nowhere with it), it now brought back to me something I hadn't remembered for years, perhaps because my grandfather had been so angry with Elliot and me at the time. There'd been an outbreak of burglaries in Limerock, and the local newspaper had helpfully described a way of opening a locked door with a strip of celluloid. So Elliot and I spent one fruitful afternoon mastering the fine art. Grandfather had been furious with the newspaper too, and wrote them letters about it, accusing them of printing a primer of crime.

Of course it had to be the simplest kind of latch, but that was what these inside doors had. I got out my billfold, and with my sewing scissors cut out the plastic window behind which my nephew Peter beamed.

Once I began to work, I became very steady, and I had all the patience in the world. I hardly knew myself. Caro, you have the makings of a great criminal, I said. But this was no time for self-congratulations. Patience paid off, the latch disengaged, and I was out in the hall. I remembered to shut the door behind me, and went across the hall to Rees's room. I'd never been in it, but I knew it was above the glassed porch. Though I expected Rees to be some time at the stone house, and Jason to stay some time at the beach, I had a superstitious fear of going downstairs. I'd started out that way so many times and been stopped.

I shuddered involuntarily when I stepped into Rees's

room; it was almost like coming into his presence. The very furniture seemed to exude a silent hostility, or worse, to menace me behind my back as I crossed swiftly to the bay window. I didn't look around at the room at all, but kept my eyes fixed on the magnificent view of sea and sky. Everything was uncannily empty out there; no boats on the sea at that moment, no gulls scaling across the blue sky, no one crossing the lawn, and I was reverently grateful for *that*.

Thanks to Jason's impeccable housekeeping, the combination screen slid up as if greased, and I stepped out on the shallow slope of the porch roof and walked down the slant. There was a broad herbaceous border under the windows, and some of the tallest plants were staked. I picked out a mass of red and white petunias as the safest spot, and jumped. As I took to the air, I remembered jumping off the shed roof at Grandfather's, scared stiff but determined to prove myself to Elliot. If he could see me now! I thought, and my feet thudded into the petunias and the soft soil beneath. I landed springily as I'd learned to do from experience in my athletic youth, only slightly jolted and startling a hummingbird away from the delphiniums, and gathered myself together for the sprint toward the woods.

With the inevitability that had become a basic element in this affair, Jason and Tim appeared outside the gate in the rose hedge. Jason was looking down at Tim, and then he glanced back the way they had come, as if to see if they'd left anything behind on the beach. If only Tim had looked back too, I could have possibly made the dash past the narrow field of vision the picket gate permitted them, since the rose hedge was high at this point.

"*Caro!*" Tim's voice soared like a gull across the lawn. "Are you better?"

I still could have escaped. But the sight and sound of the child paralyzed me; I couldn't turn away from him any more than I could have run from my own child.

I couldn't read Jason's expression from this distance, but I could see that he was staring up at the open window over the porch, the screen still pushed up. Tim hurried as fast as he could through the gate and I walked slowly across the turf to meet them. I don't know what I thought or felt then; I was so weary of thinking and feeling I must have moved like the zombie in a particularly ghastly horror movie I'd once seen.

"I'm glad you feel better, Caro!" Tim cried happily. Jason's face looked very pinched, the skin tight over the bones, lips almost invisible.

"Go on," he said in a thin, hard, and scarcely audible voice. "Get out while you have the chance. You can't hurt us any, no matter what you say. Nobody'll believe it because there'll be no proof. So hurry up. I don't condone murder."

"What about Stephen Faraday?" I asked. "What will happen to him, so there'll be no proof? That's murder, isn't it?"

"Stephen who?" His tone was dead. "I don't know what you're talking about. It was a mistake to have anyone else here, I always told him so, but he thought he could manage it. Got a God complex. I always get the lunatics." His face twisted. "I can't go, but you can. Go on, run for it!"

"What's the matter?" Tim screamed suddenly, burst into frightened tears, and wrapped his arms around my knees. "Don't go away, Caro! *Please* don't go!"

Jason tried to loosen the clinging arms. Sweat stood out on his bony forehead. "Don't think about him, Miss. He's not your business. Go away and forget him."

Tim went silent, his face pressed tightly against my legs, his arms binding me as efficiently as ropes. Jason couldn't free me, and now the sweat ran into his eyes and he swore in a long whispering stream. My own hands had no strength, but I couldn't have used force against Tim anyway.

That was how Rees found us. He came across the lawn, his hands in the pockets of his blazer. "What's going on, hm?" His eyes moved affectionately from one to the other of us, his voice easy.

Tim lifted his face and said forlornly, "Caro's going away."

"Indeed she is, and we'll miss her, won't we? But we'll make out, son. We don't allow grief here, you know." He took hold of the boy's shoulder, but he kept the right hand in his pocket and I could see the shape of the automatic through the flannel. "Come along, Timmy. Let go of Caro so we can all walk back to the house. She can't go till we've made our proper good-byes, can she?"

I did not look again at the blazer pocket, but out to sea. "Yes, let go, Tim," I said. "Then you can take my hand." Tim slowly released his grip on my legs, and then pushed his hard, confident little hand into mine. Though I gripped it very tightly he didn't try to free it.

Slowly we walked toward the house, Jason well behind. I wished there were some way I could thank him for his efforts. The sun felt very hot on my head and the light dazzled my eyes. No birds were singing. It was as if something had silenced the thrushes and whitethroats, something other than the blaze of noon when they were always quiet anyway.

The kitchen felt cold after the heat outside, and I fought a creeping cold slowly engulfing me. But I would not let Rees see me tremble, even though I ached with the effort of hiding it.

"Kiss Caro goodbye, Tim," Rees said, "and then Jason can put you in the tub upstairs and wash some of that sand off."

"You'd better go through my room, Jason," I said. "The bathroom's locked from Tim's side."

"How did you get out, by the way?" Rees asked, lounging against the counter, relaxed as Tris at his most genial.

"Oh, I picked the lock." I was proud of my jauntiness. But it didn't last when Tim came into my arms crying bitterly and clinging to me. My own nose and throat clogged. I held him tightly, feeling his wet face in my neck and the sobs that began down under his ribs and shook his whole body.

"Don't go, don't go!" he beseeched me.

"Mr. Morgan, sir," Jason began.

"That's enough, Jason," Rees snapped.

Jason went to the back door and stood looking out. Rees didn't move from where he leaned against the counter; I saw only his legs and didn't want to see his face. "Tim, darling, be a good boy and don't forget your letters," I said softly against his ear. "Don't ever forget them. You *can* read, you *can* walk—don't forget."

"No, I won't. And I'll always remember where the north star is," he hiccupped. "And you keep your rose quartz—"

"I'll keep it all my life." *All my life.*

"All right," said Rees above us. "This isn't doing anyone any good. *Jason!*" The name cracked like a whip and I saw Jason's legs coming back, not fast. Reluctantly.

"Take him upstairs and keep him, Jason."

Tim was scooped away from me and lifted up. He screamed in rage and fought furiously, but Jason was unexpectedly strong. He bore the child swiftly away down the passage toward the front stairs; the back stairs would be too narrow for carrying a struggling child in braces.

My blouse was wet with Tim's tears, and his appeals rang in my ears. I could barely retain my dignity now. When I stood up to face Rees, I had to hold onto the back of a chair, which trembled from my own uncontrollable tremors.

"It's too bad, Caro," Rees said caressingly. "We could have had a perfect marriage."

"Like yours and Valerie's?" I asked with my shaking mouth. "With me a prisoner too? No, thanks. But I'm afraid you'll find my death a great embarrassment. Two mysterious disappearances from here will make the younger Faradays ask some questions, and my brother never was quite satisfied about my taking this job." That was a lie, because Elliot had gotten over his first suspicions after he met Rees. But Rees needn't know that. I went on lying, a poor attempt to intimidate him. "Mindy told me last Friday morning he wished I'd give it up and come home."

"My dear girl," he said indulgently, "no one is going to quarrel with a tragic accident. We'd been target shooting. You were fascinated with my little automatic, and you couldn't leave it alone."

The cellar door came silently open, wide enough to allow Tris to stroll into the room. He was always pushing open doors left unlatched. Now his comradely greeting and the plumy tail raised in salute were the crowning irony. Rees, while not directly in front of the cellar door, still had his back turned to it. He didn't see the cat at first, and when Tris leaned against his legs, he was startled for a moment, and instinctively glanced down. In that instant the cellar door swung open a little more. I saw, just past its edge and high up, a lock of yellow hair, a shadowed ear, and one very active eye, which winked at me.

"Before you can rig your damn accident, you'll have to catch me," I defied Rees, and darted to another chair back, then to another, as if I were trying to edge out of the room. Rees smiled and didn't move, so I flashed a scheming glance at the passage, then back at him, and took a long step toward it; instinctively he started after me, and I whipped around to face him, pressing my back against the wall beside the open door.

"I'm pretty fast," I warned him. "Before you're through today, you'll probably have turned your son insane from terror, and then you can really lock him up for good, can't you? You can spend your days going happily from one locked room to another. When Jason can't stand it any longer, he'll leave you. And then some day the kids will get over respecting the wall, and they'll start climbing it, and what will they find? Three for the madhouse, and you'll be the one who goes in the padded cell."

He came at me with his hands shaped for my throat, and beyond his contorted face the cellar door opened all the way. In one bound Eric was huge in the room, one arm going around Rees's throat and hauling the black head back tight against his shoulder, the other hand groping in the blazer pocket for the automatic before Rees could reach it. As if it had all been rehearsed, he held the automatic out of Rees's reach and toward me. As I took it, I didn't look at Rees's face. Eric pinned one of Rees's arms behind him. The other hand could do nothing against the arm across this throat.

"Call the state police, will you, Caro?" Eric asked politely.

I laid the automatic on the counter under the cupboards near the telephone, took the instrument from the hook, and dialed the operator. Rees had become very quiet.

"If you're going to behave, Mr. Morgan," said Eric, "I'll stop mugging you." He loosened his arm, and Rees said, "Thank you. I promise that my behavior will be beyond reproach."

The operator answered and I asked her to call the state police barracks and tell them to come to Bellwood, on the Somerset road. The gates would be open for them. "There's been an attempted murder," I said. "Please bring a doctor." I didn't know what condition Stephen was in.

I hung up and turned back. I had to look at Rees then, and across the room our eyes met; his the deep blue so different from Eric's, his smile so full of infinite promise. Eric stood behind him looking as fresh and uncomplicated as a spring morning.

"Well, Caro," Rees said.

"I'm sorry, Rees," I said huskily. I *was* sorry, for so much I didn't even know where the list began.

"So am I, my dear," he said. "Because I've loved you, Caro. I still do. That makes it all the harder."

He moved like lightning, taking even Eric by surprise. One sweep of his hand and the gun went off the counter, and I thought, Now I *shall* die, and Eric too.

No, he'd gone down the passage toward the main hall and I shouted at Eric, "He's going for Stephen!" Eric plunged down the passage ahead of me, but Rees hadn't turned toward the front door. The door of Valerie's study slammed and locked behind him. We stood there panting and staring, Eric put his arm around me as if he knew what would come next.

[22]

I hung onto Eric as if to a stout oak during a hurricane, and when the shot came the oak folded its boughs around me and held me safe while the winds shrieked by. My eyes squeezed shut, my face pushed hard against his shoulder, I waited for the echoes of it to die, but the sound seemed to go on and on in my ears, as if it kept happening again and again. The only thing that could put an end to it would be Rees's appearance in the doorway, amiable and debonair, with some completely reasonable explanation of the noise.

Then over my head the tree spoke, or rather Eric did, and not to me. Something like an electric shock convulsed my brain for an instant—I thought he was speaking to Rees.

"Where's Tim?" he was saying, and from far off I heard Jason's voice, thin and distorted through the chaos in my head.

"He's playing with his dory and shells in the bathtub, sir."

I moved away from Eric's arms and looked up the stairs at Jason, blinking to clear my vision. The final reverberations of the shot had died at last, and the place had a dreadful silence.

"I told him that's what you'd want, Miss Brewster," Jason said, "and it calmed him down a little."

Miss Brewster asserted herself over the trembling shell of me. "Good," she said crisply, if not heartily.

"I guess you know what's happened, Jason," Eric said. I knew in the mental clarity that had come with the silence that he felt a profound pity for both men.

Jason's hands were squeezed together. "I have an idea, Mr. Allenby," he said in a stiff, light voice, as if on the last of his breath.

"I'd advise you to keep busy with the boy and not try to leave the house," Eric said.

"Certainly, sir," the monotone replied. "I have nowhere to go, anyway." He turned and went back along the hall. I sat down suddenly on the stairs, and Eric sat down beside me and lit a cigarette. I wouldn't look at Valerie's door, but at the shimmer of sun outside the screen, the flash of a bird's shadow. Slowly the sounds from out there began to modify the awful stillness; wind stirring through the trees, a catbird's long dissertation, a squirrel's angry chirring. What's out there, I explained to myself, is just as real as what's in here. The world doesn't come to a full stop because one person has . . .

The fact that the person who had come to a full stop this Sunday morning might well have been myself was not now credible. But Rees? That was incredible too. I must have made some sound because Eric put one arm around my shoulders, and went on smoking his cigarette and saying nothing. We had assumed that Rees had shot himself. Perhaps he'd fired the shot to fool us and had gone out the window, and—but I couldn't see Rees as a fugitive. Such conduct would be below his contempt.

He might not be dead. He might now be dying. But he would not want us in there. We had done enough damage to his plans without ruining the final one.

"Who's Stephen?" said Eric suddenly.

"He's in the stone house," I answered, still gazing at the door. "That's what I found out. When I did, it made all the difference—*Eric!*" I was fully revived at last and on my feet. "He might have done that after all! Fired a shot to fool us, I mean, and then gone out the window and around the other side of the house and down to the study to kill Stephen. Oh, *no!* If we've lost him after all I went through this weekend—" I felt like howling like a child.

"Wait a minute, now." Eric kept patting me. "I heard the fall in there. You didn't. But you just wait here, Caro, and I'll go around and look in the window." Light and swift for such a big man, he ran across the hall and out the front door. I stood there with my hands wringing each other so hard the knuckles began to snap. He came back in a moment.

"He's there," he said. He put his arm around me again and we sat down on the stairs. He drew me close in a comfortable brotherly fashion and I was glad to lean against him. I began to yawn tremendously.

"We ought to go to Stephen," I said. "Let him know it's all right—" Another yawn that seemed to come from my toes.

"We'll see to him after the police get here," said Eric. "Who is this guy, anyway?"

"He was here when Valerie died. . . . Rees said he

was to blame." I had to stop to yawn. My eyes streamed, my jaw felt loose. "He's kept him a prisoner ever since."

"Good God!" Eric at last appeared shaken. "So that's the story. Everything went through my head while I was listening to him around the cellar door, but I never guessed anything like that!"

All at once there was a small golden presence with us; Tris fell over on his head at our feet, stretched and rolled. Eric leaned down and scratched the furry white belly and Tris playfully grabbed his hand with all four feet and pretended to bite it. "That boy's been showing me the cellars," Eric said.

"How long had you been there?"

"Well, I got to the gates at ten, and you weren't there, so I rang and rang—"

"Rees turned you off." With utter disbelief I reviewed that moment when I ran for the stairs, when Rees caught up with me, with the inexorable grip and the inexorable smile.

"I was going to get into this place by hook or crook, and at first I thought about driving over to the barracks at Long Cove and getting a cruiser to come out. Then I thought, what the hell, the police would have to go over the wall too, and I didn't want to waste any more time. I didn't know what was going on out here, but I was as scared for you as I'd ever been for myself in Vietnam. So I drove on down the road a bit, parked the car close to the wall and climbed over. I followed the side wall to the shore and approached the house from below."

"But weren't Tim and Jason on the beach?"

"Yep. I came around the point and saw them. They

were back to me, feeding gulls from their hands, and the birds were making such a racket, and Tim was hollering too, that an army could have gone behind them. I made a run for the cliff path without their seeing me." He looked modestly at his big hands. "I figured if Jason came after me then, I could manage him. . . . Unless, of course, he goes armed." He gave me a one-sided grin. "I didn't think of that till afterward. Old Hindsight, I was known as."

From far off came the first warning of the sirens. I shuddered without meaning to and Eric's arm pulled me closer. "I came across to the back door and there was nobody around but Old Baseball Face here. The best old greeter there is. I snuck into the kitchen and listened. There wasn't a sound anywhere except for the clocks. The two of us were pussyfooting around down here when I heard Morgan's voice upstairs and a door shutting, so I ran down cellar. My friend went with me."

"You're two of a kind," I said, wanting foolishly to laugh. "Big, blond, good-natured, and always appearing at the exact, perfect instant. Tris made me find out about Stephen." The sirens were nearer now. I got up and went over to the wall panel and pressed the gate button. The panel was beside Valerie's door but I still didn't look at that.

"I'll go up and see to Tim," I said. "He'll want to know about the sirens. I'll have to think of some explanation."

"Tell him the police go around inspecting something or other." He got up too. "I'll go with you and take Jason over."

"I'm not afraid of him," I protested. "Jason tried to get me out of here."

"But he's a man at bay now, remember. He's likely to be in a panic with Morgan gone."

When we came into Tim's room he was dried off and in bed, playing drowsily with his shells. He had the dory loaded and was pushing it across the coverlet. At sight of me he rose up and cried joyously, "Caro, you haven't gone yet!"

"No," I said. "And I'm not going right now. But your father had to go." It was wonderful what the sight of him did for me. He was my responsibility right now, and I could forget myself.

"Oh, he always has to go somewhere." He beamed at Eric. "Thank you for my cars. Did you come in your boat this time?"

"Nope. I walked." He raised an eyebrow at me. "Where's the brain damage we've always heard about?"

"As far as I can see it doesn't exist," I said.

His face tightened and chilled. Then it warmed again for Tim. "Where's Jason, Tim?"

"He went to his room to get a pill for his headache. Listen!" he bounced up and down. "Is that fire engines? They're getting louder! They're coming *here!* Are we on fire?" He looked enchanted.

"It's not a fire engine, it's a police car," I said. "Jason's room is in the kitchen wing, Eric. You go that way." I gestured with my head. He nodded and left us.

I sat down on Tim's bed and he began showing me precious individuals among his rocks and shells, and we talked about them as the sirens screamed louder and louder through the woods and then began to die as they reached the house. Tim pranced off the bed and toward the door, wild to go see, but Eric was coming in at the same moment and I was able to hold on to Tim.

"Good thing you asked for a doctor," Eric said shortly.

"*Jason?*"

"Asleep." He ran downstairs. I wrestled a frantically excited Tim back to his bed, insisting that he must be dressed before he went downstairs. I took my time picking out his clothes, all the while making up a long and involved explanation of how the police went from door to door to see if all the dogs were licensed, and if people were careful not to build fires in dry weather, and how many people in the house were old enough to vote. When I'd worn that out, explaining why dogs should have licenses and condoling with him on not owning a dog, and telling him what voting was, I fussed so much with parting his hair that he was downright impatient with me. Then I had trouble with his braces. He looked at me with tears in his eyes and said, "But they'll be gone, and I won't *see* them!"

"You'll see them," I promised. I went out into the hall. Valerie's door was closed, and there was no one in the hall but one trooper.

"The little boy wants to come down and see a police cruiser," I called to him. "Is it all right, do you think?"

He looked up and smiled, young and tanned, immaculate in his summer uniform. "Coast is clear, ma'am."

Tim was right behind me. His lips pressed tight with determination, he swung himself rapidly down the stairs. At the foot he and the trooper gave each other mutually admiring glances. I could hear someone talking on the library telephone, calling for an ambulance. There were voices behind Valerie's door, and someone ran down the back stairs to the kitchen. Strange voices and footsteps all through the house; thus quickly had all Rees's schemes for protection and privacy been wiped out.

Tris sat on the stairs watching and listening with an air of bright interest. The police cars gleamed outside the front door. I stood in the sun, glad of its impersonal warmth striking my flesh, while the trooper showed Tim the radio in one of the cars, the circling light on the roof, and how you made the siren go. I had to know about Rees, even though I couldn't consciously think his name.

"What about in there?" I asked, while Tim was running fingers over the insigne on the car door. "In the small room?"

"Nothing anybody could do, ma'am. It was final. The doctor and Eric are up with the houseman now."

"Oh, do you know Eric? You must be the friend he mentioned." It was a relief to be so ordinary.

He looked pleased. "I guess I'm the one. Ted Chatto. We played together every summer when we were growing up. Got into more scrapes. What he couldn't think of, I did. Nothing bad—just kid foolishness." He laughed aloud. "Once we were both mad with our folks and set out to sail to Florida in this old wherry we'd rigged up. We got blown out to sea and had to be searched for and fetched home by the Coast Guard."

"That must have been humiliating. How'd you ever live it down?"

"We didn't know if we ever would. We got it from all

sides. So we slunk around the edge of town for as much as a week, till some other kids got lost on Liberty Mountain and that took the heat off us."

For these few moments, contemplating Eric as a lanky teen-ager running away from home, I'd been amused and forgetful. Then suddenly the trooper's reason for being here took me by the throat.

"Did Eric tell you about the stone house?"

He became official again. "Yes, ma'am. Two men have gone down there with a key ring they found on—" His eyes shifted toward Tim, who had got himself in behind the wheel somehow, and was being a siren. From afar another siren joined his; after that I had to get Tim away before the ambulance came. He was so in love with the cruisers, and so excited about the new siren coming—and perhaps unconsciously affected by the atmosphere around the place—that he was obstinate. It was the normal obstinacy of a spirited and intelligent child, and I was glad he was capable of it, but there was no time for it now with the ambulance probably turning in at the gates.

Eric appeared on the front doorstep all at once and said, "Hey, Tim, have you got any trains?"

"Yes," Tim said agreeably. "They're way upstairs."

"Well, how about showing me? Come on, I'll take you piggyback." He hunkered down and the trooper swung Tim up onto his back. "Hang on now! We're off for the moon! . . . Jason's out of it," he said offhandedly to me. "For good."

A little boy's happy squeals sounded from the stairs as the ambulance came up the drive. We were on the third floor when it arrived at the front door. There were two dead men waiting. As for Stephen, we didn't know yet what his condition was.

And while we played with trains in the ballroom at the top of the house, below us the strangers still came and went, and one cruiser and the ambulance finally departed.

[23]

I packed some things for myself and Tim, and Eric drove us into Somerset. His mother would welcome us there, but though I felt the presence of the older people would brace me up, I decided to accept the Websters' invitation, given at once when Eric called Helen from Bellwood after the others had gone. There would be other children to keep Tim occupied, and the dogs; and the place was far enough from town so we would be hidden away from newspaper people or the merely nosy ones while the investigation was going on.

One trooper had been left at the house to guard against the curious who could come up by the shore way. Another patrolled the wall and the gates. We left Tris behind in good hands, promising him we'd drive out every day to feed him; later we found the trip to be hardly necessary—at least for the cat's sake—because of his camaraderie with the guards. But the hour or so that Eric and I used up each afternoon for those first few days was therapeutic for me; though I dreaded the first return to Bellwood, I knew it was something that had to be gotten over with. The house was full of Rees; he was at every turn. Packing up, I would hear a footfall and think his name with my heart before my mind said, *Eric*.

A lesser ghost was Jason, but he was there too, a soundless presence in the kitchen or on the back stairs; his neat small footprints were still in the dry soil of the kitchen garden. Jason had died from a dozen of Rees's migraine capsules.

Stephen was in the hospital in Ellsworth, allowed to be seen by only his family, but he had asked the troopers about me when they'd taken him out of the stone house; when they said Tim and I were safe, he had collapsed as if he had been holding himself together only by a supreme effort. But the profound, almost comatose sleep which lasted for several days was probably the alternative to a nervous breakdown, they said at the hospital. The fact that he had not disintegrated long before this—and without any chance of recovery —was a kind of miracle. There had been several in this affair.

Jason's sister drove over from Bar Harbor to claim his body. At least he had someone to do what is euphemistically called "making the arrangements." It was a law firm who did it for Rees.

Mrs. Harper wanted to talk to me, and the county attorney called me about her, and then sent her out to the point. Helen took the children down onto the beach and left the house to me. Mrs. Harper was a thin, wiry woman who like Jason had an ageless quality, as if she'd never looked any younger even when she'd been young, but would never look any older, even when she was ninety. But she was more open than Jason—*softer* might be the word—and she had cried a good deal, though she was composed in her manner.

I gave her tea, and told her that Jason had always been very nice to me and that at the end he had tried to help me. "Even though he was so devoted to Mr. Morgan," I added.

"He had good reason to be devoted," she said bitterly, "but I wish now he'd taken his chances on the outside. If he'd come to my people when our butler, old Mr. Harris, died, he'd be alive now, and happy, not dead and disgraced. Mind you, I never knew why he wouldn't take it, until a year or so ago. He came to spend a weekend with me and he was so down in the mouth, kind of brooding, and I suppose I kept after him too much"—she fidgeted with her bag—"about why he wouldn't come with me. Finally he blurted it all out, how he wouldn't feel safe anywhere but hidden away in that place, and he'd be taking his life in his hands if he ever left the state."

I poured more tea and waited. There would be some things I would never understand in this affair, but my possible cure depended on my finding out all I could. I suppose the Brewster nose was partly responsible.

"After Korea he got working for a very nice man who went off his head and had to be put away. Then a friend of this man asked him to come to him, and as things came round it seems *this* very nice man"—she pronounced the words with bitter sarcasm—"was connected with the gangs . . . the Mafia or whatever you call it . . . and before Jason knew it he was in too deep. He knew people who came there who shouldn't have; it was thought he listened in on the phone conversations

—you see they were ignorant," she explained scornfully, "they thought he was like themselves. They didn't know he had principles. Someone died in the house in a very queer way when Jason wasn't supposed to have been home. And he knew what would happen when they found out he'd been there. He ran away, and came up to Maine. After Mr. Morgan took him on, he never left the state again. And Mr. Morgan, he played on that fear. He bought him with it, body and soul. He knew people, don't tell *me* he couldn't have found out if it was safe for Jason again!"

She stared fiercely at me, and all I could say was, "I'm sorry." *I always get the lunatics,* Jason had said to me on that last day.

"I know now what's been stabbing at Jason all this time. That poor man walled up alive down there. Jason knew it was wrong. But he was a coward, scared for his own hide. Not that I blame him too much for that," she warned me. "He was brave in the Army, he was decorated for bravery."

"And how do we know that he wasn't trying to think of a way to get Stephen out of it?" I asked, to comfort her. She nodded, her eyes filling.

Presently she thanked me for talking with her, and said she felt better—a little. But after she had gone I felt wrung out. Later I called the florist in Somerset and ordered flowers for Jason in Tim's name and mine. I sent flowers from Tim to Rees too, but none from me.

I had called Elliot up on that first day, before he could hear anything on the news, and found that he was sick with the same virus the children had had. I convinced him that I was all right and in good hands.

He drove up a few days later, and besides offering brotherly support he was able to interpret for me all the legal goings-on that took place.

Not that I really needed or wanted to understand anything. I took care of Tim, and wondered when my layer of insulation would wear thin. For I had been in love with Rees, completely and passionately committed to him, up till a week ago, and in that week he had tried to murder me, had killed himself, and had been buried. The shattered flesh lay under a stone next to Valerie. Though I had heard the shot, I had not seen him dead, and whenever I thought of Bellwood he was always there; when we went out to the house, he had just left it or was about to come back into it.

I had a mild sedative from the doctor to help me sleep at night and I hadn't yet begun dreaming of Rees. But I knew that one bullet couldn't wipe out the world I'd created out of music, flowers, summer, a persuasive voice, a smile, a tragedy. That world might have been pure fantasy, but myths die harder than the truth does, and so I felt both a revulsion against Rees and a deep grief for the loss of the Rees that he was not.

When Stephen Faraday awoke and told his story to the county attorney, the case was officially closed. It went out of the newspapers and off the radio and television newscasts. The sightseers stopped coming. But in real life nothing ever finishes with a swift clean stroke and the words "The End."

Rees's lawyers were busy now, and the trustees of Valerie's inheritance. "I'm sorry, Caro," Mr. Hayward said to me at our first meeting. "That's inadequate, but it's all I can say."

"How could you *know*?" I asked him. "And if I hadn't gone there, what about Stephen?"

Judge Carver looked twenty years older than he had that night in the Wainwright Hotel. "I'd have staked my life on Rees Morgan," he said.

And I did, I answered him silently. "Please," I begged aloud. "Let's not go back over things, let's think about Tim."

I was now asked if I were willing to be Tim's guardian. His legal affairs would remain where they were, but he had to have a home. Neither Rees nor Valerie had any surviving relatives but Tim himself, except for some very distant Martyn cousins. I could maintain a home for him at the estate's expense wherever I liked, even at Bellwood. I shook my head at that and asked about Limerock. Since Mr. Hayward and Judge Carver lived there too, Rees's lawyers had no objection.

The first thing I requested for Tim was a complete checkup by specialists. A Boston orthopedic surgeon said that Tim had been discharged as his patient about a year and a half ago, and at that time he had no more need for braces; the orthopedist who had been fitting new braces to Tim as he grew came forward to say that he must have been working, in all innocence, from forged prescriptions. It was only Tim's unquenchable spirit that had made him run secretly around his room without the braces, and thus keep his muscles from becoming utterly dependent on steel and leather.

He was not retarded; there had been no brain injury at the time of the accident. It didn't do to dwell on what his father's twisted love would have done to him. Phyllis Partridge came out with Nancy Allenby one afternoon to see Tim, and was tactful enough not to say, "I told you so." But I thought with bitter humiliation that this woman, whom I'd dismissed as a kind of crackpot, had guessed right. Yet I couldn't believe that Rees *hadn't* loved me. I couldn't believe it had all been a skillful, treacherous performance to get me completely into his hands. I still feel—and not only to save my pride—that he thought he could manage to live his two lives. But they brushed in passing and exploded in disaster.

I was thankful that I'd never blurted out anything to Mindy or Elliot on that Friday morning in Limerock. The only other person who knew about the love affair was Jason, so I was safe. If I didn't want to discuss my life there, or answer any questions but official ones, the crowd all understood; I'd been through something ghastly, I'd been almost murdered; who could blame me for silence? They were all particularly nice to Tim, who lived in a garden of delights. Though sometimes he asked when his father was coming back and when we were going home, there was always something new to think about in the next minute; the baby, the dogs, sailing, flaming marshmallows, a ride on a fat pony. And goodbye to the braces!

Finally I told him that his father had gone on a long trip this time, and he and I were going away for a while. We'd live near Peter and Bethiah—whose photographs had always fascinated him—and he'd go to school. He was silent for a few moments, staring into my face as if trying to read it. Then he said, "What about Tris?"

"Oh, we'll take Tris with us."

He was quiet again. After a while he said, "It's funny Jason went away too."

"Yes," I agreed. "But grown-ups often do funny things."

"I guess *so!*" he said in a perfect imitation of Gordon Webster. Then he went off, free of braces, to learn how to play croquet.

Before Tim and I went to Limerock, Eric and I visited Stephen Faraday in the hospital. I didn't know what to expect, and on the way I felt a sort of cringing, as if I were to meet a victim of the Nazi concentration camps, but the tall gaunt man in a dressing gown put me at ease. He insisted on my taking an easy chair by the window, and an obliging nurse brought coffee to us. His once-sandy hair was whitened, and his gray-green eyes were set in hollows; his bones stood out sharply, but they were good bones, and even like this he was ruggedly handsome and far from being a ruined man. It took only a few minutes for Eric and me to see this. But it would take time to repair the results of three years' refined torture, both mental and physical.

"Rees was in hell," he told us. "But the worst of it is that these people never know they make their own hells. It's always somebody else's fault; somebody else is going to pay. I wasn't responsible for Rees's trouble any more than Valerie was." His lips curled in a smile that never touched his eyes. "When I thought there was a chance for me, I tried to be objective and pity him. . . . Then I began to hate him. Maybe that's what kept me alive. I used to think if I hated him hard enough it would rot him to death, like gangrene. Then I thought I could will myself to death, and cheat him that way. But when I saw you walking through the woods one day I was completely demoralized; I nearly went off my head with hope."

"That must have been the day I came upon the place by accident, and then ducked back." I explained to Eric. "I wasn't supposed to be on the grounds at all that day. . . . Did you call me?" I asked Stephen. "I convinced myself it was crows."

"I remember those crows. I'd hauled myself up to look out. I was always doing that in case some brave little imp trespassed on the place. And then I heard you walking; my ears had got very keen . . . I saw you and I shouted. You didn't come back then. But when you finally did, you listened."

I remembered the cry that had waked me, and the cries that Tim and Phyllis Partridge had heard. "Did you ever shout in the night?"

"Yes. It was half madness, I think. During the days I kept my mind busy rehearsing surgical techniques, and so forth. But at night I'd lie there in the dark and get the illusion that I was buried alive in a tomb. So I'd shout to rip that damned stillness into shreds. After the last time he shot me full of Demerol to make me sleep. I don't know where he got it. He had all kinds of contacts. If you pay enough you can get anything."

He put back his head and shut his eyes, and the strain showed in long lines like seams or scars down his face. "I was afraid of becoming an addict then. Until then I could call him a fool, a maniac, and damn his eyes, and still retain my self-respect. If he'd been able to make me into an addict, he'd have been paid back for everything he fancied I'd done to him."

"But you did everything," I said, "just by existing, by keeping in touch with Valerie."

He straightened up again; when he opened his eyes his worn face became alive and young. "She'd stopped writing to me, and that was why I flew to Bangor that weekend and hired a car and drove out there. I hadn't heard from her for weeks and it bothered me. I didn't go there to make trouble, to be a nuisance to her, but to assure myself she was all right. There was an odd streak in Rees that—well, I think she married him *in spite* of it. Or maybe she was intrigued by it, I don't know." He thought for a few moments, gazing at his hand on the arm of his chair. Across the room Eric's face was politely blank. Outside the door the busy afternoon life of the hospital went on.

"When I got to the house Rees wasn't there. And Valerie was like a ghost of herself. She'd always been high-strung and sensitive, but she'd had balance and humor too. But now she was having a hard time holding on to them. . . . So that Jason couldn't report that we'd talked in secret, we walked on the lawn with Tim between us, and tried to look as if we were catching up on family news. She told me that Rees's possessiveness had become practically psychotic. She'd had to stop writing to all her friends, and turn away from the people she'd met in Somerset. She couldn't get away alone with Tim even to drive to the post office, Rees was so afraid of her running away. She was sleeping badly, she dreaded to be in his presence, yet if she flinched it was like driving a knife into him. She was *sorry* for him! That was Valerie." He looked at us with a proud and touching smile.

"I was willing to come in by boat and take her and

Tim away, or to knock Jason out then and there and take them. But she was as honorable as she was kind. Scared stiff, she still wanted to give him every chance, and she thought a psychiatrist might help, if she could only get the courage to bring up the subject. Then she looked past me, stiffened, and went white. Rees was coming across the lawn toward us. *Smiling.*"

I was as cold as if a stream of ice water were pouring gently and evenly over my head, down my back, between my breasts, over my whole body. In another moment the chills would strike. *He came smiling.* How well I knew.

Out of the corner of my eye I saw Eric get up. Moving softly in his sneakers he came across the room and leaned on the back of my chair. I felt his fingers lightly pressing on my shoulders.

"She reached down for Tim and picked him up and moved away from me." Stephen's voice was lifeless. "I put my hand out without thinking. She pulled away as if I were a rattlesnake, staring all the time at Rees. When he was within six feet of us, still smiling, she cried out something, and stepped backward." His hands went out as if he saw her falling now, and grasped at emptiness.

"Neither she nor the baby screamed. I started for the path, and Rees struck me with something across the base of the skull. I woke up in the stone house, and I was there until ten days ago. As for what happened in those three years, I've told the police and the county attorney all that's necessary. I don't intend to discuss it again with anyone. I'm Lazarus returned from the dead, and life is what interests me, not death. But you should know, Caro, what happened on one of those last nights, because you might have wondered about his bruises."

That was the night when I'd waited in my room for Something to intervene, and it had. Rees had gone down to the study, leaving the record player on to deceive me. But that night hope had given Stephen a burst of maniacal strength. Rees had turned his back for a moment, thinking that Stephen had neither the will nor the energy to move, and Stephen had jumped him.

"I tried to knock his head against the wall and brain him, but all I could do was mark him up and slow him down a bit. What I got in return was the end of me, I thought when I passed out."

"I wondered," I said, and picked up my coffee cup a bit too quickly.

[24]

In Limerock we stayed with Mindy and Elliot until I found a place of my own. When I did, it was perfect. The descendants of one of the city's old seagoing families had turned the wing of their big home into a separate dwelling. Here I would have privacy, but still not be alone at night; I found myself touchy about this for the first time in my life. There were wide lawns and shade trees about the place and the back yard opened out into fields and forest that would be ideal for Tris, and for those walks in the woods that Tim had always wanted. But at the foot of the front lawns, beyond the flower beds, other children passed constantly along the sidewalk. And *dogs.* We were a short walk from the school, and in that first autumn Tim came home from his subprimary class scuffling through dry leaves, and in the golden afternoons he rode up and down on his first tricycle.

Our Somerset friends didn't forget us. Mark and Helen Webster came several times that summer and fall. When the Lobster Festival was on, Nancy, Tamara, and the brothers Gillespie came too. But Eric was there almost every week, and you would think, at the first, that it was Tim he had come to see. We strolled in the woods, we walked along the sidewalk while Tim rode his trike, we drove down to the fascinating (to Tim) world of Main Street; we had meals or picnics with Elliot's family. Eric didn't pick up where he'd left off on that moonlit night by the gates, about wanting a chance from me, and I began to think he never would.

Not that I was anxious for him to. I wanted only this life I was living, introducing Tim to the world and the world to Tim, seeing it through his eyes, being for twenty-four hours of the day a parent. Shots, vitamins, new shoes, chicken pox, birthday parties, the glorious occasion (for Tim) of the first fist fight. It was safe, it had its cosy limits and its rewards. I wasn't Paul's Caro, Rees's Caro, or Eric's, and I didn't want to be. I'd had enough of what all that led to. And as long as Eric didn't disturb the status quo, I was as happy as Tim was to see his car drive in. He kept Tim from missing his father too much, and for me he had always been the best sort of a companion.

When school began we didn't see Eric so much. Tim was busy too, with school in the mornings, and with our afternoon walks and errands and with having someone come to play, or going to someone's house to play. But he always remembered Eric in his prayers, along with Rees and Jason.

And in Tim's prayers Rees was to me simply who he was to Tim—Tim's loving father, away on a long trip. He was not the Rees I had known.

On a fine late September Saturday, with the hills all afire with color and the big harbor an eye-hurting blue spread out before us where we lived on a slight rise above the city, Eric drove in unexpectedly. Tim flung himself into Eric's arms. I was so pleased myself that the day became instantly more beautiful.

Tim was to have his hair cut that morning, and Eric took him downtown while I got a picnic lunch together. We drove out into the country back of Limerock, and ate on the shore of a sapphire lake. Afterward Tim played at the water's edge, improvising boats and buildings as I'd taught him to do, and Eric and I talked. Eric told me about his school and some of the problems and pupils. I talked about Tim's adjustments and mine. We were comfortable in the pine-scented sunshine, listening to the birds' voices, Tim's, each other's. Eric was sprawled out on the pine needles, looking as lazy and relaxed as Tris. Suddenly he said, "Caro, what about Rees?"

He'd looked so sleepy, the attack was unfair. The very name was like a knife twisting in my stomach. My face felt cold as the blood left it. "Why do you ask that?"

"What do you think about him?" he said quietly. His eyes lifted to my face, and I had a foolish impulse to hide it so he wouldn't see if it was pale or strained. But I made myself gaze back at him. "What do you remember?" he went on. "Has he made you afraid to love anyone else? Or do you still love him?"

There was nothing I could do but to stammer foolishly, "What are you talking about? I don't know what you mean!" My hand, on the spills between us, jerked uncontrollably. He put his large one over it and held it down.

"I guessed, when I begged you that night outside the

gates to give life a chance," he said. "I couldn't say right out what I didn't know for sure. But on the last day—that morning while I listened from the cellar stairs—then I knew."

"How could you know anything?" I protested in a low, trembling voice, with a glance at the oblivious child.

"Don't you remember? No, I suppose shock knocked the whole thing out of your head." He squeezed my hand lightly, then lifted it and put it against his cheek and went on talking. "He said, 'We could have had a perfect marriage.' And you said, 'Like yours and Valerie's? With me a prisoner?' Or something like that." He held my shaking fingers tighter against his warm cheek. "Then later, when I was in the room, he said he was sorry, because he'd loved you, and he still loved you . . . it was before he got the gun. And I saw your face. I ached for you, Caro, whether you believe it or not."

I couldn't think of anything to say, and I couldn't get away from him. Was his cruelty intentional, evoking that day and those words? I couldn't accuse him, my throat was too thick. He said in this very soft voice that couldn't possibly reach Tim's ears, "I had to say this, Caro, because it's been there between us. I had to say it, before I could tell you that I loved you then and I still do. . . . Now I love you more, because of what you've been through and how you stood up to it."

"Eric," I said at last, "I don't want to talk about love."

"What, *never?*" he exclaimed. "Or hardly ever?" He grinned.

That grin restored health to the day. Nightmare was long past, there was nothing to be afraid of any more. Nothing outside myself, that was. But inside—that was a different matter. And it was time to stop being evasive. If Eric deserved anything, it was absolute honesty.

"I've made some rotten mistakes in my life, Eric," I said, "and I'm scared stiff. It would be very easy for me to imagine myself into being in love with you. I've depended on you, counted on you, leaned on you literally as well as figuratively. And I know darn well you aren't a potential embezzler, and I *don't* think you've got a sick black streak in you. But I don't want to talk about love or think about it. Is that plain enough speech for you?"

"Plain as the nose on your face," he said solemnly, and I couldn't help laughing. He could always do it to me.

"That's supposed to be a *nosy* nose. It gets me into trouble."

"It's an honest nose, and it'll get you out of trouble." He brushed his lips across my knuckles and I remembered, but only for an instant, that Rees had done that too. Then he released my hand and Tim was coming back, saying, "What are you laughing at? I'm still hungry."

It was a difficult year for me in many ways. Tim had to know at last that his father and Jason had died in an accident, but he took this well. Rees had taught him that God was taking care of his mother; now he assumed that God was taking care of his father and Jason too. Who was to say he was wrong?

For me there were nights of crashing violently into consciousness, thinking that the moonlight slanted in on me through a Bellwood window; there were times when Rees's voice saying certain familiar phrases came to me out of nowhere. There were the flashes of resemblance that Tim showed. There were the scents of certain flowers, and there was music, which could evoke an entire atmosphere until it was washed away in a breaking wave of horror.

But with Tim growing and expanding, with my renewed contacts with old friends and the new ones I'd made in Somerset, and with the balm of time itself, the bad times grew less. Eric came and went, never urging me. He kissed me when he arrived and when he left, but it was like the way he kissed Tim. Or so we made it seem.

But one night toward the end of that year we met for the first time as lovers meet. Almost without our knowing it, it had happened. Without promises, confessions, or even a glance at the past.

Tim is ten now. He's tall, and sturdy in spite of his slenderness. He's in the fifth grade. Eric's one-room school was finally closed in favor of consolidation, and he began teaching in a charming old coastal town about half way between Limerock and Somerset, where he is now principal. Tim's a swift swimmer, runner, and baseball player, and he's learning to sail with Eric in the fine summer weather. He's a good reader too, and appreciates music and poetry as his father and mother did. Incidentally, Rees's work on the mentally defective criminal was genuine. It was almost ready for publication when he died, and it is now a standard textbook in some college courses. Both Rees's and Valerie's manuscripts are being saved for Tim.

Eric and I have given him a sister in all but blood,

and he's hoping for a brother. Tris, who survives everything including the moves, graciously shares his home with a whiskery dog named Ralph, after Tim's first real chum. Stephen Faraday is married; we see him at least twice a year, and correspond in between. I don't intend to let him be cheated out of knowing Valerie's boy.

Paul is married too and doing well in another state, on his own. His mother wanted to move there to be near him, I understand, but he discouraged her.

Bellwood has been sold and another family lives in it now, but it exists only in the past tense for me, as if it came into existence when I first laid eyes on its rosy bricks and sun-dappled lawns, and disappeared on the last day I saw it; bird song and roses, honeysuckle and nicotiana, the scented white peonies, the piano and the long bronze notes of the grandfather clock—all of it borne off into space, to disappear like the fading fire of a meteorite. Gone, gone, gone.

But sometimes it is half-glimpsed in the mist like one of those enchanted kingdoms, that appear for one day in a century, when the thrushes and the whitethroats begin in the late afternoons and shadows stretch long across the grass. But the memories have lost their poison long since. So has Chopin's music, and all other things that are exquisite and innocent in themselves.

Once Rees said to me, "Sometimes the loved one becomes what the lover sees." So it was with me. I knew after a time that I had simply fallen in love with a dream, and an adolescent one at that.

Eric is no dream. He is my reality, my touchstone, my talisman. My love.

Elisabeth Ogilvie lives most of the year on the Maine Coast she describes with such enthusiasm in her novels. Born in Boston, she spent summers by the sea in Maine and eventually made her home on Gay's Island, just off the mainland.

She sold her first story when she was twenty and in 1948 won the New England Women's Press Association Award for *Storm Tide*. Primarily a writer of fiction, she has had many of her books published in Italy, France, Africa, New Zealand, and Australia. Her telling portraits of children lend her books a unique charm and understanding.